NO WAY BACK

DETECTIVE REBECCA ELLIS BOOK 5

ROBIN MAHLE

INKUBATOR
BOOKS

Published by Inkubator Books
www.inkubatorbooks.com

ISBN (eBook): 978-1-83756-399-9
ISBN (Paperback): 978-1-83756-400-2
ISBN (Hardback): 978-1-83756-401-9

1

Labored breaths masked the sound of his footfalls on the pavement. From the corner of his eye, the Penobscot River glimmered under the morning sun. A much-welcomed cool breeze kept him on pace. The rest of the riverfront landscape—lush trees, buildings, and parking lots—passed by in a blur.

Few people were on this path in the early morning hours before the city went to work. A good thing because he'd begun to run out of steam. Fewer people around who might judge. This start of his journey to wellness had been more difficult than expected. He slowed down, coming to a stop near the bridge crossing. Out of breath, he hunched over, pressing his hands against his knees.

Moments later, with lungs full of air once more, he returned to full height and cast his gaze out over the river. The beauty of the rising sun's rays reflected back at him. He cupped his hand over his brow to shield the glare. Something caught his eye. An object crashing against the steep rocky shoreline, near the pylon. With a curious eye, he wandered down the slope, each step carefully placed so as not to lose his footing on the jagged rocks. The closer he got to the river's edge, the louder the sound of a rushing current.

The pylon was surrounded by the same sharp rocks. Under the force of the current, the object crashed against it, over and over. Growing more curious, he moved closer. Was it a backpack or a computer bag? He could only see the top of it, but any closer, and he would find himself tumbling into the bitter-cold water. Never mind it was nearly July, this was Bangor, Maine. Not Miami.

He stood there for several moments, squinting to better see what was moving against the rocks. The sound of a car crossing the bridge drew his attention for a moment. When he returned his gaze, the object revealed itself.

He gasped and stumbled back, breaking his fall with outstretched hands against the rocks. "Damn it." He peered up to see that no one was around. If he slipped..."Get up, you idiot." Regaining his balance, he climbed to the top of the shoreline, just off the path. A moment of panic surged as he patted down his jogging pants, unable to locate his phone. But when he pressed against the pocket of his fleece, relief at its discovery swelled. "Thank God." He gripped the phone with both hands, fearing it might slip as they trembled, and dialed the number.

"Nine-one-one, what is your emergency?"

"Yeah, uh, I'm running along the riverfront and, uh, well, I think there's a body down here in the water."

"Sir, what is your exact location?" the operator asked.

"Behind the medical center, at the bridge. I'm down by the column." He steadied his tone. "Ma'am, you have to send the police."

"Are you in any danger?"

He surveyed the area. "No. No, I'm alone. I'm fine."

"I've made the request. Please stay where you are. They will find you."

Minutes later, sirens sounded in the distance, and he returned to the path. "I think they're here." He peered down the road. "Yes. That's them. I see lights."

"Just hold on, sir. Stay where you are," the operator repeated.

"Over here." He waved his hands, raising his tone. "Over here."

Soon, the patrol car pulled over into the nearby parking area, and an officer emerged.

"Thank you so much. They're here." He ended the call and met the man along the path. "Officer, there's someone down there, in the water."

"I'm Officer Manning. What is your name, sir?"

"Gil. Gil Runyon. I was on a jog. I stopped to catch my breath and watch the sun rise over the water." He aimed his index finger toward the bridge's pylon. "Then I saw that."

Manning peered out, as if assessing the situation. "Stay here for a moment, Mr. Runyon."

"Yes, sir." He kept his eyes on the officer's every move, taking note of his hand resting on the butt of his gun. "Careful, Officer. It's slippery."

Manning glanced back at him. "Got it. Thank you." He continued across the path and headed down toward the rocky spillway.

"You see it?" Runyon asked.

"I got this, sir."

When the officer picked up his radio, Runyon jogged toward him. "You need some help?"

Manning thrust out a hand. "Sir, stay back." He pressed the button on his radio. "Dispatch, I need a detective on scene. Looks like we got a body in the river."

———

TWO WEEKS HAD GONE by with little public traction gained on Detective Connor Bevins' incident during his time as a West Point Cadet. The blogger who had posted the image of the overturned car in the ditch apparently hadn't had the kind of impact he had expected.

Nevertheless, Detective Rebecca Ellis held the notion that this was still a ticking time bomb, and there was nothing she could do about it. Bevins had avoided her as much as possible these past couple of weeks, knowing how angry she had been to find out about this after the fact. Detective Euan McCallister had known, too, and had kept it from her, making it all the worse.

She'd believed McCallister had finished with keeping secrets from her. The whole Boston situation was over now. The furor had died down. Then this. Ellis thought she was a friend and colleague to everyone in the Criminal Investigation Division. Her standing had now been brought into question.

The call had come into Dispatch, and Ellis and McCallister were driving out to the Penobscot bridge crossing, where the responding officer waited. Her relationship with McCallister was now somewhat strained since Bevins had turned up at her house that night. The insertion of distance between them hadn't gone unnoticed. But McCallister didn't question her need for that distance; instead, he was abiding by it.

Ellis could be stubborn. A trait, no doubt, acquired from her father, retired detective Hank Ellis. How long she would hold the grudge remained to be seen. For now, she'd pushed it aside, sticking to business as usual. With the riverwalk in the distance, she turned off toward the area. "I see the unit up ahead."

Stepping out of her white Chevy Tahoe, the morning sun on her face, she slipped on sunglasses. Manning's patrol car was parked a few feet away, and as she peered out, he came into view. A light breeze shifted her short blond hair, strands now clinging to her cheeks. She tucked the rogue hairs behind her ears, waiting for McCallister to join her.

He emerged from the passenger side, his long legs stretching to the ground. A wiry figure, he smoothed the wrinkles from his shirt. "Looks like Manning's over there, talking to the witness. Better go see what he found."

"Another day, another dead body." Ellis donned a weary grin. "Someone's always gotta keep us busy."

"On the upside, it keeps us employed," McCallister quipped.

"Sure. Because nothing says job security more than finding dead people." Ellis led the way toward the scene, stepping over the handrail to meet them. "Officer Manning."

His thumbs hooked into his duty belt, he nodded. "Detectives Ellis and McCallister. You're the lucky ones, I see." He eyed the witness. "This is Gil Runyon. He discovered the body and called it in."

Ellis extended her hand. "Nice to meet you, Mr. Runyon. Did Officer Manning get a statement from you yet?"

"Yes, ma'am, Officer. I mean Detective."

She grinned and looked back at Manning. "If you're done with this gentleman, he can go."

"Copy that." He placed his hand on the man's back. "You're free to leave, Mr. Runyon, but if we have any more questions, I'll be in touch."

"Of course. Thank you."

He'd started away when Ellis overheard him mumbling, "I am never running again." Couldn't argue with his logic. She looked out over the water. "Where is it?"

"This way. Watch your step," Manning warned as they descended the slope. "I don't need any broken bones on this mission."

McCallister stepped with caution, his hands offering balance. "Don't worry, I'm a pro at staying upright."

Ellis smirked. "Yeah, with those new shoes you just bought, I'm sure you'll be fine."

Manning stopped when he reached the pylon, turning to Ellis. "When's the dive team coming?"

The body came into view. Ellis stopped to take in the scene. The victim's back floated above the water while the rest of the body remained submerged. The head or occasional glimpse of arm bobbing up and down. "Euan, can you follow up?" She turned back to Manning. "Should be soon. We called on our way here. Better to get it out quickly, or there won't be any evidence left."

McCallister stepped away to make the call.

Ellis kept her gaze fixed on the floater. "What about that witness, Runyon? Anything throw you off about him?"

"He's clear. His watch was tracking his run, and he had no problem showing it to me. Honestly, if he hadn't seen him, the poor son of a bitch might've carried on downstream for days."

McCallister returned, dropping his phone into his

pocket. "Dive team's heading here now. Should be twenty to thirty minutes."

"Okay." Ellis squatted for a better view. "The longer it's in there...Should we try to pull it out ourselves? It's not in that deep."

"You'd be risking destroying evidence," McCallister said. "I think it's best to wait this out."

Manning grunted. "I'm not going down that far. It's slippery as hell, and one of us is liable to break our necks."

"Yeah, okay." Ellis hated the idea of leaving that person to bounce around in the water like that. It could easily get pushed farther downstream, making retrieval all the more difficult. Not to mention it just didn't feel right. But waiting for the experts was the only choice. She turned her sights toward the riverwalk. "Hey, you think that coffee shop across the street is open?"

McCallister caught up to her. "Probably. Hey, Manning, will you be okay for a few minutes? We're gonna grab some coffee."

"Sure. Grab me one too? Grande, half-caff, double cream, with vanilla syrup."

Ellis restrained her grin, starting across the road. "You got it."

McCallister walked beside her, thumbing back at the officer. "Figured you would've lobbed a quick one-liner for that."

"Nah." She swatted her hand. "It would only go over his head. Gen Z, right? They're a different breed of cop. Of course, Hank would say the same about us."

"Yeah, I'll bet he and Serrano only drank black coffee. Ate glazed donuts and had roast beef on rye for lunch."

Ellis laughed. "And they'll still outlive us."

The light banter felt good. Normal. She and McCallister used to joke around all the time. Taking jabs at each other. A lot had changed between them in a short amount of time. The Boston situation had caused a small rift between them; then it seemed she was able to paper over it. Now, it was Bevins and some accident that saw a man dead and had been covered up. Maybe if Bevins had come to her first instead of McCallister. Maybe she would have felt differently. Was it possible that was the real problem? Ellis wasn't the go-to anymore. She'd always championed Bevins when no one else would. Yet he'd chosen McCallister over her. Never mind. What was done was done. She would have to find a way to get over it, and herself.

With coffees in hand, they returned to the scene. A van approached, the state police logo on the side. Ellis noticed, taking a sip of her coffee. "There's the dive team."

The van parked a few feet away from where she and McCallister stood. Moments later, a team of divers emerged from the back with the evidence tech stepping out of the driver's seat. Bangor PD was a small department, and the divers were on loan from the state police.

Ellis approached the technician. "Officer Pruitt, good morning. You guys ready to get started?"

"Detective Ellis." He shook her hand, then donned a pair of latex gloves. "Ready when you are." Pruitt had been with the department going on three years. In his thirties, he kept fit and was meticulous in his work. A lot rode on his shoulders, as he was the entirety of the CSI team.

The two divers, Pruitt, and the detectives walked down the embankment to where Manning kept watch over the body.

"Anything I can do to help?" Manning asked.

The divers zipped their dry suits and donned masks.

Pruitt helped them with their tanks and sonar equipment in the event evidence was spotted around the body. "They'll go in, remove any obstructions to free the body, and retrieve it, hopefully without causing further damage. So we'll let these guys do what they do." He gestured outward. "You two are up."

Ellis watched as they stepped into the water. She was reminded of another case earlier this past spring. The two high school students who'd been murdered, then left floating in a lake. "Did I ever mention how much I dislike water?"

McCallister turned to her, tilting his head. "Water?"

"Bodies of water, I should say. Not really my thing. Oceans, lakes, rivers. I'd rather be in the mountains."

"So you don't like snow, and you don't like water." He smirked. "I'm sorry, why do you live here?"

She couldn't help but smile. "You got me there."

Several minutes went by until one of the divers emerged, raising his mask. "We could use the backboard down here. We're ready to bring him up."

"On it." Pruitt jogged back to the van.

Ellis picked up on his words. "Him? Suppose it looks like a him."

Pruitt soon returned carrying the board. McCallister offered a hand, and the two made their way toward the divers.

The first diver emerged from the water. "Okay, we're going to bring him up." He stepped toward the edge of the embankment a few feet from where the body had been discovered. They had to slide him farther along the shoreline in order to safely bring him up to the surface, careful to avoid striking him against the rocks.

Pruitt began to document the scene, taking photos of the original location and, now, the spot where the divers were ready to carry the body to the surface.

Ellis moved closer. "Anything we can do?"

The diver raised his hand. "We got it from here, Detective."

She returned to McCallister, shrugging away her offer. "Feeling a little helpless here."

"Join the club."

The divers began to move the body to shore.

Ellis stepped closer for a better look. "Wonder how long he's been in there."

McCallister joined her, looking on. "Won't know till the coroner checks him out. The clothes are mostly intact, so it doesn't appear he's been in there for too long."

"And the condition of the body," Ellis added. "Not seeing a lot of damage from marine life. Gotta be only a day or two, at most."

The divers made it to shore, placing the wet body on the backboard.

Pruitt waved them over. "You two want to come take a look?"

Ellis walked on, stopping a few steps from the victim. The bloated face and body, purple, veiny skin. She gasped, a sudden recognition sparking in her mind. She stumbled back.

McCallister reached out to steady her. "Hey, you all right?"

Officer Manning moved in. "Detective Ellis?"

Ellis waved away their concern, regaining her balance.

"I'm fine. It's okay." Her eyes blinked hard, and her heart pounded in her ears. "I—uh—I know who that is...That's Carter."

Manning turned to her, a question on his face.

"Carter," Ellis repeated. "My brother, Carter."

2

The Pentagon was the last place Detective Connor Bevins thought he'd be today. But his father, Jack Bevins, was a top aide to the chairman of the Joint Chiefs of Staff. To get his attention, this was where he had to go.

Their relationship had always been more like a business arrangement. Bevins' mother, who'd divorced Jack when Connor was only five, had been the nurturing one. But Jack, he was the one who'd put his son on the path to a successful career in Washington. Not unlike the one he himself enjoyed. Everything had gone to plan until Bevins' final year at West Point, which was the reason he was here now. Someone else had learned his secret. It was only a matter of time before the rest of the world found out. Not only would it destroy the young detective's career, but his father's too.

Bevins waited in the lobby. The twenty-five-year-old had gotten by on his looks for most of his life. While his father's money and influence carried him through his career. But the fact of the matter was, he loved his job. Loved the people he worked with. And after confiding in Ellis and McCallister, he'd come here to tell his father.

Sharp footfalls sounded behind him. Bevins turned to see they had come from Major General Jack Bevins. He stood at attention, tugging on his suit jacket. Though he was no longer a cadet, his father demanded respect. "Sir."

With hands clasped behind his back, Jack looked him up and down. "Hello, son."

Jack had always been an intimidating man. "Sir, I'd like to follow up on the call I made to you a couple of weeks ago."

"All right. Let's go to my office." Jack rotated sharply on his right heel and headed toward the elevators.

Bevins joined him, and the two rode the elevator to the third floor. Jack said nothing and continued into the hallway until he reached his office. Bevins had been at the Pentagon before, and it never ceased to impress. Rich pecan-wood tones. Highly polished terrazzo floors. The Pentagon was the largest office building in the country, housing thirty thousand employees, both military and civilian. The self-contained facility had a pharmacy, a food court, and a bank. It served as the headquarters for the Department of Defense, along with the Army, Navy, and Air Force. This was the prestigious environment where Bevins was supposed to be working until he'd made his one fatal mistake.

He followed Jack inside the luxurious office. A large mahogany desk was positioned between two tall windows. The American flag stood on the left with the Army's flag on the right. Hand-carved bookshelves spanned the walls and were filled with everything from historical novels to tomes on strategic military practices.

"Have a seat, son," Jack said, sitting behind his desk. And

when Bevins sat down, Jack continued, "Seems as though we have ourselves a problem."

He clasped his hands in his lap. "Yes, sir. To my knowledge, nothing more has been posted on the situation."

"Sounds to me this…blogger…is waiting to hear from you. Or me." Jack steepled his fingers, resting his arms on the chair. "Wouldn't be too hard to figure out he's looking for money to keep from exposing us further."

"I don't know, sir. He doesn't seem motivated by money so much as making me appear as though I'd gotten away with something. To show that people with money often tend to get away with things others don't."

Jack appeared to have taken offense. "Well, if this sorry individual thinks you have money, then he's most certainly barking up the wrong tree. Everything you have, you have because of me."

"Yes, sir. I'm aware of that." It was a fact Bevins couldn't deny. His beloved Mustang. His apartment. Even his job. It was all because of Jack. Even if he earned his own money now, his father had got him to where he was today instead of living out his life behind bars.

"So what is it you think I can do in this situation, son?" Jack asked.

"I don't know, sir. Except to say that while this particular blogger doesn't have a large following, it would only take a few other more influential people who'd seen what he'd posted to share it. Then, I think, we'd be confronted with a situation."

"You haven't answered my question, Connor," Jack pressed. "What am I supposed to do about this? Seems to me I've done a great deal already, yet here we are. You understand what this would do to both of us?"

"I do, sir, which is why I'd like to be the one to confront the blogger, to find a way to discredit him and his source. We don't know how he got that image. I'm not even sure the military police had photos of the scene."

"I was certain the MPs did not," Jack said. "Then again, someone did and offered the image to this person for reasons I have no doubt we'll find out soon enough."

"Of course. So, I'll do what I can to make it seem that the image was AI generated. A deep fake."

Jack nodded along with a downturned mouth, seeming to consider his son's plan. "That could work, but then there's concern that others might decide to look into it themselves."

"Yes, but they won't find anything. You made sure of that. With your buy-off, sir, this is how I'd like to proceed."

Jack tilted his head, fixing his steely gaze on his son. "And if it doesn't work?" He waited a moment before continuing, "If it doesn't work, I'll have no choice but to separate myself from the situation. You understand what that means, yes?"

Bevins fixed his eyes on his father. "Yes, sir. I understand completely."

CARTER'S BODY was being loaded into the coroner's van. Ellis stood by, a range of emotions coursing through her. The worst part? She was going to have to tell her father.

McCallister placed his hand on her shoulder. "I'm so sorry, Becca. Are you sure you don't want to just head home? I can take it from here."

"No. I'll follow the van to Augusta and talk to the medical examiner there. I'll formally identify the body." She turned to him. "He did this to himself, Euan. I didn't even know he was out of rehab, but clearly he shouldn't have been."

"There's no evidence to suggest an overdose."

Ellis pursed her lips. "Come on, you saw the body. I saw no signs of trauma other than from being in the water."

"But we don't know how he ended up there."

"You're right. We don't." She looked back over the river. "But I suspect he OD'd and whoever was with him pushed him into the river so he wouldn't be held accountable. Either that, or Carter simply fell in. Regardless, I suppose eventually I expected something like this to happen. And now that it has, I have to figure out how to tell Hank."

Officer Manning approached them. "Detective Ellis, they're ready to head out."

"Thank you. I'll follow."

He nodded. "I'm sorry, Detective. If there's anything—"

Ellis raised her hand. "I appreciate it. But there's nothing anyone can do for my brother now." She looked at McCallister. "You mind getting started on the paperwork, and I'll meet you back at the station?"

"Sure. I'll catch a ride from Manning."

"Thanks." Ellis returned to her SUV and climbed inside. She stared through the windshield as the doors closed on the coroner's van and the technician drove away. Her eyes were drawn to McCallister, who looked back at her. He'd been right to suggest she leave the scene. Sergeant Abbott would've insisted on the same thing. And when McCallister returned to the station, Abbott would learn what had happened. However, she had every inclination that this was not a murder investigation. Knowing her brother, it would prove to be an overdose case.

There would be no reason for Abbott to suggest she step

aside. And she wouldn't dare let Hank be the one to ID his son. He was still fragile as far as she was concerned. Only months had passed since his stroke, and while Hank would insist otherwise, she wasn't going to put him at risk.

The pain of learning the news would be hard enough. Maybe he would insist on seeing Carter regardless. Either way, this was what needed to be done first. She would deal with her father later.

As Ellis drove on, her phone pinged with an incoming alert. An email from Detective Alcott, the man assisting the feds on her ex-husband, Andrew's, fraud investigation. The one she'd decided to help with so that he wouldn't spend time behind bars thanks to the actions of his fiancée. But right now, it was the least of her priorities.

So many things seemed to be coming at her all at once. She worried about Bevins. She worried about McCallister and Andrew. Now, worst of all, she would worry about how Hank would take the news of his only son's death. No matter how often Carter screwed up, or whatever behavior he engaged in, it was as though Hank was willing to overlook it all. She wished she had that ability. Even now, she was angry with Carter over what his death would do to Hank.

Ellis soon arrived at the coroner's office. The van had already driven around back to unload the body. "Just get this over with." She climbed down from the driver's side and headed toward the entrance. Walking inside, she checked the time and made her way to the front desk.

The woman behind the desk smiled. "Detective Ellis, good afternoon."

"Hi. Listen, uh, I don't suppose Dr. Rivera is available? He's not out to lunch, is he?"

"Oh, no, ma'am. He eats lunch in his office on most afternoons. Too busy to leave."

"That's probably not a good thing," she replied. "Can I see him, please? It's about the body that was just brought in."

"Of course. I'll call him now." She picked up the phone.

Ellis stepped away and scrolled through her emails. She happened on the one that Alcott had sent and began to read. "Damn it." It seemed the FBI was ready to charge Andrew. "What the hell am I going to do now?"

"What's that, Detective?" Dr. Rivera asked as he drew near.

She pocketed her phone and turned to him. "Oh, nothing. Sorry about that, Doc." She offered her hand. "Thanks for coming out."

"Of course. This is about the male corpse they just brought in?"

"Yeah, it is." She steadied herself. "We pulled him out of the Penobscot this morning near one of the bridges. I need to officially ID him, if I could."

Rivera drew in his brow. "That's usually reserved for family, Detective, as I'm sure you're aware."

"I am aware." She felt a twinge of grief clutch her chest. "Unfortunately, he is family. He's my brother."

"Oh, I see." Rivera shoved his hands in his pockets. "I'm so sorry. And you say you fished him out?"

"Yes. He was discovered by a jogger this morning. It appears that he may have overdosed. I didn't notice any trauma elsewhere." Ellis gestured toward him. "Of course, you're the expert, but I'd like to officially ID him so we can have the body released for burial."

"I see. Please follow me. I believe he's in room two."

Rivera turned around, heading back into the wide corridor beyond the double doors.

Ellis trailed him as he entered the autopsy room.

Rivera walked toward the most recent body to arrive, which was shrouded in a white sheet. "I, of course, haven't had a chance to take a look, but you say you believe it was an overdose?"

"I do." She moved toward him. "Carter was an addict, and he'd been confined to a rehab facility, so it was a shock to find him floating in the river. I'll be contacting the facility after I leave here to discuss that. And as I said, I didn't note any other trauma."

"Let me take a look." She nodded, and Rivera pulled down the sheet.

The faint smell of wet fabric hung in the air. A hint of disinfectant from the facility layered over the acrid odor of the river.

Rivera appeared stoic, his face a mask of concentration as he began to inspect the corpse.

Ellis joined him, studying the body of her brother. His skin, a sickly purplish gray. Bruises on his arms and legs. Most likely caused by the constant battering of the current. The river's water had swelled his ankles in death. As she inspected Carter's body further, she tipped her head back and took a deep breath.

Rivera noticed her reaction. "We can stop if you'd like, Detective."

"No. I'm fine. What do you think?"

"I'm sorry?" he asked.

"About the cause of death." Ellis crossed her arms. "I know nothing's official yet, but given what you see here, what are your thoughts?"

"We all know how it works. A body will sink first once water enters the lungs. Then decomp happens…"

"And the body floats to the surface again." Ellis nodded. "So Carter had to have been dead a day, maybe two, before he floated back up."

"I won't know if drowning was the cause of his death until I do the autopsy. And given your input, I'll obviously run a tox screen." Rivera raised one of Carter's arms and studied it for a moment. He then moved to the other arm. "I don't see track marks."

"Check between his toes."

Rivera moved toward the feet and gently separated the big toe from the others to look in between. "Nothing here from what I can see." He glanced at her again. "But you said he was in rehab. That could mean he was clean."

"It could, except that I know my brother. *Knew* him. Someone clearly released him, and he went right back to his old habit. How soon can you get me a report?"

"Detective, you know the drill." Rivera covered Carter's body again.

"Yeah, sure. I understand."

"But I will do what I can for you and your family," he added.

"Thanks, Doc. I appreciate it." Ellis gazed at her brother's shape under the sheet. "Jesus, Carter. What the hell did you get yourself into?"

Ellis returned to her Tahoe, sitting in silence for some time, trying to wrap her head around how Carter had gotten out of the rehab facility. Hank had pulled a lot of strings to get him in there in the first place. And not even Hank could've gotten him out. Although Carter's stay there was almost up. Maybe Hank had stepped in?

She was pulled from her thoughts when a call rang through. It was Abbott, which meant McCallister had told him what had happened. She answered the line. "Hey, Sarge—"

"Becca, where the hell are you?" Abbott cut in.

She closed her eyes. "Augusta."

"Jeez, you didn't—"

"I had to ID him. I wasn't going to let Hank do it." Ellis pressed the ignition. "I'm getting ready to head back to the station now. We can talk about—"

"Go home, Becca. Go see Hank. Tell him, okay? Don't delay, you understand me? He won't forgive either of us if you do."

She pressed her lips and nodded. "Yes, sir."

"And don't come in," he added. "Not today. Not tomorrow. Look, Becca, I know how you felt about your brother, but he was still your brother. Take some time, would you? Do it for me. Better yet, do it for Hank. He's going to need you right now, more than ever."

The sarge was right. This was going to hit Hank hard. The man had already lost an ex-wife to murder and a second wife to cancer. Now this. "Yes, sir. I understand." She ended the call.

Ellis pulled out of the parking lot and drove on, back to Bangor to see her father and deliver the news. Guilt weighed on her as she experienced some relief at his death. Carter had done so much harm to himself, and to Hank, and now it was something she no longer had to worry about.

On the other hand, it also meant that Hank was all she had left of her family. There was no one else. Her mother had been an only child. Hank's older brother had been killed in Vietnam. It was just her and her dad now.

For a moment, she considered calling Piper. Her best friend since high school, Piper Dixon was always there when she needed her. But maybe it was a conversation better had in person. Right now, Ellis needed to process what had happened and prepare to tell Hank.

Her throat tightened as tears welled. She blinked them away. They weren't for Carter. They were for Hank. She needed to get those tears out of her system now because she was going to have to be strong for him. As strong as he had been for her in the aftermath of her mother's murder.

She reached his house, parking behind his old Chevy truck. It had turned into a warm day. Ellis felt almost stifled by the heat as she emerged and walked toward the front door.

Hank had spent most of his time at home since the stroke. Ellis had paid for a nurse to stop by every day to check on him, but those visits were over now. Mostly due to Hank's stubbornness. He didn't get out much anymore to see his friends, all the dinosaur cops he'd relied on all his life.

Ellis opened the door. "Dad, it's me."

He stepped into the hallway holding a butter knife—he must've been in the kitchen, preparing lunch. His kind face was lined with age, his warm smile raising his full cheeks. "Hey there, kid. What are you doing here? Shouldn't you be at the station?"

She forced a half-smile, gazing into her father's loving eyes.

He wiped his hands on a dishtowel that hung over his shoulder and tugged on his pants, which sat below his waist. He'd aged since the stroke, looking older to her now than his sixty-three years would suggest.

"Hey, Dad. Fixing lunch?" She walked toward him.

"I am. You hungry? I can make you a sandwich."

Ellis placed her hand on his forearm. "I'm not hungry. Why don't you come sit down in the living room? I need to talk to you a minute."

But he wouldn't budge. His face hardened. His smile faded. "No. No. You tell me right here. I've been around long enough to know what this is, Becca."

His eyes reddened and glistened with tears. She was certain he'd been in this very position plenty of times in his career, even if not with his own family. "Dad..." she whispered.

"Oh God." His heart shattered before her. "He's gone, isn't he? My boy is gone."

3

Ellis had only ever seen Hank cry once before, and that was when Carter's mother passed away. Now, she sat on the couch, an arm wrapped around him while he sobbed. Her heart broke for him. The hardened cop felt frail in her arms. No words could make his grief better. All she could do was be there.

It didn't take long before he pulled himself together, as always. Never wanting anyone to believe he was weak. Now, they sat in silence. The only sound came from Hank's ragged breaths and occasional sniffles.

He sat up straight, wiping his eyes with a tissue from the coffee table. He looked at Ellis with confusion. "How the hell did he get out of rehab without me knowing?"

At that moment, Ellis realized how similar the two of them really were, as she'd asked herself that very question. "I don't know, but it's something I'll work on finding out. I went to the coroner's office already. Did the paperwork, ID'd him. He'll be released to you when the autopsy is finished."

"Serrano let you do that?" Hank's eyes darkened, and his lips pressed together. "He let you ID your own brother?"

Ellis raised her hand in protest. "I didn't give him a chance to stop me. In fact, I don't know if the sarge has told him yet. I already got an earful from Abbott. Euan and I had been called out to the scene. From there, I followed the van back to Augusta."

Hank shot her a look. "You were there?"

"Dad, Carter was found in the Penobscot, not far from the Riverside district. The responding officer followed protocol. Euan and I were called to the scene. We had divers come out and retrieve the body." As she relayed the details of how she'd found her brother, Hank covered his face with his hands, tears streaming down his cheeks again. "It wasn't until he was brought to the shore that I saw his face."

Hank looked at her with compassion, taking her hand. "I'm so sorry you had to be the one, Becca. That's not right. That's not right at all."

"Honestly, I'm glad I was the one called out."

Hank tilted back his head, gazing up at the ceiling. "Do you think someone killed him?"

"I don't think so. There were no obvious signs of trauma apart from the bruises he'd sustained in the water. No bullet or stab wounds. But we'll have to wait for the coroner's report. My first thought was that he probably OD'd, then went into the water—but how, we don't know yet."

Hank swallowed hard. "That doesn't explain how the hell he got out of the facility. You can't just walk out of that place. He was serving out the remainder of his sentence."

Ellis nodded. "I know, and that's what I need to work on. But that's for tomorrow. Right now, I'm here for you, okay?"

Hank looked down, a smile evident on his cheeks. "You're

too much like me, kid. I know you shouldn't be the one to deal with this." He set his sights on her again. "But I wouldn't trust anyone else."

ELLIS WAS on her way home after Hank had insisted she didn't need to stick around to care for him. The real reason was so he could grieve in private, though he would never admit it. Knowing she needed to give him the space to handle this in his own way, she hadn't pushed back.

Now, with the humidity rising on this warm summer day, she turned on her windshield wipers to clear away the building mist.

Her phone rang; it was McCallister on the other end of the line. She answered, "Hi."

"Hi. Where are you?"

"Driving home from Hank's. You?"

"Sitting outside your house."

The two-lane road stretched ahead of her beneath the shade of overhanging trees. "Euan, I told you I'd be fine. You didn't need to—"

"Yes, I did. You shouldn't be alone right now, Becca. Neither should Hank, to be honest, but I know the apple doesn't fall far from the tree."

Her lips pulled back in a tender smile as she made the turn onto her street. "No, it doesn't." Drawing closer to her house, she saw his car alongside the curb. Ellis parked in her driveway and stepped out, making her way up the path toward her front porch.

McCallister sat in one of the Adirondack chairs, a six-pack on the table beside him. "How's he doing?"

Ellis raised her shoulder in a lopsided shrug. "About as good as you'd expect. Then again, it's Hank, so..."

He wrapped his arm around her and pulled her close. "I'm so sorry, Becca."

She leaned into him, feeling the warmth of his body and the steady beating of his heart. For a moment, she considered giving in to her emotions. Letting him soak them up, letting him make them go away. But that wasn't who she was. Instead, Ellis pulled back, turning to her door and unlocking it.

They walked inside, and Ellis dropped her bag on the floor at the entrance. "I'll take one of those beers."

McCallister closed the door behind them and handed her one. "You eat anything yet?"

"No." She took the bottle. "I'm not hungry right now." Ellis walked into the living room, dropping onto the sofa. She popped open the bottle and curled her leg under her.

McCallister took a seat beside her.

They sat in silence. A hint of afternoon light spilled in through the front window. Shadows descended the walls. No television. No music.

Ellis sipped on the bottle. "I told him I'd stay the night, but he insisted I leave. I don't think he wanted me to watch him break down more than I already had."

"He's an old-school cop," McCallister said. "Breaking down in front of others, that's not how they do things."

"Believe me, I know." Ellis peered through the window at the tree in her front yard. The lush green leaves swayed in the gentle breeze. "Dr. Rivera's going to do the autopsy and the tox screen."

"How soon for results?"

Ellis shrugged. "Who knows? But in the meantime, I

have to figure out how Carter was released from the facility without Hank knowing about it. He's the court-appointed guardian. This never should've happened."

"Wasn't he scheduled to come out soon?"

Ellis nodded. "He was, but not this soon, and definitely not without calling his family."

McCallister set down his bottle of beer. "How do you plan on handling this? Do you think this was an accident or a drug overdose?"

She rubbed her face. "I have no idea. But I can't imagine why my brother was there. I can tell you that he would've called Hank the moment he was released because he would've needed money or a place to stay. The fact he didn't tells me he was planning something." Ellis took a swig of her beer. "I know the kind of person my brother was, Euan."

"What are you saying?"

Ellis exhaled. "I'm saying that where my brother was concerned, bad things always seemed to happen. Only this time, the bad thing happened to him."

———

As it turned out, Ellis had been affected by Carter's death more than she could admit. Now, in the middle of the night, McCallister in the bed next to her, she was grateful for his presence. A brief disagreement over whether he should stay, and then she gave in, ultimately not wanting to be alone tonight.

The irritation she'd felt toward him these past couple of weeks melted away, at least temporarily. Looking back, she'd been hard on him. Maybe too hard. The reality of the loss made everything else seem trivial.

As much as she'd been angry with Carter, disliked him even, she'd never wished him dead. More for Hank than for him, but the fact of the matter was, Ellis hadn't gone through this kind of loss in a long time.

She padded out of her bedroom, unable to sleep. Her mind's eye consumed with visions of her brother's dead, bloated body. Ellis sat on her couch, darkness surrounding her. Tears spilled down her cheeks.

Carter was eleven years younger than her, meaning they were never very close. The age gap was too great. And as Carter grew older, he'd turned to drugs, and she was already a cop by then. The two lifestyles mixed like water and oil. She thought back to the Aldrich case, and how years earlier, a young Carter had stood by, watching the young Ben Aldrich nearly drown in Pushaw Lake. He was selfish. Always bringing trouble with him. That trouble usually landed on Hank's doorstep. Would the same happen now?

Ellis wiped the tears from her face and took a deep, steadying breath. She couldn't change the past or bring Carter back to life, but she could try to make things right for Hank. Focusing on how Carter had ended up in the Penobscot was now her priority.

But as she sat there, lost in thought, a sense of dread weighed her down. This case was personal, and it conjured memories of her past that she had tried hard to bury. Memories of a time when she, too, had been lost and broken, trying to find her way back to the light. She had made it back. Carter hadn't.

Tomorrow, she would contact the rehab facility for Carter's records. Where had he gone when he was released? Who had been the last people to see him alive? And why hadn't Hank been called?

Hank's words swirled in her head—maybe she was too much like him after all. Then again, that kind of resolve brought cases to closure. Brought justice to those who needed it. But did Carter need justice? Had he been in the wrong place at the wrong time, or had he done this to himself? Only Dr. Rivera would be able to answer whether Carter had overdosed, and then the picture might become clearer.

But then, in the darkness of her living room, it occurred to her. "Security."

The riverwalk had cameras everywhere. Most of them on the nearby businesses. She had no idea where Carter had gone into the river, or how far it had taken him downstream, but CCTV from the surrounding area would be a hell of a good place to start looking.

THE LIGHT of a new day had dawned, leaving Ellis feeling determined to peel back the truth about what had happened to Carter in the moments before he wound up in the river.

McCallister had left early this morning, heading back to his apartment to get ready for work. She felt mild relief, not wanting to be asked about her feelings, or whether she'd slept, or any number of those questions people asked when they were otherwise at a loss for words.

Now, she drove straight to the riverwalk to start to gather whatever video evidence existed, hoping to see Carter captured somewhere, seeking out images of her brother that might bring resolution and closure.

Stepping out, Ellis felt the cool air coming off the river. The sun shone brightly, and she slipped on a pair of sunglasses. Behind her were buildings. Offices, medical centers, cafés. Ahead was the pathway where people biked and walked. Only a few feet from where Carter was found, Ellis scanned the area in search of security cameras that pointed toward the walkway. The nearest one, attached to the side of the building that faced the water.

A security guard stood behind a desk at the front entrance as Ellis made her way inside. "Good morning. I'm Detective Ellis. I'd like to take a look at your security footage from the camera on the river's side."

The guard eyed her, tilting his head. "Don't you need a warrant for that?"

She grinned. "No, actually I don't. That camera faces a public space. But since a man was pulled from the river yesterday, I thought you could help me figure out how he ended up there without it causing you too much trouble."

He glanced down, seemingly embarrassed. "Sorry, Detective. Of course I can pull the footage for you."

Ellis followed him to the elevators, and they rode up to the top floor. They reached the server room, where several video displays were mounted on the wall.

The man sat down. "Do you have a timeframe?"

"Yesterday, early morning." She raised a finger. "Actually, let's go back a couple of nights. I don't know when it happened, but let's cast a wide net."

"Yes, ma'am." The operator went to work and retrieved the footage she'd requested. "This was from the night before last at about midnight." He glanced at her. "Far enough back for you?"

"We'll see."

He got up from the chair. "Go right ahead. Press the keys to fast-forward, stop, reverse. Whatever."

"Got it, thanks." Ellis went to work reviewing the footage. The camera had a view of about fifty yards in either direction and out over the river.

As she fast-forwarded through the files, nothing out of the ordinary stood out. Just a few people walking along the sidewalk. Some cars passing over the bridge. But as she slowed down the video and scrutinized it more closely, something caught her eye. A figure. It was hard to make out any details, but the person was wearing a hoodie and appeared to be walking near the water's edge, well beyond the footpath.

Ellis rewound the footage and watched it again. This time, she noticed the person stop, climb over the handrail, and peer down toward the water. After a few moments, the figure turned and fell out of the camera's view. Several minutes passed, but the person didn't appear again. Not on these cameras.

"The timing works." Ellis paused the video and took a screenshot of the figure.

The guard leaned closer. "Sorry, ma'am?"

"Nothing. I think I've seen all I'm going to see." She stood again. "Thank you for your time."

"Yes, ma'am."

"I'll show myself out." Ellis left the room and headed into the hallway again. Down the elevator, she carried on through the lobby and walked outside, glad of the air and light.

There was no way to identify the man in the hoodie, but a lone person, walking to the river...well, it could have been Carter.

She jumped into her Tahoe and headed to the station. But as the morning waned, a call to Hank was in order. "Hey,

Dad. I was on my way to the station and wondered if you wanted me to come by first? Have you eaten?"

"I'm okay, kid. I'm up. Had my coffee. Don't need anything else right now. Don't worry, I'm doing all right."

That seemed unlikely, but she would respect his wishes. "Okay, then I'll stop by after work, as usual. And, Dad?"

"Yeah?"

"I'm fine to start making the arrangements."

"No, ma'am. He was my son. It's my responsibility. Go on now. Get to work, and I'll see you later."

The call ended. Ellis somehow felt worse than if she hadn't called him. His abrupt conclusion to the call suggested he was putting on a front. She heard it in his voice. But he was a stubborn man, and she wasn't going to change him.

Ellis arrived at the station and entered the lobby. By the look on everyone's faces, word had spread. "Damn it," she whispered.

Dispatcher Liz Varney was at the front desk. She looked at Ellis, her face solemn. "Good morning, Becca."

"Morning, Liz."

"I'm—I'm so sorry—"

Ellis raised her hand. "Don't be. Please. I appreciate it, but I'm okay."

Liz shrugged. "Yeah, sure."

Ellis felt the eyes of the officers on her as she passed them and reached the steps.

At the top of the landing, Sergeant Abbott stood with his hands on his round hips.

"Sarge." She nodded.

"You shouldn't be here, Becca." He peered at her over his

reading glasses before taking them off. "What are you doing?"

"My job, Sarge."

"Your team can pick up the slack. I told you this yesterday."

Sergeant James Abbott was a big man. Just turned sixty-one. And right now, his kind brown eyes bored into her. He ran a hand over his thinning hair, seeming to understand he wasn't going to win this argument.

"I went down to the river this morning," Ellis began. "I figured pulling surveillance video from the spot where Carter washed up might shed some light."

Abbott folded his arms over his broad chest. "And?"

"And I saw someone. Couldn't tell you whether it was Carter or not. But I'd like to get with Forensics and try to find out."

He creased his brow, licking his lips as if preparing to try to prevent her from doing what he must've thought certain she would do—get to the truth. "It'd be best to wait for the coroner's report."

A half-smile tugged at her lips. "Yes, sir, it would, but as you know, I'm not one for waiting around."

4

The person Ellis had seen on the surveillance video presented her with two scenarios. Either it had been Carter before he jumped or fell into the river, or it had been someone who'd seen him in the water after the fact and simply walked away.

Before facing her team inside the bullpen, it was best to bypass all the condolences and head straight down to see Computer Forensics Officer Leo Brown. As far as she was concerned, the man's talents verged on genius.

Forensics was located on the first floor near the back of the building. Ellis didn't stop to say hello to the guys in Patrol, nor to Sergeant Moss on her way. Instead, she marched on, pushing through the double glass doors. Inside was Elliot Harding at his desk. "Hey, Elliot, is Leo in?"

He peered up at her, displaying a youthful smile and big hazel eyes. "Morning, Becca. He's in the ballistics lab. I'll go get him." He pushed away from his desk and started toward the back corridor.

It seemed he didn't know about Carter, or if he did, he

kept it to himself. Ellis waited, looking at the computer screens and various equipment that surrounded her. Soon, she heard footfalls, and moments later, Brown appeared, walking ahead of Harding. The full-bearded, stout forensics expert offered a nod as he approached.

"Morning, Detective," Brown said. "What can I do for you?"

Ellis retrieved the flash drive. "Wondering if you can enhance an image for me. Looking to ID the guy on here."

Brown took it from her. "Let's see what we've got." He inserted the flash drive into the computer at his desk.

Ellis leaned over his shoulder. "Timestamp is 2:34 a.m. yesterday morning. No one else appears before or after."

"Got it." Brown forwarded the video to the point in time. He narrowed his gaze, leaning toward the screen for a moment. "This guy in the hoodie?"

"That's the one."

Brown pulled back, crossing his arms. "You're not giving me much to work with here."

Ellis nodded, lowering her gaze. "I understand. But it's either my brother, Carter Ellis, before he fell into the water, or someone who saw him floating there and did nothing." She raised her eyes to him again. "Anything you can do would be appreciated."

"Jeez. I'm so sorry for your loss. I'll do the best I can and get back to you ASAP."

"I appreciate it, Leo, thanks." Ellis turned around and headed back into the hall, toward the lobby once again. She reached the stairs and hesitated, knowing the time had come to face her colleagues. Had they been given advance warning? Probably. Hopefully. She didn't think she had it in her to rehash yesterday's events.

Climbing up to the second floor, she walked into the Criminal Investigation Division's bullpen. CID was where her team worked. And now, she was about to see them for the first time since learning that her half-brother had been found facedown in the Penobscot.

Chatter stopped. Phone calls ended. And all eyes were on Ellis.

Gabby Lewis was the first to walk around her desk. She took Ellis's hands. "Becca, if there's anything I can do..."

"Thank you, Gabby. I'm okay for now."

Bevins came up behind her, laying his hand on her shoulder. "I'm sorry, Becca. Even sorrier you had to be the one to find him."

"It's okay, Connor. I just need to carry on as usual and figure out what happened."

That was when Fletch stepped in. Lori Fletcher was on her way to the top, and everyone knew it. She was fierce and loyal. For a woman who'd just turned twenty-eight, she was as strong, if not stronger, than Ellis had been at that age.

"Hey, Becca, you sure there's nothing we can take off your plate?"

Ellis glanced past her for a moment. McCallister was at his desk, his eyes fixed on her. "No, I'm okay. I appreciate it, guys, but really, the best thing for me is to just do my job."

Detective Bryce Pelletier, a dear friend to Ellis, who'd once admitted his love for her, appeared from beyond the corner.

Ellis smiled. "Morning, Bryce."

"Becca, I'd say I'm surprised to see you here, but I'm not." He donned a tender smile. "Anything I can do?"

"No. I was just telling everyone it's best for me to keep

busy. But I appreciate all the support. You guys are the best." Ellis carried on toward her desk.

As she sat down, she couldn't help but feel a pang of guilt for not having a better relationship with Carter before he passed. But nearly eleven years of bad blood couldn't be erased, even in death. She shook her head, trying to clear her thoughts, when McCallister rolled his chair over to her.

"Becca, you don't have to push yourself so hard. Take some time off if you need it."

Ellis looked up at him, her eyes softening. "I appreciate your concern, Euan, but I need to keep busy. It's the best thing for me right now."

He nodded, appearing resigned. "Okay. I got it. But if you need anything..."

"I know."

BEVINS HAD RETURNED this morning from his visit to his father in DC. The only solution being Jack's insistence that he not get involved, which left Bevins to proceed with a plan of his own.

The time had come to talk to the sarge about it. After dealing with the Boston fallout, this wasn't likely to go over well. Fletch would go ballistic when she found out. And Ellis? He'd gone to her when it was first discovered, praying for a solution. But she had none to offer. In fact, she'd become distant since it happened, angry that he'd kept it from her in the first place. And now, with the death of her brother, he wouldn't dare ask for her help.

Bevins headed toward Abbott's office down the hall, past

the stairs. He walked inside to find him at his desk, staring intently at his phone. "Sarge?"

Abbott looked up at him. "Connor, come in."

He closed the door. "I, uh, I need to talk to you about where I was yesterday."

"You mean with your dad in Washington?" Abbott nodded. "I'm aware, son. Sit down."

"You're aware? How?" Bevins took a seat.

"You think your father and I haven't already talked?"

Bevins pursed his lips. "Right." It should've come as no surprise Abbott knew. After all, it was Jack who'd got him this job. "Sir, I suggested to Jack that I handle this on my own. He agreed."

"And how do you propose to do that?"

"If I can find this blogger or contact him in some way, I can work to discredit him." Bevins shrugged. "Make him look like he was using a deep fake."

Abbott nodded, appearing to consider the plan. "I get where you're coming from, all right. But tracking down this person, calling them a liar and whatever else...well, I think that's a recipe for a lawsuit, maybe worse."

"What else can I do?" Bevins pleaded. "He has something that shouldn't exist. He's out to destroy me and my dad."

"He got the information from someone. That's the real problem," Abbott replied. "Son, you're a good detective. I don't want to see your career ruined because of this, but trying to cover up the cover-up? Not a good idea. For you, your father, or this department."

Bevins nodded, feeling ashamed. "You knew about this, yet you hired me anyway. Why?"

Abbott folded his reading glasses and set them down on his worn oak desk. "That's a hell of a good question, and I'll tell you, it's because I believe in second chances. And I'm not entirely sure what happened is really what happened. Listen, son, I met your father through a friend. This friend was someone I trusted. So when he asked for my help, I was ready and willing to offer it." He glanced away for a moment. "After talking with Jack for a while, I figured the kind of man he was. And then I read your file. There was something about you...let's just say I knew you and Jack were two very different people. That was why I hired you."

Bevins narrowed his gaze, parting his lips as he prepared to speak, but then thought it best not to pull on that thread. "I have to at least contact this blogger. Find out how he got the information. Talk to him. Get a feel for what else he intends to do."

As if dealing with her brother's death wasn't enough, Ellis had almost forgotten about the email sent over by Detective Alcott. She'd learned that his case against Andrew and his fiancée was solid. Alcott's email had suggested the feds were ready to make a move.

McCallister was working at his desk. Ellis had caught sight of him from the corner of her eye, yet he remained on his own tasks. She checked her email and opened the message from Alcott. After reading it, she lowered her gaze, defeated. The feds were ready to bring charges. So was the state.

She got up and headed toward the break room, feeling McCallister's gaze on her. Once inside, she made the call. "Detective Alcott, it's Ellis. Sorry for the delay in getting back to you."

"You read my email, I assume."

Ellis rested her elbow in her hand as she spoke, peering through the break room window. "I did. As you know, I'd been hoping to hear back from Andrew with copies of the transactions."

"Doesn't sound like he's come through, Detective. I gave you my word I'd keep you up to speed. You were to do the same."

She wasn't about to mention the death of her brother. To be honest, Alcott wouldn't have cared in the first place. "It's a delicate situation. But I will contact him now in the hope he was able to retrieve the information you need."

"If Andrew Cofield has managed to come up with proof none of that money went to him, I'll be all ears. I suggest you contact him before I do. You have till the end of the day." The call ended.

"Goddam it." She let out a sigh before dialing Andrew's number. When he answered, she jumped right in. "You're out of time, Andrew."

"Good morning to you, too, Becca."

"I just got off the phone with Detective Alcott. He says they're ready to file charges. That could mean you'll be in cuffs by the end of the day." She meandered around the tables. "Do you have what we talked about?"

"Some of it. Myra's been cautious. I think she suspects I've accessed her laptop," he said. "When I looked again a few days ago, much of the data had been erased."

"Shit." Ellis raked her hand through her hair. "Send me what you have. I won't be able to help you get in again. I already owe my guy for the favor," Ellis said, referring to how she had helped Andrew hack into Myra's personal laptop through a program Leo Brown had used in the past. Was it legal? Hell no, and Brown made sure she knew that, but he'd helped her, nonetheless. He'd remotely installed the software used to access her data. But it sounded like Myra had suspected she was being tracked.

"Will it be enough?" Andrew asked. "It shows the money going into her account. None of it ties to me, just like I told you."

"Send it to me. I'll take a look and figure out how to present it to Alcott. There may be a way to conceal how the information was obtained. But it'll prove your innocence."

"Thank you, Becca. Really. I know you've put your ass on the line for me."

He had no idea. Not only was it her ass, it was Brown's ass as well. Like Bangor PD needed more scandals. Ellis told herself she was doing it to keep Andrew out of jail. That his fiancée was the actual crook, and this was the right thing to do. But time would tell whether it would be enough. "Don't thank me yet. Send it to the server link I gave you. Not to my email."

"Got it."

"I'll be in touch." Ellis ended the call, laying her palm on her forehead. At times, the weight of others' burdens was almost too much for her to carry. But she carried it anyway.

She returned to her desk without saying a word to anyone. Only moments later, a text arrived. Ellis thought it would be from Andrew, but the caller ID revealed it was Brown. He wanted to see her. "Brown's got something." She looked at McCallister. "I'm going to run downstairs and see if he was able to get an ID on that guy."

"You want me to come with you?" McCallister asked.

"No. I got this for now." She carried on downstairs and along the corridor that led to Forensics. Upon pushing through the glass doors, there he was, appearing to have been expecting her. "You have something?"

Brown waved her back. "Could be. Come on. I'll show you." He walked back to his desk, sitting down and tapping on his keyboard. "I ran facial-recognition software and cross-referenced it with our database of suspects, along with crime scene photos from all the investigations that have been entered into the system."

A flicker of hope ignited within Ellis. "And?"

Brown leaned back, gesturing to the screen. "Take a look." He waited a moment while she walked around to peer at it. "Eighty percent match to a guy named Tyler Beck. Former inmate in Maine's correctional facility, temporary resident at Cochran House Rehab Center."

"The rehab center where Carter was." She furrowed her brow. "Eighty percent match? What was he charged with?"

Brown pulled up the report. "The records indicate Tyler Beck had a history of drug-related crimes. Mostly small stuff."

"Can I take a look?" Ellis leaned over him to read the screen. She scanned through the details, and one thing immediately stood out. "There it is."

"There's what?" Brown asked.

She smiled, nodding with renewed confidence. "This is what I needed. Your eighty percent is enough."

Ellis spun around, but Brown called out to her. "Wait, Becca. Who is this guy? Why was he at the river?"

She stopped and turned back to him. "I don't know the *why* yet, but he might've been there when my brother died."

Ellis made her way back into the corridor. What she'd left out with Brown was the fact that Tyler Beck had been in jail around the same time as Carter. Hardly definitive that they knew each other, but given the man just so happened to be walking by and just so happened to be looking into the river when her brother might've been floating around—well, it seemed worth following up.

She returned upstairs, heading straight for her desk, and entered the name Tyler Beck into the database.

In his familiar gesture, McCallister rolled his chair toward her. "Did Brown ID the guy in the security video?"

"Yes. I'm looking him up now. Looks like he might have known Carter. Served time with him in Warren and lived in the same rehab facility, Cochran House."

"Any idea where this guy's at now?"

"I'm working on it," she replied.

A few moments later, the computer screen flashed with the results of her search. Ellis scanned through the information. "Tyler Beck was released from prison only six weeks ago and is currently on parole. He was at Cochran House on his release, but not anymore. Now, he's at a state-run halfway house."

Without wasting another moment, Ellis grabbed her keys. "I need to track him down. He could be a witness. But first, I need answers from the rehab center as to why the hell Carter was released." She preempted any effort on his part to tag along. This was hers to figure out. At least, for now.

Within moments, Ellis was out the door. She felt alone despite her team offering support. Something drove her... compelled her...to deal with this on her own. The weight of her brother's death, adding to the other burdens she'd chosen to carry.

Heading north on the 95, it was still busy with commuters. However, the place wasn't far, and she jumped off the exit toward Stillwater Avenue.

Carter's court-ordered stay at the facility was thanks to Hank. While he'd been set to be released soon, it wasn't supposed to be like this. Hank should've been notified. Now, Ellis was about to learn why he wasn't, and she would be demanding to know who the hell had authorized Carter's release in the first place. And if she got more details on Tyler Beck in the process, then all the better.

Ellis parked near the front of the building. With Cape Cod-style architecture, a soft gray exterior with white shutters and dormer windows, it seemed well-funded, almost like a condominium. She wondered what it was like on the inside. And then it occurred to her—all this time Carter had been here, she hadn't visited him once.

Inside, she had her badge ready. "Good morning. Detective Ellis, Bangor PD."

The man wore a friendly smile. His bearded chin and thick black hair made him appear more like a security officer than a front desk attendant. Maybe that was intentional. "Good morning, Detective. How can I help you today?"

"Two things." She held up her fingers. "First of all, I'd like to know who released my brother, Carter Ellis, before his time was served. Secondly, I need to know if Tyler Beck was a resident here with him, and when he was released."

The man looked down, almost fearful of her now. "As far as our residents go, Detective, I'm afraid I can't offer that information. Regarding your brother?" He peered up at her as if asking a question.

"Yes, my brother, Carter Ellis. He was recently released. Now he's dead." She wore a serious gaze. "Anyone here know how that was allowed to happen?"

5

Bevins tried to focus on the job, but in the back of his mind, he knew that a reckoning was coming. Could he stop it? And if so, what kind of person would that make him?

He never should've listened to his father in the first place. Jack had convinced him he could bury the accident. And Bevins had believed him. Barely twenty-one at the time, he'd believed Jack had the power to make it all go away. And it seemed he did—for a while.

Now, could the blogger be tracked down? And if so, what could Bevins possibly do? Force him to take down the image? This was a bell that couldn't be unrung. If this blogger gained traction with his story, the Bevins family name would be ruined. Jack would certainly lose his job. And jail time wasn't out of the question—for either father or son. Though Bevins suspected Jack had enough friends in high enough places to, at the very least, save himself.

He opened his laptop and pulled up the blog post. He knew the blogger's handle. He'd watched the video. Now it was time to find this person. What would happen once he did, Bevins had no idea. But someone gave this person the photograph. One that shouldn't even have existed. So, who had done this? Was someone after Jack Bevins, and this was how they were choosing to come at him?

Bevins turned off the volume on his computer and played the video once again. This blogger was young, maybe even younger than him. Arrogant. A guy who thought himself a do-gooder for exposing corruption. And in this case, tragedy. Was he doing this for fame or righteousness? Bevins couldn't be sure, but for now tracking down his IP address was the best way to find him, assuming he wasn't smart enough to use a proxy server.

He looked up to see McCallister heading toward him. Bevins closed the laptop. "Hey. What's up? You need something?"

McCallister perched on the corner of Bevins' desk. "Listen, I know you talked to your dad about all this. And I know you're struggling. I can see it." He looked around at the rest of the team. "Your best shot at getting to the bottom of who contacted the blogger is finding out what really happened to your buddy."

"What do you mean?" Bevins creased his brow. "He was stuck inside the car. I left him for dead."

McCallister folded his hands in his lap. "Connor, listen to what I'm telling you. Look, this won't be easy, but if you can, find out what happened to your vehicle at the time. Mechanical issues. An animal in the road. Whatever it was that caused it to flip. Get more information on how they recovered your friend, what injuries he sustained...That way, you might stand a chance at defending yourself. Because that's where this is headed."

"First of all, I wouldn't know how to go about doing any of what you're suggesting. And secondly, there is no defense."

"There is if you weren't at fault. Did you screw up by letting your dad try to hide it? Yeah, you did. But you were a scared kid. Your dad, a powerful military official. What the hell else were you supposed to do?"

"What are you saying?" Connor challenged. "That my dad tried to scrub it all without knowing the truth?"

McCallister raised a shoulder. "I'm saying he did what he thought he needed to do to protect both of you. The truth may not have factored into it. Getting answers could mean letting go of this burden you've carried, that or stepping up and taking responsibility for it. It's your choice, Con."

Bevins considered his colleague's words. Funny that it had never struck him that way before. Had his friend died on impact? Was the accident truly his fault? In all the confusion, he'd never bothered to notice. In the icy grip of fear, he'd run, calling his father to plead for help. And Jack had come to the aid of his son. But how? Was there more to this than he knew? "I want to know the truth," he said. "And I'll accept whatever consequences that brings."

McCallister returned to his feet. "Then the first thing you need to do is get in contact with local law enforcement—"

"It happened in West Point," Bevins cut in. "The MPs are in charge over there."

McCallister pursed his lips. "That must've been how your dad was able to keep it under wraps."

"He held a different position at the Pentagon then, but yeah, he pulled strings...a lot of strings." Bevins opened his laptop again. "But I can see how far I get. Records of the accident shouldn't exist, but I think I know who to contact to take a look for me."

McCallister lifted a brow. "You have an insider?"

"I did. I think he's still there, but I'll have to find out." He regarded McCallister a moment. "Thanks, Euan."

"You can thank me when this is all over. But listen..." He aimed a finger at Bevins. "You need help on this, I'm here, you got that?"

Bevins grinned. "Copy."

———

A MIDDLE-AGED WOMAN approached the desk, seeming intent on rescuing the man Ellis was lobbing her questions at. "Excuse me, can I help you?"

Ellis restated what she'd told the man. "I need to see your records on Carter Ellis."

The woman pushed up her glasses. "Our patients' records are private, Detective. Unless you have a court order or—"

"The patient in question is dead," Ellis cut in, making her point crystal clear this time. "And I'm his sister. Our father, Hank Ellis, got him his place here. So, please, I need to speak with someone who can tell me why my brother was released when the only person with the authority to sign him out was our father."

The woman shuffled through a folder on the desk, her hands now unsteady. And when it seemed the folder offered no solution, she looked at Ellis, her lips twitching. "Excuse me one moment. I'll go tell the manager you're here and see if she can help."

"Thank you." Ellis waited in the lobby, peering at the

pamphlets that rested on the desk. Each one seemed to offer help in a few short paragraphs on dealing with friends, family, and partners who were struggling with addiction. In hindsight, some of that information might've been useful to her.

The same woman reemerged, though now with another at her side; she appeared steadier and more reassured.

"Detective, I'm Phyllis Dobbs. I manage this center." She held out her hand. A woman of about sixty, tall, thin, gray hair cut short. She appeared professional, not as easily rattled as her staff.

"Detective Ellis, I'd like to talk to you about—"

"Carter," she jumped in. "Your brother. Yes, I'm aware. Please, let's talk in my office." She started back.

Ellis trailed behind as they walked along the first floor toward the right side of the building. Several offices lined the hallway. The one at the end seemed to belong to Dobbs.

"Through here, please. Take a seat." Dobbs gestured for Ellis to enter. "Can I get you something to drink? A cup of coffee?"

"No, thank you. I'm fine." Ellis sat down in the black vinyl chair with chrome armrests.

"All right then." Dobbs rounded the desk, taking her seat. "First of all, let me say that I'm so sorry for your loss."

"Did you know Carter?" Ellis asked, not interested in soothing this woman's conscience.

"Of course. I make it my business to get to know everyone here. And your brother was here for several months."

"Yes, he was. What I'd like to know is, who authorized you to release him?"

The woman peered down her nose and typed something

on her computer. "According to the file, Carter's court-ordered time here had been completed. He was free to go. Prison records indicated the release date per the agreement Mr. Hank Ellis and Mr. Carter Ellis signed." She turned her screen so that Ellis could view it. "That date was three weeks ago."

How was that possible? Hank would've known about this. "Can you print that off for me? I'll need to include it in the investigation."

"Yes, of course."

While she waited for Dobbs to do this, there was one other thing she had to know. "What can you tell me about Tyler Beck?"

Dobbs returned a curious gaze. "As you know, he was a former patient. I'm afraid that's all I can tell you about him."

"When was he released?" Ellis noticed the woman's brow narrow, as though considering whether she could reveal such details.

"He's a potential witness in the death of my brother. If you're unable to offer further information, I'm happy to get a warrant." Ellis never liked throwing that in people's faces, especially when they were trying to be helpful, but something had gone awry, and Tyler Beck might know what that was.

Dobbs cleared her throat. "He was released a few weeks ahead of your brother. Sent to a halfway house for transitioning back into society. As your brother would have been."

Ellis grabbed the report. "Thank you for your help." She walked out of the facility. Carter's early release and Tyler Beck's appearance at the riverwalk were too coincidental to ignore. She needed to find him.

As she stepped into her car, she dialed Pelletier's number.

He picked up after a couple of rings. "Hey, Becca. What's up?"

"Can I ask a favor?" Ellis started the engine.

"Yeah, of course. What is it?"

"I'm looking for a man named Tyler Beck. He was in the Cochran House Rehab Center with my brother. I understand he's at a halfway house now. Any chance you can run a background and get a location for me?"

There was a brief pause on the other end of the line before Pelletier responded. "What's going on? Why do you need to find him?"

"It looks like this guy Beck was at the riverwalk in the early morning hours before the call about Carter came in. I'm pretty sure they knew each other. I need to know why he was there and if he knows what happened."

"I'll run it now and get back to you. You sure you want to do this? Any one of us can run this down for you, Becca. It doesn't have to be you."

"Yes, it does. Thanks, Bryce. I'm heading back to the station. I'll see you soon." Just as she ended that call, another arrived. She answered, "Ellis here."

"Detective, this is Dr. Rivera. Do you have a moment to talk?"

"Yes, sir, I do. I'm surprised to hear from you. Does this mean you have labs back?" Ellis headed back onto the 95, driving south toward the station.

"I have some preliminary information for you, yes."

"Well, don't keep me in suspense, Doc. What'd you find out?"

"The tox screen indicated opioids in Carter's system at the time of his death."

Ellis sighed. "Why doesn't that surprise me? He'd come out of rehab only weeks earlier and obviously went right back to using again."

"But that's not all, Detective," he continued. "As you know, I saw no indication of bruising around the neck. However, markers were discovered in the brain suggestive of hypoxia."

"Hypoxia? That's suffocation, right?"

"A lack of oxygen to the brain, yes. In addition to the immunochemistry markers in the brain, I also noted petechial hemorrhages of the conjunctivae. The little red spots found on the skin. As well as pulmonary edema."

"Which means?" It was a good thing Rivera couldn't see the frustration in her face.

"While Carter did have opioids in his system, they were not enough to be the primary cause of death. Although I have more to work through for a final determination, I wanted to let you know that my current findings suggest hypoxia. Suffocation. Detective, I believe Carter died from suffocation."

"And it was meant to look like an overdose?" she asked.

"That, I'm afraid, I can't tell you."

"Right. I'm the detective. I have to figure that one out. Listen, Doc. Thank you. I know you pushed this up to the top of the pile, and I appreciate it. More than you know."

"Of course. I hope to have the final report issued in the next week. If anything changes, though I doubt it will, I'll let you know immediately."

"Thank you. Goodbye." She ended the call, staring at the

road ahead. The exit approached, and she almost missed it. "Shit." Ellis veered off, still in a haze of emotion. She had been certain Carter had done this to himself, but now? Was it possible he'd been murdered? Who would've done it—and why?

She arrived at the station, marching to the stairs and climbing with purpose. Confusion replaced what had been a sense of detachment over the loss of her brother. She needed to talk to Abbott.

Abbott glanced up at her as she appeared in his doorway. "Becca, you all right?" He removed his reading glasses and narrowed his gaze. "Come in; sit down. Tell me what happened."

Ellis dropped onto the chair. "Much more than I expected. I just got a call from the coroner."

"Rivera already has results?"

"Preliminary, yes, sir." She licked her lips, her fingers tucking hair behind her ear. "Sarge, Rivera says the primary cause of Carter's death was hypoxia. He had drugs in his system but, according to Rivera, not enough to kill him."

Abbott let out a sigh.

Ellis steadied her voice, realizing now that not only had her mother been murdered all those years ago, but now maybe her brother had been too. "Suffocation. How could that have happened if not at someone else's hands?"

Abbott leaned back, lacing his fingers together over his desk. "It is possible he passed out from the drugs, accidentally smothering himself in a pillow or bedding. Maybe someone he was with got scared, thinking they'd get blamed. Took him down to the river...What makes you think someone else did it?"

She considered his question. The suffocation could easily have been of his own doing, but then how had he ended up in the Penobscot? No one would've gone to that much trouble unless they'd killed him. And what did Tyler Beck have to do with it?

"Well, Sarge, I suppose you could be right. But drug addicts, they know to be careful about positioning themselves in a certain way. On their sides as a way to keep from choking on their own vomit. And Carter was an experienced addict. He knew these things. The man in the video I found? His name is Tyler Beck. He served time with Carter and was also transferred to the same rehab facility."

Ellis aimed a steadfast gaze at Abbott. "This can't be ignored, Sarge. I need to know for certain whether or not my brother was murdered."

"Becca, come on." Abbott leaned back in his chair. "You're too close. Don't ask me to let you do this when you know I can't."

She rested her elbows on her thighs. "Hank deserves to know the truth, and he would want it to come from me. He deserves my full attention on this, no matter the outcome."

"For God's sake, Becca." Abbott glanced away, a sigh escaping his lips. "Fine. But you'll be working with Euan on this, you got it? I let you run this alone, and, in the event your hunch about murder is right, the DA will have my ass. Any defense lawyer worth his salt will claim conflict of interest. And they'll be right. But if you do this with a partner, then we can legitimize it in the eyes of the court should it come to that."

"Fair enough." She nodded. "It'll be me and Euan. Done." Ellis got up and headed out of Abbott's office. But before she roped McCallister into this, she needed to see Pelletier.

On her return inside the bullpen, Pelletier looked up from his desk, waving her over.

She made her way toward him. "Bryce, you come up with a location for Beck?"

He wore a closed-lipped smile and held a file in his hands. "Your boy, Beck. He has quite the history."

"I'm aware. He served time with Carter and then was with him in rehab. What I need to know now is a location. Where is this guy?"

"The address for the halfway house is in the file." He firmed his grip on it. "I read this guy's sheet, Becca. We're talking a possible connection to a Mexican drug cartel. If your brother was connected to that..." He shook his head.

Ellis took the file. "Yeah, well, it is what it is. I appreciate you getting this for me. I owe you."

He nodded. "I'll hold you to it."

She clicked her tongue and winked at him before heading over to her desk. Looking at McCallister now, he seemed to have picked up on the conversation. Now was the time to bring him into the fold.

Working with him again after doing a pretty good job keeping him at arm's length meant she'd have to set aside her disappointment about how he'd handled the Connor situation. A momentary lapse in judgment last night didn't erase what had happened. Was she being too hard on him? A man who'd helped her more times than she could count? Probably.

And just when the team was feeling like a cohesive unit again, could she hold this against him? She hadn't held Bevins to the same standard, so why be so hard on him? It was a question she didn't want to know the answer to.

"Hey." She handed over the file. "Abbott wants you and me on this."

McCallister glanced at it. "On what?"

"Carter. Preliminary cause of death was hypoxia, not drugs. While I can't be sure Carter was the cause of his own death, I can't be sure he wasn't. It's possible someone suffocated him to death. We start by talking to Tyler Beck, the man in the security footage at the riverwalk. So what do you say? You and me working together again. You good with that?"

He smiled. "Always."

"Then let's go find Beck."

6

C hances were good that if Tyler Beck had anything to do with Carter's death, he wouldn't be hanging around town. Let alone at the first place anyone would think to look for him—the halfway house. Nevertheless, he was still a man on parole with limited options, so Ellis and McCallister headed in that direction now to cover their bases.

Ellis kept her gaze on the road ahead. "I hope we aren't wasting our time."

"If Beck isn't there, and he's gone dark, it could add weight to the theory Carter was murdered. At the very least, it makes the guy look guilty as hell." McCallister checked his phone. "Map says we're only a few minutes away. If Beck's not there, we'll find someone willing to talk."

"Yeah, I hope so." She pondered whether she'd cut Carter too much slack. His cause of death, as Abbott had pointed out, still could have been of his own doing. But too many other things leading up to it didn't jibe.

McCallister nodded ahead. "Make a right here, Becca."

"Got it." She made the turn, arriving at an older neighborhood. Single-level homes. Small, dated, looking worse for wear. The street was lined with trees, their leafy canopies shading it as she drove. Front yards were overgrown and weedy. Shingled rooftops appeared a hodge-podge of colors from patchwork repairs over the years.

"It's the third on the left," he added.

Ellis rolled to a stop in front of the house. The green wood siding was faded and chipped. The front yard was fenced in with a low chain-link, and the paint on the porch railing had peeled. It was a state-run home, so its current, unloved condition didn't come as much of a surprise.

She cut the engine and unbuckled her seat belt. McCallister reached out for her arm. She looked at him. "What is it?"

"Listen, Becca, I know you're not impressed by how I handled things with Connor. And this probably isn't the right time, but I have to tell you that he'd asked me to keep it quiet. I chose to respect his wishes. I guess I'm bringing this up now because I want you to let me back in. Not out of grief or sadness over your brother, but because you want me here." He peered at the home. "I want us to be a team again. We can figure out what happened to Carter together."

She looked away for a moment, feeling the weight of this relationship bearing down at a time when another ounce just might break her. "Is Connor going to be able to get out of this?"

"I don't know...He's not asking for your help or mine. He's handling this on his own. I guess we'll have to wait and see."

Ellis opened her door. "I want us to be a team again too."

She stepped down onto the sidewalk, turning her sights on the house.

McCallister joined her as they walked toward the front porch, through the unlocked chain-link gate. Ellis knocked on the door. Within moments, it opened.

Behind it stood a middle-aged man with a stubbled beard, wearing a T-shirt and khaki shorts, looking like he already knew they were cops. "What do you want?"

A warm welcome if there ever was one, she thought. "Detectives Ellis and McCallister. Bangor PD. We'd like to talk to you about Carter Ellis and Tyler Beck, if you have a moment."

"Sorry to disappoint, but neither is here." The man started to close the door.

Ellis thrust out her hand. It seemed he didn't know about Carter. "Do you know where we can find Mr. Beck? Carter Ellis is dead, and we believe Beck might know something about that."

The man hesitated, eyeing Ellis. "You're related to Carter Ellis?"

"Yes, sir. He was my brother."

He cast down his gaze. "Sorry about that. I didn't know he was...anyway, come in. His things are here."

Ellis walked inside the dusky house, noting the drawn curtains in the living room. A single light was switched on over the nearby kitchen sink. A couch and loveseat were positioned in front of a small television, and a few men sat on spindle-backed chairs at the table.

"What is your name, sir?" Ellis headed into the living room.

"Oliver Rice," he replied. "I run the home."

"What can you tell me about Carter and Tyler Beck?" She took a seat, McCallister dropping down next to her.

Rice sat down across from them. "I run a tight ship here. We have rules and curfews. Carter and Tyler shared a room. Both adhered to the rules. I got no trouble from them." He rubbed his thumb into his palm. "I didn't know Carter was dead."

"We found him in the Penobscot," Ellis said matter-of-factly. "And we suspect Beck might know what happened to him, or maybe he even saw something. That's what we're trying to find out."

"Tyler moved out a couple days ago."

Ellis raised her brow. "How was he allowed to move out?"

"Paperwork came through. I didn't question it." He paused a moment, as if considering his next words carefully. "There were rumors about what Carter and Tyler were into when they came here."

"What kind of rumors?" Ellis asked.

"That they were dealing. They both seemed to have money all the time."

Carter had had drugs in his system when he died, suggesting he was using again. But Ellis wondered…"Was Carter still clean, that you were aware of?"

"It wasn't my job to know that. They had parole officers who conducted regular drug tests. If they were using, the POs were supposed to send them back to Cochran House or back to jail, depending on their deal."

"But Carter was only here for what, less than a month?" Ellis continued. "Based on your experience, do you believe he was using?"

Rice appeared reluctant to answer.

McCallister chimed in, his voice calm but probing.

"What about after Tyler left? Did anyone else show up looking for him? Or for Carter?"

"No. No one gives a shit about these guys. Any of them. Just their POs; they're the only people who show up."

As far as Ellis was concerned, this conversation wasn't going anywhere. She needed to get to the point and move on. "So you don't know where Tyler Beck is?"

"No, ma'am. I'd tell you if I did. Best bet is for you to reach out to his parole officer. See if he's made contact. Other than that, as far as I'm concerned..." He shrugged. "I did what I could for those two. I'm sorry about your brother, sincerely."

Ellis rose from the couch. "Could you show me Carter's room?"

"Of course. Like I said, he shared with Tyler." Rice got up and headed into the hallway. "It's down here."

Ellis followed with McCallister beside her.

Rice reached for his keys to unlock the door.

She narrowed her gaze. "You have a key to the room?"

"Oh yeah. I have keys to all the bedrooms. This is a halfway house, Detective. These men don't yet have the full freedom of life on the outside." He opened the door and turned on the light.

She glanced at McCallister, her hackles raised. "Would you mind if we take a look around?"

"No, ma'am. You go right ahead." Rice thumbed back. "I'll, uh, I'll just go hang out in the kitchen. You need some garbage bags or something? Figure you'll want to take his things with you."

Ellis surveyed the messy room. She could smell her brother. That lingering hint of musky cologne he wore mixed with a hint of weed. "Not today, thanks."

"Sure thing, Detective. Well, take as much time as you need."

When he left, Ellis stood inside the room. A couple of twin beds. Both unmade. Rickety old dressers. Fast-food wrappers.

McCallister took in the scene. "They weren't clean freaks."

"Carter never was." She walked ahead. "I think this was his side. There's a picture of his mom and Hank. Well, I guess we should look for a laptop or phone. Anything that might answer some questions, huh?"

"I suppose so." He moved toward her. "This can't be easy, Becca. We can have someone else do this."

"No. I mean, maybe someone else can bag everything up, but it should be us looking to see if he left anything we can use as evidence behind."

"All right." McCallister carried on searching the room.

She felt Carter's presence all around her; she couldn't help imagining him sitting on his bed, a needle in his arm. Imagining him dealing drugs and working with Tyler Beck and, maybe, members of a ruthless cartel. It occurred to her that Hank had been right. At the time of Carter's arrest, Hank had insisted prison was the worst place for him. Ellis had pushed back, wanting Carter to serve time for what he'd done, believing it would set him on the right path. Now he was dead. Either having suffered from his own mistake, or because someone else had made him pay for one.

Her emotions caught in her throat as she went through his things, finding nothing but inconsequential remnants of her brother's life. She couldn't contain her sobs any longer.

"Hey." McCallister drew near, wrapping an arm around her. "Listen, I don't see anything. No tech. Why don't we get out of here? Come back another time? We need to find Beck, right? Let's shift our focus to that."

Ellis cleared her throat, a little embarrassed. "Yeah, okay. Let's get out of here."

They returned to the front room, where Rice stood with his back against the kitchen sink, waiting. "Thank you for your help, Mr. Rice." She nodded at McCallister. "We're going to head out, but, uh, we'll be back another time to collect Carter's belongings."

"Yes, ma'am." Rice walked them to the front door. "They'll be safe here till you do."

Ellis stepped outside, raising her face to feel the warmth of the sun, and taking a calming breath.

McCallister stepped out to join her, and the door closed behind them. "Come on. Let's get out of here."

They walked along the path, and a car that hadn't been there when they arrived caught Ellis's attention. "Black Lexus. Ten o'clock."

He shifted his gaze almost imperceptibly as they returned to her SUV. "Curious."

Ellis pressed the remote to open her door and got inside. Once McCallister climbed in, she regarded him. "Looks like a fed to me."

MOST OF THE team was away from their desks, each working their own cases. Abbott hadn't assigned Bevins anything since all this came out, probably fearing he wouldn't be around to see it through. Nevertheless, he was going to do everything in his power to make sure he stuck around for a long time. And that started with a phone call.

With the phone at his ear, Bevins glanced through the window inside the bullpen. The line rang...

"DES, how may I direct your call?"

The West Point Directorate of Emergency Services, or DES, handled law enforcement for not only the academy, but the town as well. They were the military police, and Bevins had a contact inside. Or at least, he used to.

"Yeah, I'd like to speak with Captain Chris Murphy, please."

"Who's calling?" the operator asked.

"Detective Connor Bevins. Bangor Police."

"One moment. I'll connect you."

Bevins waited, listening to staticky soft rock elevator music in the background. "Go, Army." He rolled his eyes.

When the line picked up again, a voice sounded. "Connor?"

Bevins smiled. "Yeah, man, it's me. How you doing, Murph? Wasn't sure you'd still be there."

"Oh yeah. I'm here. I'm doing good, brother. It's been a long time. What's going on?"

It felt good to talk to someone from his West Point days. Chris Murphy, or Murph as he'd always been referred to back then, had graduated the year he was supposed to graduate and was already a captain. Bevins felt a twinge of jealousy. "I wanted to ask you about something. Something about what happened before I left the academy."

The line went quiet for a moment. "I'm not sure I know what you're talking about."

This was where Bevins had to be careful. If Jack had pulled the right strings, and Captain Murphy needed to keep his mouth shut, well, this conversation was going nowhere fast.

"Yeah, uh, that's fine. Hey, are you still living at the same place?"

"Sure, man. But I got married last year, so the wife is there with me."

"Married?" Bevins raised his brow. "That's great, man. Congratulations."

"I would've extended an invite..."

"No, don't worry about it." Bevins already knew that associating with him was frowned upon by those at the academy. "I'm still here in Bangor, working as a detective in CID."

"A detective? Congrats. I'll bet it's nothing like Army CID," Murphy replied.

"To be honest, it's not all that different. But hey, you know, I was thinking, maybe we could catch up soon? I could give you a buzz on your day off? Why don't you drop me your digits?"

"Absolutely. That'd be great. Or, you know, I'm usually home after six, so anytime, man. I mean that. I'll give you my email, and we can exchange numbers."

Bevins smiled, realizing Murph was still an ally. "I'll take you up on that. Shoot." He grabbed a pen and jotted the info down on a sticky note. "Listen, I'll let you get back to it. We'll talk soon, man." He ended the call.

The first step had been taken. Murph hadn't changed at all. Nothing slipped past this guy. Even now, his cryptic words, intended to prevent eavesdroppers from hearing his phone number, had been as smooth as silk. The Army recorded conversations, whether or not they were supposed to. The question remained, could Bevins get the information he needed without landing his buddy in hot water?

In the meantime, Bevins had tracked down the blogger and had left him a message about the possibility of meeting up. And now, coincidentally, an email from him had just arrived. As Bevins opened it, he smiled. "This day is looking up." He snatched his keys and headed out.

The blogger didn't reveal his location. Instead, he said he'd drive to meet Bevins. That meeting was slated to happen within the hour.

Bevins drove out to the riverwalk, only a few minutes away. The sky was clear with idyllic temperatures warming the air. A few clouds floated above as he stepped out of his Mustang, smoothing down his tie and shirt.

The café was straight ahead. Bevins figured this guy already knew where he worked, so picking a nearby spot upped the odds he could make the appointment. Although he would've met him anywhere, it was best not to seem too desperate. Even if he was.

Caution was in order because Bevins' first instinct was to punch the guy's lights out for what he'd done. But could he be blamed? The blogger was putting out a story of potential corruption. Would he be easily swayed from his agenda?

As he arrived, Bevins opened the door of the café. When it closed, the sound of the river, the birds, and the cars faded, replaced by light music and clanking silverware. A picture of the blogger was on his website, so Bevins knew whom to look for. He kept his eyes peeled for the young man in his twenties, on the thin side and average-looking with short brown hair.

There he was. Sitting at a table for two, sipping on an iced coffee. Bevins approached. "Asher Daly?"

The man pulled his gaze from the window. "Detective Bevins. Please sit down. Thank you for meeting me on such short notice."

Bevins pulled out a chair to sit. "I should be thanking you. I appreciate you making the drive."

"How could I not?" He wrapped his lips around the straw and slurped his drink. "You're the subject of one of my most popular posts."

Bevins worked hard to maintain his cool, keeping in mind the guy was doing what he thought was right. And when the server came around, he ordered himself a Pepsi.

"I could ask what's on your mind," Daly said. "But I have a feeling I already know. So the question is, why are you coming to me?"

Bevins waited for the server to return with his drink. He slowly peeled away the paper from the straw and dropped it inside the glass. Finally, he took a long sip, intentionally drawing out the process. "Well, I should start by asking how you got that photograph."

"Of the accident?" Daly raised his brow. "Why do you want to know?"

"Why?" Bevins raised his brow. "Because it was a matter for the Army. Not intended for public knowledge."

"A matter for the Army?" Daly nodded. "Seems to me it was a matter for you and your dad to try to cover up. What about the kid who died in that car, huh?"

"He was my friend. It was an accident," Bevins replied. "Nothing more."

"Oh, I think there's a lot more to it than that. Especially considering the guy who died." Daly shrugged. "No one seems to know who he was. That's strange, don't you think?"

Daly was different than how he behaved on his blog. Less arrogant, but still somehow annoying. Bevins leaned forward, his eyes narrowing. "You think you know something, don't you? Something that nobody else does."

Daly smirked. "Maybe I do, maybe I don't. But it seems like you're the one with something to hide, Detective. You should check with your dad. He probably knows where the photo came from."

Bevins clenched his jaw, frustration bubbling beneath the surface. "Look, I get you want to be popular, have influence. Gain followers, whatever. But this is something you have no idea about. It's not a political statement. It's not a statement about Big Brother. This will ruin lives."

Daly turned serious. "And whose lives are we talking about? Yours? Your father's? What about the life of the person who died?"

"The information you have is classified. Having it in your possession is a felony. Sharing it will only compound your troubles." Bevins leaned back, ensuring his badge was on full display.

Daly fixed his gaze on Bevins. "I am a reporter, Detective. And as such, I have sources that I must protect."

"A reporter." He scoffed. "A real reporter would verify claims. Obtain multiple sources. You're nothing more than a hack who's peddling false information. Dangerous information, at that."

A glint of satisfaction appeared in Daly's eyes. "I'll tell you how I got the photo if you tell me the truth about what happened. I'll get your side of the story out there for all to hear."

Bevins released the tension in his clenched fist. He took a deep breath, composing himself. "There's not a lot of love lost between my father and me." He considered Daly's proposal, but could this guy be trusted? And if he put his cards on the table, would it even matter at that point how

Daly got the photo? The story would be out there. His life and his career would be over.

"How about you start with the fact that your father helped you cover up the death of your passenger?" Daly said.

There had to be another way. What did this guy want? Money? Fame? Followers? Status? Bevins had to offer him something more valuable than this story. Something that would shut him up about all of it. "You call yourself a reporter. Fine. If that's what you really want to be, I can help you with that. I can get you recommendations. I can get you hired wherever you want to work—in exchange for dropping this."

Daly returned a half-cocked smile. "How do you propose to do that?"

"You said yourself, my father is a powerful man. He knows people. So the deal stands. Drop the story and you'll get to write your own ticket," Bevins replied. "You help me, and I'll help you. Your choice."

7

Ellis kept her eye on the rearview mirror and on the car behind them. They had remained in front of the halfway house for a few minutes, and so had the black Lexus. "What do you think?"

"He doesn't seem to want to do anything until we leave, so we could go ask what he's doing here," McCallister said.

Ellis opened her car door. "Exactly what I was thinking." Stepping out, she waited a moment for McCallister to catch up, and the two headed back toward the car.

The man inside kept focus on them, seeming to gauge whether they would continue his way. As they drew near, he stepped out. He looked to be about thirty to thirty-five. Short brown hair. Stocky guy, muscles bulging under his shirt. "Afternoon."

Ellis rested her hand on her waist, her badge visible. "Afternoon. Detective Ellis." Thumbing to McCallister, she continued, "Detective McCallister. Bangor PD. And you are?"

"Agent Sean Kroll, Drug Enforcement." He held up his

badge. "Good to meet you, Detectives. I was wondering how long you'd planned on sitting there."

"DEA, okay." Ellis glanced away, wearing a smile. "I figured you for a fed of some kind. Can I ask what you're doing here?"

"I could ask you the same thing."

"We're investigating a suspected murder," McCallister cut in. "You? Looking for an easy target for your bosses by hanging around a halfway house?"

Kroll grinned. "Not exactly." He regarded Ellis. "Whose murder?"

"Doubt you'd know him."

Kroll nodded. "Well, we could stand here and trade jabs, or we can sit down somewhere and have a talk. Because I have a feeling we might be looking into the same thing. You two have some time right now?"

Ellis turned to McCallister, who nodded. "I think we can make that work." She eyed Kroll. "Lead the way."

They headed back to her Tahoe, and after entering, Ellis pressed the ignition. "What the hell is the DEA doing here?"

McCallister buckled his seat belt. "We're about to find out."

When Kroll pulled out in front of them, Ellis trailed. "You think Beck is a DEA informant? It would explain why he hasn't been seen in days."

"Anything's possible. And if he is, Kroll might have some idea where we can find him. Might know about Carter too." He turned to Ellis. "Let's keep our cards close to our chests. I'm not sure we want to tell him Beck was nearby shortly before your brother was found."

"We'll let him open up and see if he's got information we

can use." Ellis followed the car ahead for another mile or two. "Looks like he's pulling into that diner."

"Suppose I could use some lunch," McCallister said.

"Same here." She parked next to him, and the two stepped out.

Kroll approached them, gesturing outward. "After you."

Inside, they followed the host to a booth that faced the parking lot. It was a small place, booths lining either side of the walkway. A few too many hanging plants and brass fixtures, but otherwise, it seemed decent enough.

Taking a seat opposite Kroll, Ellis waited for McCallister to slide in next to her. "Okay, now that we're here, let's talk. Agent Kroll, we're looking for Tyler Beck. Any chance you know him?"

Kroll picked up the menu, his shirt pulling taut around his biceps. "Beck's been on our radar, yes. We figure he's got some involvement in a trafficking operation here in Bangor."

"Any idea where he can be found?" McCallister asked.

"I know he was living at the halfway house. In fact, I was preparing to meet with the guy who's in charge there to see what he knows."

Ellis rested her arms on the table. "We're looking for him too. So, you hadn't spoken to anyone at the halfway house yet? How'd you know Beck had been there?"

Kroll sighed, his eyes darting between Ellis and McCallister. "Look, Detectives, if you're investigating a homicide, it might be a good idea to share some details with me too. Could be we have something else in common."

"Beck is a potential witness to our suspected homicide." Ellis recalled McCallister's suggestion of holding off on certain facts. But Kroll clearly wasn't going to offer up intel without some in return.

Kroll set down the menu as the server arrived. "Yeah, I'll take a cheeseburger and Coke."

"BLT for me, please," Ellis added.

McCallister handed her his menu. "Same here, thanks."

The server jotted down their order. "Great. I'll be back shortly with your food."

Kroll waited for her to fall out of earshot, aiming his gaze at Ellis. "Here's what I do know. Trafficking activity in Bangor has tripled in the past two years. Most of what flows in is being trafficked by the Mexican cartel pushing north up into the Canadian border. I'm here because we suspect Tyler Beck had a connection. Someone in prison, most likely, where we know he'd also served time. I'd like to find him or that connection."

Ellis figured McCallister probably had a better handle on the drug trade here in the city. Not so long ago, he'd worked a case of multiple overdoses, eventually hunting down the supplier. But where had Beck gotten his supply from? That seemed to be where the DEA wanted to step in. "So you're saying that Tyler Beck may have been involved in some kind of drug ring inside the prison?"

"It's a strong possibility," Kroll replied. "We've been monitoring their activities for months now. It seems like they were facilitating the trafficking of drugs from within the prison and coordinating with their contacts on the outside. Then when they ended up in the halfway house, things may have come to a head."

Ellis leaned back in her seat, absorbing the implications of Kroll's words and how they related to her brother. If Beck had been involved in a cartel operation, had Carter been too? If so, were they the ones who killed him?

"Listen." Kroll rested his elbows on the table. "Tell me who your suspected homicide investigation involves, because if you're looking for Beck, then your victim may also be part of what I'm working on. And if that's the case, we should consider some kind of joint operation."

Ellis had no experience working with the feds. She had no idea what that kind of operation would look like. All she wanted to know was whether Carter had been murdered, and if he had, then by whom.

"It'll take some coordination between my assistant special agent-in-charge and your boss," Kroll continued. "But we might need each other on this. You two open to that?"

She regarded McCallister and realized that an unspoken agreement had been reached. Ellis turned to Kroll again. "We might be able to help each other out."

THEY'D RETURNED to the station, having no more information about Tyler Beck's whereabouts than when they'd left. But now that they'd learned about the DEA's involvement, the game had changed.

Ellis and McCallister appeared in Abbott's doorway. "Sarge?" she asked. "You have a minute?"

He sat up in his chair. "Course I do. Come in."

Ellis took her seat and launched right in. "Sarge, the DEA's got their hands all over this case."

Abbott tilted his head. "Carter's investigation?"

"My guess is, yes, because they knew about the guy we were looking for," McCallister cut in. "Suggesting they know a hell of a lot more than we do. Agent Sean Kroll just so happened to be at the halfway house when we arrived. We came out...the guy was still there. So we had a chat with him." He nodded at Ellis to continue.

"He was looking for the man I'd seen in the surveillance video, peering into the river."

"Tyler Beck," Abbott confirmed.

Ellis shot an uncertain glance at McCallister. "Yes, sir. How'd you know?"

Abbott tapped on the phone that lay on his desk. "I already got a call from the DEA's assistant special agent in charge in Buffalo. Their man was heading back on the four p.m. flight."

"Their man, Kroll." Ellis nodded. "Why are they involved, Sarge? Kroll says Mexican cartel."

"Increased trafficking bleeding over into Bangor," Abbott replied. "We haven't been completely blind to that. Moss and his narcotics team are becoming well-versed. What'd this guy have to say about Beck? Did you mention Carter?"

"We didn't tell him about Carter." Ellis shrugged. "And he didn't have much of anything on Beck, or if he did, wasn't willing to offer it up. What do you think about going in on this with them, Sarge?"

Abbott sighed, rubbing his temples with his meaty fingers. "Damn DEA. Always thinking they can waltz into our jurisdiction and take over. But this time, they might actually be onto something. Certainly, yes, if it helps with figuring out what happened to Carter."

Ellis leaned forward, her eyes narrowing. "Can we trust Kroll?"

McCallister scratched his stubbled chin. "He's holding

back. Same as us. But it might be in our best interest to work together."

Abbott firmed his jaw, cementing his apparent resolve. "Here's what we'll do. I'll agree to their suggestion of a joint task force, of sorts. We need to make sure our interests align and that they're not hiding anything from us. We're still going to investigate Carter's death, but we need to find a way to work with these guys. Beck seems to be the key, and his connection to Carter might shed some light on what happened to him."

BEVINS INSERTED his key into the front door of his apartment, the metallic click echoing in the quiet hallway. Stepping inside, he dropped his keys and wallet into a bowl on a table near the entrance.

He walked through to the living room, peering out at the trees that surrounded his building. Their lush green leaves rustled gently in the evening breeze. The summer sky had finally surrendered to night. Bevins checked the time. "Eight o'clock. Murph should be home by now."

After the unexpected meeting with the blogger, he was no more certain what the man would do, even after his offer. It was a solution Jack would easily get behind, but would Daly go for it? Daly had left after insisting he'd only take it under advisement. Bevins scoffed. "Take it under *advisement*." He shuffled into the kitchen, opening the fridge for a bottle of beer.

His buddy Murph was his best hope for information. Daly hadn't given him a name or even a hint about how he'd got hold of the damning photo. Bevins wasn't going to sit back, not knowing what direction the blogger would take.

He picked up his phone and dialed Murph's number. Each ring echoed in his ear like a timer counting down.

After what felt like an eternity, Murph's deep voice filled the line. "Hey, man. I'm glad you called." His voice was gruff but warm, a welcome sound amid all this uncertainty.

Bevins sank into his sofa, its plush black cushions molding around him. "I figured I picked up on what you meant. Sounds like I was right. I'm grateful, man. Truly."

"I know you are," Murph replied with a chuckle. "I can guess what this is about."

"Yeah..." Bevins trailed off, the words catching in his throat. "Someone got hold of something that, should it gain traction, is going to ruin me and my dad. But rather than turn tail, I'm looking for answers."

"Oh, man." Murph sighed. "I don't know if I have the answers you need. You know how it works."

"I just need the report," Bevins pushed on. "I know it's been years, but do you think it's something you can track down?"

His friend went quiet for a moment. "Man, I have no idea whether it even still exists. You know your dad. When he takes care of things...he really takes care of them."

Bevins released a bitter laugh. "Tell me about it. You think you can do some digging without raising any red flags? Look, I know what I'm asking is a lot—"

"I know you do," Murph cut him off gently. "But who is this for? You or your pop?"

Bevins hesitated a moment, his mind racing with unsaid thoughts and unasked questions. "If I can get to the bottom of it, then I think it'll give me closure, you know? As far as my dad? Well, that depends on what you find."

"Why are you doing this now, brother?" Murph asked. "I thought things were going well there in Bangor. You're like, a big-time detective."

He laughed. "Not big-time, no. But the thing is, like I said earlier, word's gotten out. And it's going to destroy everything I've built here." He paused again. "I had a good friend of mine remind me that maybe all isn't as it seems."

8

It was in the quiet that it had hit Ellis, coming in a constant flow of waves. Some strong like a tsunami, some gentle and rolling. Sitting on her couch under the light of the side table lamp, she felt Carter's loss. Not only the loss, but the guilt for how she'd treated him over the past years. Really, since his mother had died.

A part of her wondered if it was because he'd felt the same pain she had—losing his mom. Taking away the one thing that had belonged exclusively to her—grief. Of course, to compare the two events was impossible. But looking back on it all now...the kid had needed help, and she'd done everything she could to work against him. Not Hank, though. He was and would always be a good father. Now, and she almost crumpled under the weight of it, she was investigating what appeared certain to be Carter's murder.

Abbott was right; she was too close to take this on. In hindsight, she and McCallister should've turned Carter's room upside down. Instead, he'd whisked her away, leaving behind her grief amid the debris of her brother's final days. That was their relationship getting in the way of their partnership. Nevertheless, she wasn't going to remove herself from the case now. Not when the DEA had stuck its nose into their business.

A notification arrived on her phone, and Ellis glanced at it. "Oh my God." She jumped off the couch to grab her laptop, returning to her seat and opening it. Andrew had sent a text, wondering why she'd said nothing about the information he'd uploaded to the server.

The whole thing had escaped her thoughts. Ellis logged into the secure server and opened the files. Financials. He'd sent over the company's financials, bank statements. And then more bank statements from Myra's account and his. She pored over the information, searching for proof that Andrew had taken none of the money Myra had siphoned off.

There it was. Ellis drew back her shoulders. "An email. Holy shit, where did you get this?" But was this going to be enough? Alcott had said she had till the end of the day. Was she too late?

She glanced at the time. It was already after eight o'clock. She quickly typed a reply.

> Have you heard from the detective or the FBI?

Ellis waited only a moment for his reply.

> No. Did you see it? I'm outta time, Becca.
> Help me, please.

> I'll call Alcott now. Hang on.

She pressed the detective's contact, and the line answered after a single ring.

"I was about to give up on you, Detective," Alcott said. "Tell me you have something. Your time's up."

"I have evidence Myra Cook deposited money from the clients at her and Andrew's investment firm. I have their financials that show some of these same amounts as expenses."

"We know what we have on her." Alcott grunted. "What do you have to prove Andrew played no part?"

"I have his bank information—"

"So do I, Ellis. Try harder."

"And an email."

The line went silent for a moment. "I'm listening."

"It's from a client to Myra. The client is insisting his investment portfolio didn't match up with the statements the firm sent him. Andrew sent the attachments from the client as well, showing the discrepancies."

Alcott went quiet again. "Why hasn't this client come forward already? Surely, such an allegation would've been brought to the attention of the executive officers."

"Hang on." Ellis pulled away her phone to type the message to Andrew. She waited a moment, and then he replied.

> Look at November, last year's bank statement. Myra deposited the money. It came back out in February, when the client called her out.

Ellis smiled and returned to the call. "I have Myra's bank statements that show the money from that client was deposited into her personal account; then when she got caught out, she returned it months later."

"How did you happen on this information, Detective Ellis? I've been working with the feds for months, yet you've been involved for a mere few weeks—and you uncover this?"

She couldn't reveal Brown's part and knew this could come back to bite her. But it depended on Alcott and how far he would push it. "Detective Alcott, I have proof Andrew Cofield wasn't involved in this, no matter what Myra Cook was seeking to lie about to secure herself a deal."

"So that's how this is going to go, huh?" he asked. "Send me what you have. If you're right about this, then we'll start talking about how Mr. Cofield can assist us further with our investigation into Myra Cook."

"You won't book him on charges tonight?" Ellis asked, determined to press her point.

"Tonight? No. But I'll get back with you as soon as I can to see where things are at. Good night, Detective Ellis. I'll be on the lookout for that information."

"Good night." Ellis ended the call and typed a rapid reply to Andrew.

> Alcott agreed to take a look. I'm sending everything over to him now. Do yourself a favor, stay as far away from Myra as possible.

> Thank you, Becca. I know what this could've cost you.

She scoffed to herself, but didn't reply. "It still could."

ELLIS DIDN'T LET Hank in on all she'd learned from Agent Kroll. Not until she could be certain they were on the right track. Now, this morning, as she'd arrived at the station, McCallister seemed to have been waiting for her.

"Kroll sent over his files," he said. "Have you taken a look yet?"

Ellis dropped her bag at her chair. "I saw the email come through, but no, I haven't read it."

McCallister rounded his desk, walking toward her. "He's coming into town to stay for a while. Says his people agreed to the joint investigation."

"Which means Abbott did too," Ellis replied. "But no information on Beck's whereabouts? He's who we need to find right now."

"Nothing yet. Kroll said he'd arrive by midafternoon. He'll be checking into a hotel near us, so we'll be able to coordinate our efforts."

Ellis opened the files on her laptop. "Looks like he's been investigating a connection to the prison in Warren for a while." She looked at McCallister. "Maybe we should see what we can find on our own there before he arrives. I get this guy's DEA and all, but if drugs are coming in from the north, filtering through Warren, and then someone on the inside is controlling how they get onto the street here...isn't this something we should get a handle on?"

McCallister nodded. "So, what are you thinking?"

Ellis checked the time. "It's a long drive, but it might be worth talking to whoever was in Carter and Tyler Beck's circle. We can be back before Kroll arrives."

"Can't hurt."

Within moments, she'd gathered her things again and

was prepared to leave when Detective Gabby Lewis appeared.

"Gabby, hey."

"Hey, guys. Listen, Becca, I know you have a lot on your plate with your brother and everything..." She trailed off but only for a moment. "And I overheard a little about what you have going on with the DEA. So I was thinking, I could work on obtaining the financial records of the Cochran House Rehab Center. Given that it's a state-run facility, those financials should be available to us."

"What do you hope to find?" McCallister asked. "If they're into something, kickbacks or whatever, they won't leave evidence of it on their books."

"No, you're right. But I can look to see how many people are getting referred there from Warren compared to other facilities. Could spot an imbalance. Check to see that the funds match the beds. Things like that." She shrugged. "I'm just saying, this must go beyond a random couple of guys, especially if the DEA is involved."

Ellis nodded. "We'd love the help, Gabby. But I thought you were working on something right now?"

"It's peanuts compared to this. Besides, I'm about ready to hand it over to the DA for prosecution." She eyed them. "Let me see what I can dig up. This is big. Maybe bigger than anything our department has been involved with. I don't want the DEA taking all the credit, you know?"

Ellis raised the corner of her mouth. "I hear you. Thanks, Gabby. Euan and I are going to make a run at the prison. Try to talk to those who hung around Carter or the guy we're looking for, Beck. So if you want to run on the financial side of this, we're happy for the help."

Lewis smiled. "Consider it done. You know, I left Chicago

for a lot of reasons, but this? The drugs and the cartels...were the biggest ones. We have to find a way to cut off these guys at the source...the money. I want to help make that happen."

"Then we'll catch up with you when we return," Ellis replied. "Thanks again, Gabby. We're glad to have you on board."

She tossed a nod at McCallister, and the two carried on toward the stairs, descending into the lobby. "I still feel like Kroll knows a lot more than he's letting on." Ellis pushed through the doors and strode toward the parking lot.

"It does feel like we might be his pawns while he works with the queen." McCallister walked around to the passenger side of her SUV.

Ellis unlocked it, and they stepped inside. The day was warm, bordering on muggy. She started the engine, flipping on the air conditioner. "Then let's get what we can before he moves in."

"Agreed."

It was an hour and a half from Bangor, south to Warren, where the correctional facility was located. Carter had spent about three months there before Hank pulled strings to get him sent to Cochran House in Bangor to serve out the remainder of his sentence. That sentence had been commuted by someone. Someone with connections that went far beyond anything Hank possessed.

As they drove on, silence surrounding them, Ellis felt McCallister's eyes on her. In the weeks that had passed since the night Bevins came over, a night that was supposed to have been a celebration for having solved their previous investigation, it had been one blow after another.

She stole a glance at him and saw the tension etched on his face. It mirrored her own internal struggle. The events of that night had cast a shadow over their relationship, leaving them both grappling with their emotions. They had been partners in more ways than one, but now their personal connection had turned fragile.

"Euan." Her voice fractured. "I haven't forgotten what you said about Bevins. Keeping your word with him."

"I don't want to push it. Not with everything else going on." McCallister hesitated a moment. "I just need to know if you still want me in your life. It hasn't felt like it in a while. And I know the other night...I've been trying to give you the space you need."

"I appreciate it, really, I do." Ellis kept her eyes forward, fearing what her expression might reveal.

He turned away, almost as if to shield his emotions from her. "Right now, I know your focus and mine is on finding out what happened to Carter. So that's what we'll do."

The silence between them felt a little easier until they at last arrived at the Maine state prison in the city of Warren, south of Bangor. A circular drive led to the entrance. In the center, an island of greenery and blooming summer flowers. A large flagpole with the state and US flags stood in front of the concrete block building. A pitched roofline in the center, it was otherwise linear with square columns. Only when the rest of the facility behind the façade came into view did its function become obvious.

Ellis stopped in the visitors' lot and cut the engine. "The only question now is, will anyone here talk to us?"

McCallister opened the door, glancing back at her. "Suppose that depends on what we have to offer them."

"If we have nothing?"

He smiled, raising his shoulder in a lopsided shrug. "As they say, we'll cross that bridge..."

"Right." Ellis climbed out and peered up at the clear morning sky. She took a breath to soothe the tension in her chest. Keeping herself detached and maintaining a neutral perspective was growing harder by the day.

They reached the double-doored entrance under the cover of a concrete overhang. Inside the lobby, officers sat at a long desk behind plexiglass with metal detectors blocking the entrance to the halls.

Ellis displayed her badge as she reached the desk. "Good morning, Detectives Ellis and McCallister. Bangor PD. We're looking to speak with the known associates of both Tyler Beck and Carter Ellis. They served time here together, and Carter Ellis was released about four months ago."

The man behind the admin desk typed in something on his computer. "Detectives, I'm going to have to get my boss to come talk to you. I can't release information like that without his approval."

"Thank you. We're happy to wait," McCallister replied.

They stepped away while the officer made the call.

A moment later, a tall, bulky man in a suit appeared. His receding hairline and salt-and-pepper beard suggested he was in his fifties. "Detectives. Associate Warden Bill Fenton." He outstretched his hand. "Nice to meet you. You've come a long way for something that we might've been able to resolve with a phone call."

"A conversation with inmates is ultimately what we were hoping to accomplish," Ellis replied. "Would that be possible?"

"Follow me. I'll see what I can do."

They trailed the warden back to his office after going through security and checking in their weapons. Once inside, he closed the door. "Tyler Beck and Carter Ellis."

Taking a seat at his desk, he narrowed his gaze and peered at Ellis. "Any relation?"

"Carter Ellis was my brother."

"Was?" Fenton's expression softened. "I'm sorry to hear that."

"Yes, well, we're here to find out who was in Carter and Tyler Beck's circle. Their friends. Anyone we can look at as a possible connection."

Fenton raised his chin. "Connection to what?"

Ellis felt hesitant to say much more, specifically as it related to the DEA's involvement. The cartel's reach was far and wide. No telling who was compromised. "Anyone who has an idea as to who wanted my brother dead. Maybe someone else who was recently released."

"Sir," McCallister cut in, "we'd like to talk to these people, and we are pressed for time. Will you authorize it?"

Fenton seemed to consider it a moment. "Of course. Anything I can do to help. Can't say they'll be willing to say much to you, but I don't have a problem with you trying." He opened his desk drawer to retrieve two visitors' badges. "Let's get you cleared, and I'll have the guards show you back."

They were ushered into a waiting area, Ellis still having no idea who they were about to see. She watched the comings and goings of staff. "How long do you think we'll have to wait here?"

McCallister looked around the entirely blank space. "I have no idea."

"Detectives?" A guard meandered toward them, his thumbs hooked into his duty belt. "I'll take you back now."

Ellis got to her feet, raising her brows at McCallister. They followed the guard to a room marked for visits.

"Right through here, please." He opened the door to reveal two men inside.

Ellis studied them a moment, her thoughts neutral with still no introductions having been made. "Thank you."

The large room housed tables with attached benches. Painted concrete walls and a few reinforced windows for light. Two other guards were posted in the corners, standing at attention.

The two men sat across from each other, their eyes darting between Ellis and McCallister. One of them was young with a thin frame and sunken cheeks. His clothes hung loosely on his body. The other man was older, heavier, his face etched with lines and tattoos.

Ellis took a seat next to the younger man while McCallister positioned himself opposite the inked man. "Gentlemen, I'm Detective Ellis, and this is Detective McCallister. We'd like to ask you about Tyler Beck and Carter Ellis. We understand you two knew them. Were you cellmates at any time?"

The younger man raised his leg over the other, slumping back in his chair. He glanced at the older one, seeming to wait for him to talk first.

This was going nowhere fast, so Ellis fixed her sights on the younger man. "Carter Ellis was found floating in the Penobscot River in Bangor a couple of days ago. And now Tyler Beck has gone missing. We're here because we'd like to know if you two were aware of anyone who might have wanted Carter dead. Did Beck have a beef with him?"

The older man crossed his powerful arms. "Why would we say shit to you?"

Ellis shrugged, turned her lips down. "You help us. We

help you. That's how this works." What help that might be, she had no idea, but McCallister seemed to play along.

The man eyed her, tilting his head. "Lady, no offense, but I'm no snitch."

"Being a snitch implies you know someone did something wrong. I'm simply asking you if, in your time here, you picked up on anyone who disagreed with Carter or Tyler. Or if you saw the two of them at odds."

The younger guy darted a side eye at the other inmate before looking at Ellis. "Carter and Tyler were friends. As far as any beef, lots of people in here have beefs. Only a few have the means to make someone pay for it once they're on the outside."

"They kept their heads down. Did what they were told and got out," the older man added. "That's it. That's all there is to say."

Ellis nodded. "Did as they were told. Okay." She glanced at McCallister. "I think we're done here."

McCallister got to his feet. "Yeah. Doesn't seem like these guys know anything else, so there's not much we can do for them."

They'd started toward the door when the young guy called out, "Hey. Wait."

Ellis turned around, looking at him as though she had the upper hand, even if she didn't.

"My parole hearing is next week. I've been denied once already," he said.

Ellis walked back toward them. McCallister beside her. "Hey, whatever you saw, I'm listening. What's your name?"

"Adrian Perez."

She nodded. "I'm willing to write a recommendation to the board if that's what it takes."

The older inmate swatted his hand almost petulantly. "Man, that ain't gonna do shit."

Ellis lifted an eyebrow. "Guess you won't know unless you try."

Perez appeared to consider his odds. "Beck, Ellis, and a few other guys...they all had the same lawyer, and they all got out within a couple months of each other."

Ellis knew Carter's lawyer had been court-appointed. To her knowledge, no lawyer had come here. They would've had no reason to when Hank stepped in to get him transferred to Cochran House. Unless a call from a lawyer had prompted Hank. She hadn't been involved in that.

"That lawyer got those guys put into some cushy rehab place." Perez raised his chin. "Must have been a damn good lawyer. Ain't none of those guys had that kind of cabbage for one."

"Okay, thank you for the information." She now carried on back to the door, where a guard stood watch. "We're ready to go."

"You gonna write that letter for me?" he called out again.

She turned back. "I'll keep my word, Mr. Perez."

The guard opened the door, and the detectives were led back out into the corridor, returning to the prison lobby. Without a word, Ellis walked outside, heading back to her Tahoe. She sensed McCallister's uncertainty.

"Who do you think could've provided a lawyer for those guys?" she asked, unlocking the vehicle.

He shrugged. "More importantly, I'd like to find out who the other prisoners were. We need names. If they're on the outside, we might be able to make the connection to Carter." He stepped into the passenger seat.

Ellis closed her door and pressed the ignition. "I have a

feeling we'll find them at Cochran House, too." She started to pull out of the parking lot. "I need to contact Carter's parole officer. Whoever it is, he or she could help us tighten up our timeline as to when he was killed."

McCallister opened the file in his computer bag. "Should be in here. Hang on." He went about searching through the information as Ellis drove on. "This is it. Name's Joe Mattson. I have a number here too."

"Let's give him a call," she replied.

He dialed the number, and the line rang twice before it was answered.

"Mattson speaking."

"Mr. Joe Mattson, this is Detective Euan McCallister, Bangor PD. I've got you on speaker here with Detective Rebecca Ellis."

"What can I do for you both?"

Ellis glanced over before she spoke. "You're the parole officer assigned to Carter Ellis?"

"I am."

"Then you know he's dead."

Mattson turned quiet a moment. "I was only recently made aware of that, yes, ma'am...Ellis? You're a relative?"

"I'm Carter's sister," she replied. "We're heading back to Bangor now after questioning some men at the state prison who also knew my brother. When was the last time you saw Carter?" She drove onto the highway, waiting for a response.

"He checks in every Friday at three p.m.," Mattson replied. "When he didn't show up this past Friday, I contacted the halfway house. Mr. Rice there said he hadn't seen Carter. That was when I issued a bench warrant."

Ellis narrowed her gaze. "When was that?"

"Would've been first thing Monday morning. I try to give these guys some rope, but it usually bites me in the ass."

She shot a look at McCallister. "That would've been the day before we found him."

"We'd have to check our database for the warrant," her partner replied. "Unless Carter had been stopped for something, our guys wouldn't have known about it."

"Mr. Mattson, who told you Carter was dead?" Ellis continued.

"I'm also the case manager for one of his associates at the halfway house. I had a meeting with him on Tuesday. A kid named Tyler Beck."

Ellis felt her face drain of color. "You saw Beck two days ago?"

"Yes, ma'am."

Her grip tightened on the steering wheel. "Do you know where he is now?"

"I assume at the halfway house." His confident tone faltered. "At least, that's where he's supposed to be."

9

Something unexpected had happened when Detective Gabby Lewis requested financial information on the government-funded Cochran House. She was told the only information available to the public was the annual budget. It turned out, if she wanted anything more, it would require a warrant.

Never one to let a setback like this dissuade her, Lewis headed over to the nearby courthouse. On her arrival, she stood at the front desk, warrant application in hand. "Morning."

"Detective Lewis," the clerk said, "what can I do for you?"

"Hey, Tony, I'm in a bind. Hoping Judge Russo is available." She held up the application. "Need to ask her to sign off on a warrant."

"You don't have an appointment?" Tony asked.

"No, sir, I sure don't. This here is a last-minute hiccup."

He picked up the phone, returning a smile. "Let me see if she has a minute to spare."

Lewis tapped her fingers on the counter. "You're a lifesaver." She waited while he made the call, and she was pleased to note that the look on his face suggested she wasn't going to leave here empty-handed.

After hanging up, Tony returned his attention to her. "Judge Russo can see you now. You're lucky. She's in between cases at the moment. You don't have much time."

Lewis revealed a bright smile. "I owe you." She started away. "Next time you get a speeding ticket..."

Tony laughed. "You'll clear it right up, will you?"

Lewis turned around and winked at him. "Okay, maybe a drink sometime, yeah?"

"You got it, Gabby."

She arrived at Judge Russo's office, knocking on the door. The judge was known for being a stickler for procedure, and she would want something Lewis didn't yet have—clear evidence.

"Come in."

Lewis opened the door.

Judge Russo peered up, her eyes crinkling at the corners, donning a grin. Evelin Russo was tough, but fair. In her late fifties, she'd served as a state prosecutor for twenty years before being appointed to the bench. Her full blond hair was cut just above her shoulders, and her style exuded elegance. "Detective Lewis, what brings you here today so unexpectedly?"

"I'm here to ask for your signature on a warrant, Your Honor," Lewis replied. "I'm looking to obtain financial records relating to the Cochran House Rehabilitation Center. It's integral to our investigation into the death of Carter Ellis."

"I had heard about that." The judge leaned back in her chair. "How's Becca doing?"

Lewis sighed, setting down the application on Russo's desk. "You know how she is, ma'am. Never letting anyone get close enough to see."

Russo nodded, then picked up the document, slipping on her reading glasses. "Yes, well, what grounds do you have for looking into this facility?"

"Your Honor, we have reason to believe that there may be illicit financial activity. Mounting evidence suggests several formerly incarcerated individuals, including Carter Ellis, had been transferred to Cochran House to serve out the remainder of their sentence."

Russo continued to read the application. "I thought it was Hank who managed to get his son transferred?"

"Yes, Your Honor, that is true. However, a handful of other inmates had also been transferred. I don't yet know the connection, which is part of the reason for this request."

Judge Russo set down the application. "Gabby, I trust your instincts, you know that. But I need something more than the suggestion of a connection. What else do you have?"

Now would've been the time to contact Ellis in the hope that she had gotten more details after visiting the prison. But it was too late for that. "Preliminary reports indicated Carter Ellis's death could be a homicide. Detective Ellis accessed surveillance video in the vicinity of where his body was found that revealed a man named Tyler Beck. Beck was also at Cochran House, both men having been moved to the same halfway house within weeks of each other. Both had also served time together in Warren."

Russo chewed on her lower lip, nodding thoughtfully.

This wasn't looking good, Gabby thought; she really needed to press her point. "Your Honor, we suspect a possible money trail or a kickback scheme from the prison to Cochran House. It's a longshot to be sure, but it's something Detective Ellis feels presents a strong lead. And so do I."

Lewis knew that her reputation preceded her. Her work in cyber money laundering and other financial crimes had been solid. But would it be enough for Russo to take a chance?

Russo sighed. "I must caution you that obtaining a warrant with what little you've provided would be unusual. You'll need solid evidence to convince me and the court that it's necessary to breach the privacy of Cochran House's financial records."

Lewis pressed her lips together, her determination unwavering. "I assure you that we are working diligently to gather all the necessary evidence."

"And when you have it, I'll be happy to reconsider." Russo handed back the application. "However, I'm unable to grant your request at this time. I suggest you and Detective Ellis continue your efforts in collecting additional details to demonstrate this link you suspect between Cochran House and any illicit financial activities."

Lewis straightened her posture, her eyes locking with Judge Russo's. "Your Honor, I understand the constraints and significance of obtaining a warrant—"

"I won't change my mind, Gabby," she cut in. "Come back when you have more."

WHEN BEVINS'S PHONE RANG, he hesitated to answer. The caller ID read "Murph." But here at the office, ears were all around, and he wasn't ready for everyone to know the severity of this situation. However, on surveying the bullpen, only Fletch was at her desk. The others were working on active investigations.

If Murph was calling, he had something. Could Bevins risk Fletch learning what he'd done, or could he be discreet enough to keep it from her? The call couldn't be ignored, so he answered. "Hey, Murph. What's going on?"

"Connor, you have a minute? I think I got what you're looking for."

Bevins shot a glance at Fletch, whose eyes were focused on her laptop. "Hang on." He walked out of the bullpen and made his way into the break room. "Yeah, man, what'd you find?"

"Believe it or not, I tracked down your car," Murph replied.

Bevins rocked back on his heels. "Are you shitting me? You found it?"

"I found it. It's in some junkyard upstate. MPs signed it over not long after the accident."

Realizing the implications, Bevins felt fear clutch his chest. "Wait, are you alone?"

"Course I am. Look, the report itself, I'm having trouble locating, but I don't know, maybe the car will help you out."

"Yeah, absolutely. Holy shit. I can't thank you enough for this, man."

"Don't thank me yet. I'll keep working on my end, but get yourself up there. I'll text you the address. Don't tell anyone there who you are, you got it? I mean it, brother. It could come back on me."

"Yeah, of course. Not a peep."

"I'll be in touch when I find out more," Murph said. "Take care, man."

The call ended. Bevins stood in stunned silence. This was the first step to uncovering the truth, the real truth. Maybe, he considered, Jack had told him the truth, but Jack looked out for himself, and saving his son's ass would always be a secondary consideration.

THEY'D SPENT MORE time in Warren than anticipated, so when Ellis and McCallister returned to the station, it was no surprise to see who awaited them.

Upon entering the bullpen, Ellis regarded the DEA agent as he leaned back against her desk. Beefy arms crossed, wearing a wide smile as though he ruled the roost. Before he'd even opened his mouth, he was pulling rank. She'd begun to understand Abbott's dislike for the federal authorities. Turning to McCallister, she whispered, "He beat us here." But before he could respond, Ellis offered her hand as they approached him. "Agent Kroll, I hear you'll be sticking around Bangor for a while."

He accepted her greeting. "For as long as it takes, Detective Ellis." Kroll reached down for his computer bag. "You have a place I can set up shop for a while?"

"Yeah, of course." McCallister gestured toward a nearby empty desk. "We keep a spot over here for visitors. This do the job for you?"

"Perfect."

Most of the team had their eyes fixed on them as they spoke to the agent. Ellis realized it was time for introductions. "Hey, guys," she began. "As you heard from the sarge's briefing yesterday, Euan and I will be working closely with DEA Agent Sean Kroll, who's visiting us from Buffalo."

"Good to meet you all." Kroll nodded. "I'll be sure and stay out of the way. So don't mind me. I appreciate you letting me take up some space." He set down his things.

McCallister tucked his hands into his pockets. "We'll let you get settled in, and then we can huddle up and start putting together a plan."

Kroll sat down. "Sounds great."

Ellis was returning to her desk when Lewis approached, her face masked with disappointment. "Let me guess, you didn't find anything suspicious in Cochran House's financials?"

"Apparently, only certain details are available publicly," Lewis replied. "And not the kind of details that would reveal any wrongdoing. So I applied for a warrant. Took a trip to see Russo."

Ellis raised a brow, knowing the judge's reputation. "How'd that go?"

Lewis shook her head. "Russo's being a hard-ass on this one. I need something to show her this is legit. A trail of some kind suggesting a connection might exist between Cochran House and the prison. Tell me you guys came up with something I can use."

Ellis glanced over at Kroll, who seemed busy organizing himself. Should she pull Lewis aside to discuss this further? Probably. She got up from her desk and nodded for Lewis to follow.

Once they reached the hall, Ellis continued, "One of the inmates said that more than a few guys got out at around the same time, including Carter. Though I know Hank's involvement there, so that's something to consider. Said they went to Cochran House thanks to the interventions of a lawyer none of them could afford."

"No other place? Just Cochran House?" Lewis set her hands on her hips. "There's at least half a dozen facilities between Warren and here."

"I know. Big red flag there. I still need to figure out the timings, because maybe when Hank was looking to pull strings to get Carter transferred, someone came along and aided in that effort."

"The same person or persons who aided the others," Lewis replied.

"Maybe." An idea began to take shape. "That's where we need to be looking, then. Those other men who got transferred."

"Prison records. We find out who's been transferred there and under what circumstances. Those are the guys we want to focus on." She aimed a finger at Ellis, a slight smile on her face. "You get enough people being transferred there as opposed to other facilities, that might be enough for Russo to reconsider."

"I couldn't agree more." Ellis placed her hand on Lewis's shoulder and led her back into the bullpen. "Thanks for going to see her. That was above and beyond. I appreciate it."

"Keep me posted," Lewis replied, "and you can be sure as hell I'll secure the warrant."

As Ellis headed back to her desk once more, Kroll marched toward her. "Sorry, did I hear you correctly? You're seeking a warrant? This about the case?"

She shot a glance at McCallister, letting him know that her efforts to keep this contained had failed. "Yeah. We're running on a lead."

Kroll turned up his palms, surprise on his face. "Care to fill me in?"

Lewis must've overheard the comment and cut in. "We're looking for financials on Cochran House. Suspicious activity reports. Anything like that to understand whether there's a chance the people running the facility are getting kickbacks or other monies flowing through."

"I see," he replied, hands on his hips.

Kroll didn't know about the prison visit, but it was clearly too late to keep the lid on the warrant. They were supposed to be working together on this, but Ellis wasn't willing to offer up details too easily. "You don't think that's a good idea?"

"I think if you're planning on making a move like that, then we should talk about it as a team."

She felt slightly heated by his remark. "You weren't here. We got a hunch and ran with it. Unless you already have this information, we think it's worth looking into. And since we've only just partnered up on this, then from here on out, consider yourself in the loop."

"Good. Thank you. And no, I don't have that information. But I can show you what I do have." He returned to his desk, grabbing his files. "Should we dig into this now?"

Ellis followed him. "No time like the present. Hey, Gabby, stick around, would you? Probably a good idea for you to be in on this, too. Euan?"

"Yep." He got up from his desk.

Kroll walked over to the whiteboard and grabbed a marker. "The Sinaloa cartel moved into Canada a few years ago." He wrote down the name. "They worked with an already established organized crime unit there called the Wolfpack. The Wolfpack essentially invited the cartel to move north of the border—to more strategic locations with easy access to Chicago and New York. Not to mention Europe. Our northern border has seen a four hundred and eighty percent increase in fentanyl seizures over the last three years."

"Jeez." Ellis crossed her arms. "And so, some of that is coming here, into Bangor?"

"Yes, ma'am, it is. From here, it's being transported to other cities. Bangor seems to be a growing hub of significant drug activity."

"We're obviously aware of the fentanyl crisis here in our city," McCallister said. "In fact, I worked a case not long ago that saw the conviction of a high-ranking supplier."

Kroll nodded. "I've read the file. Congratulations. It was a clean bust. So you've already felt the effects here."

Ellis thought back to that investigation; it was one that saw McCallister shot in the shoulder. She didn't want to think about how that could easily happen again. Now it seemed that Carter might have been caught up in something bigger than the activities of a low-level, low-life drug dealer.

Kroll returned the marker to the tray. "I've had eyes on the Cochran House facility for some time as a flow-through environment from a leader I suspect is orchestrating his operations from behind bars. I can help you and your team, Detective Ellis." He reached for another file and handed it to her. "In there, you'll find the names of everyone at Cochran House, including Carter Ellis. The information I have on them. Who I suspect they're tied to...all of it...right there."

So he already knew about Carter. Of course he did. Ellis took the file from Kroll's outstretched hand. As she flipped it open, she saw a list of names, each one accompanied by a photo and a detailed background report. She couldn't believe the extent of the surveillance that Kroll had already conducted. "How did you manage to gather all this information?"

He grinned, a glint of satisfaction in his eyes. "Let's just say the DEA has access to more than you realize, Detective. But right now, what matters is what we do with this information."

Ellis inhaled a deep breath. "As I'm sure you've already figured out, Carter Ellis was my brother. The reason we were at the halfway house when we saw you was to ask where we could find Tyler Beck."

"You think your brother was murdered, correct?" Kroll asked, his tone brusque.

She glanced at McCallister. "That's how it currently appears. We're still waiting on the final autopsy report."

McCallister perched on the edge of his desk. "Since we've now laid our cards on the table, we need to be careful. It looks like this goes beyond Carter Ellis. The more we dig into any kind of cartel business, the higher the stakes—for everyone."

Kroll aimed a finger at him. "No truer words, compadre."

"I get that." Ellis fixed her gaze on Carter's picture in the file. "But if there's even a chance that this information could lead us to the people behind my brother's death, then I'm willing to take that risk."

Kroll nodded. "I suggest we consider paying a visit to the people who knew Tyler Beck. Someone knows where he is."

"We're looking into the names of those who were transferred out of Warren and into Cochran House over the past several months," McCallister said. "Beck was among them, as was Carter. So, whoever else went with them, there's a good chance they might know where Beck can be found."

Gabby Lewis chimed in then, her voice filled with concern. "Let me see what I can dig up on him. Checked into any hotels. Used any credit cards. I can make a run at the Department of Transportation and see what they have. Unless he's a ghost, we'll find him."

Ellis turned to her. "You've got your hands full with the warrant situation. We can get a jump on Beck's whereabouts while you work on that. The warrant will be critical."

"I do have a last-known address for Beck. Only recently popped up, and I haven't had a chance to run it down yet," Kroll jumped in. "Place belongs to his mother. I was going to head there after the halfway house, but I bumped into you two instead."

"Can't hurt to go check it out," Ellis said. "See if she knows where her son is."

"Where's it at?" McCallister asked.

"South of town, heading toward Augusta." Kroll checked his watch. "It's still early. I don't think we should waste another minute."

"We'll go," Ellis cut in. "Gabby's going to need help. Maybe you can do something to help her get that warrant." As she regarded him, it seemed Kroll was trying hard to hide his dislike for her idea, but she wanted to do this. "You said yourself—the DEA has resources we don't."

"I did say that." He turned back to his desk. "Yeah, okay. I'll stick around here and see what I can do to assist Detective Lewis."

Lewis nodded. "I can use all the help I can get."

Ellis headed out, offering a grateful glance at Lewis. She and McCallister walked downstairs and carried on through the lobby. Outside, as they made their way into the parking lot, she stopped cold. "What do you think about Kroll?"

McCallister blew out a long breath. "Not sure yet. He seems to know a lot about what's going on in Bangor, but not a lot about how it might involve Carter or Tyler Beck. So I can't say how this is going to play out."

"Seems to me he'll only keep us in the loop if it suits him." She reached for her car keys.

McCallister placed his hand over hers. "I'll drive. You drove all the way to Warren and back."

"Yeah, okay." Ellis trailed him to his black Ford Interceptor and stepped into the passenger seat.

As he got in and started the engine, he eyed her. "I do want to say one thing, if Tyler Beck is tied in with the cartel, and he had anything to do with Carter's death, I think they would've gotten him out of town pretty damn quick, or..."

"I don't want to think about the alternative." Ellis buckled her seat belt. "Are we wasting our time going to the mother's house?"

"No, I just want to temper expectations." He drove off.

The sounds of tires on the road and the occasional rush of cars passing by filled the silence. This left Ellis unable to stop thinking about how Carter had gotten himself in so deep that he felt he couldn't come to her. Or maybe he was afraid to get her involved? Afraid for whoever was after him to realize he had two cops in his family. Had Carter in fact protected her and Hank—and paid the price for his loyalty?

"This is the place, just up here," McCallister said. "No car in the driveway."

"Well, we're here, so we might as well see what we've got." Ellis stepped out of the car after he parked curbside.

The neighborhood was middle class. Modest homes. Nice yards. Pretty much cookie-cutter, suggesting Tyler Beck had come up in similar fashion to Carter. It made Ellis feel almost grateful she didn't have kids. It didn't seem to matter if you had hardworking parents who served as positive role models. Kids were going to turn out however they were going to turn out.

They reached the front door, and McCallister knocked. Several moments passed before it finally opened.

A woman in her late forties stood cautiously behind it. Her petite frame, narrow shoulders, and big brown eyes combined to create a somewhat frail appearance. "Yes?"

"Ma'am, we're with Bangor Police. I'm Detective McCallister; this is my partner, Detective Ellis." He held out his badge. "We're looking for Tyler Beck. Are you his mother?"

"I am. What is this about?"

"We have reason to believe that your son may be connected to an ongoing investigation," he replied. "We need to speak with him as soon as possible. Is he here?"

The woman's eyes widened, alarm flickering across her face. "I...I haven't seen Tyler in weeks. He lives in a halfway house—"

"We're aware," Ellis cut in. "We have been there already. Do you have any idea where else he might go if not here? Any friends he could be staying with?"

The woman's brow furrowed, the lines on her forehead deepening. "I'm sorry. I don't know. Tyler doesn't speak to me often. I wish I could help. All I can say is that he changed a lot after he got out. He'd been sent to Cochran House Rehabilitation for a while. I thought it would help him." She shrugged. "Maybe it did. Like I said, he doesn't talk to me much."

"Okay." Ellis handed over her card. "Thank you for your help, ma'am. If you hear from him, we'd like to know."

She and McCallister were heading back toward his car when the woman called out, "What did he do, Detectives?"

McCallister turned around. "Nothing that we know of. We just want to talk to him, so if you do see him..."

She looked at the card again. "Yes, of course."

Ellis walked on, hearing the door close behind them. "Well, that was a bust."

McCallister grunted. "Our window of opportunity to find him might have just closed, along with that door."

10

Bevins rolled out of bed, his feet landing on the soft rug at its side. He rubbed his eyes and glanced at his bedroom window. The rising sun peeked through the blinds, its rays slicing through. For a moment, he considered his plan, hesitant that he might discover something meant to stay hidden. But the time for burying his head in the sand was over. Peering at his phone on the nightstand, he picked it up and texted Abbott.

> Need the day off. Gotta go to NY. It's important.

Within moments, a response arrived.

> Do what you gotta do but get back soon. We still need you here.

He didn't need to elaborate. Abbott already knew what Bevins was up against. He had precious little time to figure a way out of this before the world came crashing down around him. It still might, but at least he would have answers.

When Jack had stepped in, all he'd done in the years since was pretend none of it had ever existed. That Bevins hadn't killed his friend that night thanks to his own negligence. But now that his past had returned to the present, he was older. Wiser. And he wasn't about to leave it to Jack to fix things again. This was his responsibility now.

Bevins stood and lengthened his body in a long stretch. His well-formed muscles were enhanced by the deepening of his breath. For a young man who'd come from wealth and power, who was attractive by anyone's definition, he'd come to realize none of that mattered. It had once, but not anymore.

Those things were important to his father. But Bevins's team had each other's backs. Always. That was what mattered.

He stepped into the shower, letting the hot water dilute the sin of his past mistakes, if that was possible. Bevins had become a new man. A better man. One who still had much to make up for. He would own up to his mistake—if that was where this was headed.

Stepping out, he dried off and dressed in jeans and a T-shirt. He wasn't going to represent the department. No point in looking like a cop. And Murph had insisted he do his best to keep a low profile. Sniffing around for a vehicle the Army might have helped conceal might be the kind of behavior that got a man noticed.

He made his way into the kitchen, pouring a cup of coffee into his travel mug. A final glance around his apartment and a sip from the fresh brew, and he was off.

His beloved black Mustang awaited him. The reason he'd bought it, or rather Jack had bought it, seemed so juvenile now. Still, it would get him to his destination. The airport. Then, on to upstate New York, where he would visit the junkyard and, he hoped, see again the vehicle that had changed the course of his life.

———

HOURS LATER, under a cloudy midday sky, Bevins had reached his destination. Ahead of him was the entrance to the junkyard. He walked toward the gate. An open padlock hung on the closure, and all he had to do was push inside. Several feet ahead was a small building. A couple of windows on either side of a door. A sign in one of the windows that read "Open."

Bevins pushed on the creaky door, the smell of oil and rust permeating the air inside.

A grizzled old man with a scruffy beard sat behind a cluttered desk. He was assembling what appeared to be part of a car engine. His fingernails were stained with grease. The man glanced up, squinting at Bevins through a pair of thick glasses. "What can I do for ya?"

Bevins stepped inside, letting the door slam shut behind him. The mild thud caused him to flinch. "I'm looking for a specific vehicle." He reached into his pocket and retrieved the photograph. "It's an older Toyota Corolla. White. 2018 model year. You wouldn't happen to have something like that around here?"

The man eyed the photo. "You looking for parts or something?"

"No, sir. The vehicle itself."

"You some sort of detective, son?" He cast a wary gaze, removing his glasses.

That felt a little on the nose, but Bevins suspected it was

only a casual inquiry. One the man had probably used plenty of times before. Nevertheless, Murph's words echoed in his mind. "No, nothing like that. Just looking for the car."

The old man's chest rose and fell with deep, raspy breaths as he fixed his gaze on Bevins. The silence grew uncomfortable before the man pushed back in his chair. "I might have what you're looking for. But it ain't gonna be easy to find. This place is a maze—a boneyard of metal."

At long last—progress. "I'm willing to search every inch if I have to. I got no other place to be."

The old man chuckled. "Well, son, I hope you've got a good pair of boots on." He rounded the desk and motioned for Bevins to follow.

He'd never been in a junkyard before. Rusted hulks sat on top of one another like carcasses left to rot. Random parts lay in rows on the ground. The crunch of gravel beneath his feet echoed through the narrow paths.

"So, what is it you need from this Corolla?" The man glanced at Bevins with curiosity.

What could he say that didn't involve the truth? "My brother had that car back in the day. He wrecked it and has been trying to rebuild it since. So I guess I am looking to see what I might be able to salvage from what you have."

"You are looking for parts, then. You should've said. I have a good grasp of the inventory around here."

"Sure, but like I said, you know, I'm not sure what I'm looking for until I see it."

"Uh-huh." The man seemed unconvinced.

To be honest, Bevins was struggling to convince himself. He followed the man deeper into the labyrinth of twisted metal, bare tires, and various mechanical parts strewn around.

Soon, the old man checked the time. "Listen, I gotta be getting back. I'm gonna have to point you in the right direction from here. You'll find her down that way about another few hundred yards. Take a right ahead and keep going till you see the next section. Stop and she should be there on the left. But I will say, it's easy as hell to get lost out here. So keep your bearings."

"I'll be fine. I can use the map on my phone to get back."

"All right then. Good luck, son." He turned around and soon disappeared into the labyrinth.

Bevins followed the directions and eventually arrived at the row the old man had mentioned. He looked to his left, searching around for the car. And when a glint of sunlight reflected off a piece of chrome, he looked down. There it was. "Oh my God." A wave of powerful emotion overcame him, the events of that night flooding back.

The bitter tang of regret lingered on his tongue as he stared at the battered wreckage. But could this really be the one? He retrieved the picture. The one that his friend had taken days after Jack bought him the car for school. After careful examination, yes. "This is it. I think," he murmured to himself. Looking nothing like it had in its early days, but the interior matched. The exterior, though rusted and chipped, was otherwise the same.

The night of the accident consumed his thoughts. Autumn had arrived. School had been in full swing. It was his second year at West Point, and he'd felt like he owned the place. Everyone knew who his father was. He'd had their admiration and respect.

After a night out drinking, he and his friend, Lance Curry, needed to get back to the dorm before curfew. It seemed to happen in an instant. Bevins couldn't recall much except that the car had spun out of control. He remembered Lance's face contorted with fear, mirroring his own, most likely.

The screeching tires, the sickening thud as they collided with the guardrail, then flipping over into the ditch—it played on an endless loop inside his mind. He remembered the cold sweat that trickled down his forehead as he desperately fought to regain control of the vehicle, but it was far too late.

In his panic, Bevins had made a choice—a choice that would forever haunt him. He had scrambled out of the wreckage, leaving behind his friend trapped and helpless. He had abandoned Lance, deserting him to die in that twisted wreck.

"I'm so sorry I left you, brother." His voice faltered. "I should've stayed. I should've helped you."

Bevins kept his gaze fixed on the rusted wreck of a car. Murph said it had been transferred here not long after the accident. Jack had left it here, hoping it would rust away and be forgotten. He wondered why it hadn't been crushed. Maybe the old man wanted to part it out first and didn't follow through on destroying it. Regardless, it was a welcome oversight.

Bevins retrieved his phone and walked around the vehicle, snapping pictures from every angle. Maybe the department's forensics analyst, Officer Seavers, could somehow reconstruct the accident, find the cause. He was an expert in that kind of thing. But was the car too damaged, too rusted, too exposed to the elements for so long? Only one way to find out.

He returned his phone to his pocket and marched back to the office. It took twenty minutes, and he'd almost gotten completely lost, but finally, he entered. "Thank you, sir, for letting me take a look. I did find it. Is it possible for me to purchase it—and haul it away?"

"The whole damn thing?" The old man scratched his chin, seemingly puzzled. "Son, for the right amount of money, you can do what you want with it."

———

FEW THINGS BROUGHT the kind of smile onto Lewis's face like the one she wore right now.

Ellis watched her approach, waiting for what she was certain was good news.

"I got it." Lewis set the document on the desk with a resounding thud. "Russo authorized the warrant on Cochran House."

Ellis needed this news after striking out yesterday in her efforts to find Tyler Beck. The kid's mother's claim she hadn't seen him in weeks. "Based on what new information?"

"After you two left yesterday afternoon, Kroll gave me the names of the people who'd been sent from Warren to Cochran House over the past six months. Including Carter, there were seven. Twice as many as those who had been sent to other facilities. It was enough to convince Russo to sign off. She called me in this morning to pick it up."

Things were looking up, both from the financial perspective as well as now being able to contact those other people. One of them had to know where Beck was.

McCallister rose from his chair. "Gabby, you got it?"

"I sure did."

Kroll was at his desk, seeming to have overheard the conversation. Ellis looked at him. "Can we get current addresses on these people? Do we know where they are right now?"

"The warden offered me that information," Kroll replied. "Following up with Cochran House might offer us the best chance at getting a list of their current residents. And the warrant should allow for that. I'm happy to work with Detective Lewis to track this down. It's critical we talk to these people."

"I agree," Ellis said. "They all have something in common, and one of them might know where Beck is." She considered whether saddling Lewis with Kroll was a good idea. A part of her still felt he was holding back. But they needed the manpower. They needed to divide and conquer. "Okay, yeah, we'd be grateful for the help. There's lots more we can do now to track him down."

"Such as?" McCallister asked.

"I keep thinking...Beck was seen at the riverwalk in the middle of the night before Carter was found. Yet he seemed to vanish from the area after that." She shook her head. "He didn't walk there, so we should see if we can spot his vehicle in the vicinity."

"Check out the nearby parking lots and structures for any signs of him," McCallister cut in.

"Right. Try to pick him up somewhere around that time getting into a car...then we'll know what he drives, and we issue a BOLO. Have every cop in the city keeping eyes out for it."

"I'm on board with that. His background didn't pull up a vehicle reg., but he had to be driving something," Kroll said.

"Exactly." Ellis grabbed her keys, eyeing McCallister. "We could head out now?"

"No point in waiting." He got up, slipping on his suit jacket.

"I'll keep you posted on our progress here," Lewis called out.

"Thanks, Gabby. We'll catch up later." Ellis led the way through CID, stopping at the landing that overlooked the first-floor lobby.

McCallister caught up to her.

"If we don't find a vehicle, all we have to rely on is whatever Gabby and Kroll dredge up with the financials," she said.

"I think they stand a good shot at tracking down those people. Probably better than we have at finding a vehicle."

"I guess we'll see." She jogged down the steps with McCallister at her side.

"You don't seem to have much faith in Kroll," he observed.

Ellis reached the lobby and marched toward the exit, pushing her way outside. The morning sun was shrouded in light clouds, cooling the summer air. She held the door for McCallister. "We'll check out that bank first. It's right in front of the public parking lot. They'll have cameras for sure." She kept moving, glossing over his comment.

They walked into the parking lot and climbed into her SUV. The riverwalk was only a short distance away, and she drove ahead to the north end, where Carter had been found.

Arriving at the bank, the two stepped out, heading toward the entrance. It was nearly empty with only two tellers inside. One of them offered a warm smile, her hands clasped on top of the counter. "Good morning. How can I help you both?"

"Detectives Ellis and McCallister, Bangor PD," Ellis said as they both flashed their badges. "We'd like to review your CCTV footage."

"Oh, okay." She appeared slightly confused for a moment. "Let me get my supervisor for you."

A few minutes later, a middle-aged man in a suit came out to greet them. "I'm Robert Greene, branch manager. How can I help Bangor's finest today?"

"We'd like to take a look at the security footage you have around the area of the public parking lot," Ellis replied. "It's in connection with a suspected homicide that occurred a few days ago."

The man wore a bemused expression.

"There's reason to believe the suspect's vehicle may have been captured on your cameras," McCallister added.

Greene's face now turned grim. "A homicide, I see. Well, we'll certainly do everything we can to assist. If you'll follow me, I can take you to our security office and pull up the footage you need." He led them through a set of doors opening into the back and down a hallway to the security room.

Greene ushered the two detectives into the small office. The front wall was lined with monitors displaying various camera angles from around the bank. A long table was in front, with three chairs.

"Have a seat," Greene said. "What specifically are you looking for on the footage, again?"

Ellis sat down. "The parking lot. But I wouldn't mind taking a look at any video you have around the riverwalk. I have the timeframe in question."

Here at the bank, they were several yards upstream from

where Carter had been recovered. The riverwalk itself only stretched half a mile, but public access went much farther with several business and shops in the area. Taking the time to review all the footage wasn't realistic. So they had to pick and choose, hoping something would turn up. This bank made sense as a starting point because it was located in front of a favored public parking lot.

Greene sat down at the computer and opened up the security software. His fingers flew across the keyboard as he entered the date and time parameters.

"Okay, here we go." He scrolled through thumbnail images from different camera views. "I'll move us to the specific times..." A few more keystrokes and he'd arrived. "All right. I'll leave you two alone to take a look. Please let me know if you need more. We keep recordings for thirty days on-site."

"Thanks." Ellis moved around the other side to view the screens as the man left. "We'll start at around the same time I saw Beck on the riverwalk."

McCallister pulled a chair around to join her. "Let's take a look."

They viewed the footage, which appeared black and white at that late hour of the night. Bugs, bats, and all kinds of night creatures flew in front of the lens, offering their own sort of horror show. But between all that, they kept their eyes on the monitors.

"We've got a few cars in this lot," McCallister said.

"All the bars and restaurants would've been closed at this time of night." Ellis continued to view the screen. "Could be a case of people too drunk to drive, catching rides home and leaving their cars till morning."

Several more minutes passed by when Ellis sighed. "If he was in this lot, he didn't return to his car for some time after I'd seen him." But then she stopped cold. "There. That guy getting into the Jeep Cherokee. Dark hoodie. Skinny. That's gotta be Beck."

McCallister squinted at the image. "Can you make out the plate?"

She searched for the zoom button. "Here, let me see if this helps." A moment later, the image appeared clearer. "I see it now." Ellis jotted down the number. "This is it."

McCallister held up a hand. "We think. But we have to be thorough. There are more places to check."

BY THE TIME they'd finished reviewing footage from the public parking cameras, most of the day had passed, and only the one sighting had given them any hope of a lead. Still, Ellis counted that as a win. They had a plate and a guy stepping into that Jeep who looked a hell of a lot like Tyler Beck.

What Ellis couldn't figure out yet was why Beck had gone to the riverwalk in the first place. Had he been there to confirm Carter was there? Were they supposed to meet up that night?

They didn't know enough to be able to rule him out for Carter's death. But the more they learned about connections to the prison and the cartel, and now with the DEA's involvement, the more it seemed Beck could be on the run for his life.

"We've got a hit." At her desk, Ellis brought her fist to her chest and pumped it once, a small sign of triumph. "The Jeep Cherokee is registered to Beck's mother. And we've got him on camera near the crime scene."

"After the fact," Kroll replied, dousing her excitement. "Better than nothing, though. Good work. Let's get that BOLO issued and see if we can track him down. We're still waiting on Cochran House to hand over the files on that list of names we got."

Lewis got up from her desk. "Hey, something else here for you." She held a folder in her hand and set it down on Ellis's desk. "Based on the warrant, I was able to retrieve the tax filings from Cochran House, their bank statements, and their nonprofit filings."

"And?" Ellis asked. "Tell me you found a lot of money going to them that shouldn't have been."

"At first glance, nothing jumped out," Lewis continued. "The transactions seemed routine—payments for the mortgage, utilities, employee salaries. But I dug deeper. Every month, there were small deposits at first, but then totaling several thousand dollars, all from a holding company called Pine Valley Partners."

"You didn't mention their name," Kroll said to Lewis as he turned back and walked over to them. "Pine Valley?"

"Yep," Lewis said. "I just found it. You know them?"

"We suspect they're a shell company for the cartel in Canada. So, what...they're funneling money through the facility?" he asked.

"Maybe that's how they're able to ensure certain former inmates get transferred there," McCallister said. "It's a kick-back in disguise. Donation, maybe?"

"No way that much money is going to pass off as dona-tions," Lewis replied. "IRS would've straight up flagged it."

Ellis glanced at Kroll. "Any chance there's an IRS agent tied to this too? In place to let this kind of money slip under the radar?"

Kroll folded his arms over his beefy chest. "Anything's possible."

11

B e on the lookout—*dark blue 2010 Jeep Cherokee, plate—LDOJ123.* That was the information Ellis had sent over the wire.

As the day drew to a close, no sightings of the vehicle had yet been reported. Encouraging details had emerged regarding Cochran House, though, thanks to Lewis, but it was Beck who had been in Ellis's sights. She was sure he held the key to Carter's final days.

Agent Kroll, however, appeared to hold different priorities. His interest seemed focused only on uncovering a deeper cartel ring that had infiltrated the city, with suspected connections to the prison.

While she studied the details Lewis had provided, McCallister appeared at her desk. "Did you coordinate the BOLO with Moss?"

She peered up at him. "I did."

"Good. Then we just have to take a back seat and wait till something pops. If Tyler Beck is still in Bangor, they'll find him."

"And if he isn't?"

"Then we'll figure out a plan B. We always do," he replied.

McCallister was nothing if not pragmatic. A trait Ellis appreciated in this moment. It was one that complemented her own dogged determination. "Thanks for the reminder." She gave Kroll a sideways glance as he studied the case board. "What about him?"

McCallister pressed his hand against her desk, leaning down. "We're stuck with him until this is over," he said in a low voice. "But he could still be useful." He checked the time, furrowing his brow. "It's late, Becca."

She nodded. "You keep checking your watch."

"Yeah, I—I thought Connor would be back by now."

"Where is he?"

He perched on her desk. "Upstate New York."

"Why on earth is he there?"

"He's looking for answers." McCallister glanced at the young detective's desk. "I mentioned to him there are always two sides to a story. One side that blogger wants to tell, and the other is the truth. He went to figure out if those two sides are, in fact, the same."

Ellis thought back to the moment she'd watched that video. The arrogance of the blogger, the shock of what had happened. She'd turned her back on Bevins, insisting he figure it out for himself. McCallister had offered more practical advice. No wonder Bevins had chosen to confide in him and not her. "You're suggesting his father is hiding something?"

"I suggested he find out. This could mean a lot more than Connor losing his job."

"I'm well aware that he could face prison." Her attention

was drawn to the hallway. Officer Triggs rounded the corner, heading toward her with purpose. His arrival was unexpected.

He reached her desk, setting down a sheet of paper. "We got a hit on that BOLO. It was sighted only minutes ago, pulling into a parking lot of the bus terminal near the airport."

Ellis snatched the paper, scanning it quickly. "Who's near enough to grab him?"

"Already on it," Triggs replied. "They're making the stop now. What do you want to do?"

"Agent Kroll," she called out, "we got a hit on Beck."

He stepped away from the case board, heading over. "We need him brought in ASAP."

"Yep." She turned back to Triggs. "Make sure your guys bring him in, along with his vehicle."

"Copy that." Triggs spun around, disappearing again beyond the corridor.

Ellis steadied her thoughts, focusing on how best to handle this new development. "Let's prepare to have a sit-down with him."

McCallister nudged her, drawing her attention. He tossed a nod toward Bevins, who'd just returned. "Go on. I'll catch up with you two."

Ellis kept an eye on Bevins as he walked to his desk. Something had changed in him, but this wasn't the time to deal with it. Instead, she gestured outward. "Agent Kroll, let's head to the interview room now and get ready."

She and Kroll passed by Bevins. A tilted smile formed on her lips. "Glad you're back, Connor."

He returned a slight nod. "Me too. I'll catch up with you later."

She led the way toward the stairs and descended into the lobby.

Kroll walked beside her, clutching the handrail. "So, what's his story?"

"Whose? Connor's?"

"Detective Bevins, yes."

Ellis stopped as they reached the bottom step. The lobby echoed with chatter and footfalls on the tile floor. "He's dealing with some personal issues right now."

"And that takes precedence over his work?"

Frustration surged in her chest. "He's a good detective, Agent Kroll. There are times when we all have to face down the demons of our past."

He locked eyes with her. "And have you faced down yours, Detective Ellis?"

———

MCCALLISTER HAD BECOME MORE than an ally, he'd become Bevins' closest friend. A time was, Ellis and Pelletier had each other to lean on. The two had been practically insepa-rable, and Bevins had envied that. Lewis had her kids to look after, and while she was loyal to a fault, he never felt comfortable going to her with problems. And then there was Fletch. She cared about the team, but always saw them as a single unit, a team representing a department, rarely as indi-viduals.

Bevins had been the new guy until McCallister came along. He'd once viewed him as competition. Not anymore. And now, if it hadn't been for him, Bevins would've allowed himself to be swallowed up by the scandal brewing, running to his father for help.

Now, McCallister stood at his desk. "So, how'd it go? I was getting a little concerned I hadn't heard from you."

Bevins retrieved his phone, opening it to the images. "I found the car, if you can believe that. I wasn't sure what I'd hoped for, but I don't think it was this. I took pictures of it, thinking maybe Seavers can do something. In fact, I think I'll have it transported here."

McCallister peered at the screen. "This is the same car?"

"Oh yeah." Bevins nodded. "The old guy who ran the junkyard still had the records. It was delivered by Army personnel right after the accident, just like my friend told me. Came straight from West Point." Bevins swiped through his gallery of images. "Now, I have to compare it to the photo the blogger posted to see if it's the same car."

"You don't think it is?" McCallister asked.

"It's hard to judge based on this wreck, but I figured that's where I'd start. I know it's rusted as hell, but maybe there's something Seavers can tell me about it. If he could help me determine if there was a mechanical failure or anything like that..." Bevins looked up at McCallister. "Maybe there is another explanation."

ELLIS HAD WRITTEN HER NOTES, agreeing with Kroll on a line of questioning that would help her determine how much Beck knew about what had happened to Carter.

Kroll had his own agenda, seeking details about possible cartel activity, but it seemed she'd been able to get them into some kind of alignment for now.

Inside the interview room, a text arrived on Ellis's phone. "He's here." She looked at Kroll, who sat at the table in the center of the room. "Triggs is bringing him back now."

The door opened, and Ellis turned to see McCallister. "Perfect timing. Beck is on his way." An unspoken understanding of what lay ahead rested between them, including the need for an update on Bevins' situation.

Ellis held herself responsible for learning the truth about Carter. Her assumption about her brother had been all but proven wrong. Only the small detail of a final confirmation from Rivera was needed. Now, Hank deserved to know who had killed his son.

Moments later, the door opened, and Triggs ushered Tyler Beck inside. "Take a seat."

Ellis observed the young man. He was about Carter's age. Thin, clean-shaven. Fear appeared to have gripped him.

Triggs led the handcuffed man to a chair. He then looked at Ellis. "If you need anything..."

"Thank you. We've got it from here."

Ellis settled into a chair across from Tyler Beck as Triggs closed the door behind him. McCallister joined her, and now, all three fixed their sights on the young man. His nervous energy obvious, he refused to meet their gaze.

She glanced at her colleagues before beginning, "Mr. Beck, I'm Detective Ellis. This is DEA Agent Kroll and Detective McCallister. We'd like to ask you some questions about Carter Ellis and how he ended up dead in the Penobscot River a few days ago."

Beck's gaze finally met hers, his pale eyes wide with apprehension. "I don't know what happened." The tremor in his voice suggested otherwise.

"In case you didn't pick up on the name, Carter was my brother. You both served time together in Warren, then were transferred to Cochran Rehab Center and on to the halfway house sometime later."

Beck shrugged. "Yeah. Doesn't mean I know what happened to him."

"We have you on security video at the river in the early morning hours before his body was found," Ellis continued. "You were on the pathway, peering into the water where he was left crashing into a pylon." She felt an unexpected rumble of emotion. "Why were you there? How did you know he would be unless you were the one who put him there."

"I like to go for walks. That's all. I—I didn't know that was him. Something caught my eye, and I went to look. But I didn't know it was even a body—let alone Carter."

"You go for walks along the river in the middle of the night?" Kroll interjected. "And it just so happened that a man you knew was floating around, dead."

Ellis was losing patience. "Let's try this again, Mr. Beck. What was your relationship with Carter Ellis?"

Beck shifted in his seat, eyes darting between the three of them. "We weren't that close. Like you said, we served time together. Went to rehab together, but..."

McCallister leaned forward, his piercing gaze fixed on Beck. "I know why Carter Ellis was sent to Cochran House. How'd you come to find yourself there? I've seen your file. You aren't an addict."

Beck paled. "I don't know. They said I could go there, that it'd be a way of shaving off some time I still had left in Warren. So that was what I did."

"They said. Who? The prison? Was it a deal worked out with your lawyer? Why'd they choose you?"

The kid remained silent. Fidgeting with his fingers.

Ellis was approaching the end of her rope, then remembered this was supposed to be about Carter. She was letting Kroll's case edge into her psyche. "Were you two working for a dealer? Someone associated with the Sinaloa cartel? Did they kill my brother?"

Beck stared at the table; his shoulders slumped in defeat. "Look, me and Carter, we weren't exactly model citizens. But I don't know anything about any cartel. That shit's way above my pay grade." He raised his eyes to meet hers. "All I know is that Carter would disappear, sometimes for days, when he got transferred to the halfway house."

"Didn't you have a curfew there?" Ellis asked.

"Yeah, but no one there gave a shit, all right? Rice always went on about how he ran a tight fucking ship. No, he didn't. The guy didn't care. Just wanted the money that came with running that place." Beck ran a hand through his stringy hair, taking a calming breath. "Look, a few days before he... Carter said he was going to meet someone. Wouldn't tell me who. And I didn't ask. That wasn't how things worked between us."

Ellis thought about the timing. Rivera had yet to determine the exact date of Carter's death, meaning he could've been in the water for days. So whoever he met with could be his killer. "And when he didn't return...you didn't find that strange?"

Beck's lips trembled. "I don't know. I guess so, yeah. That's why I knew to go check out the riverwalk because that was where he said he was going. I figured he'd been gone a long time, you know? When I got there...I didn't call the cops because I'm on parole. I left the halfway house without approval. I didn't want to go back to jail."

"So Carter told you he was going to the riverwalk?" Ellis

tried to make sense of Beck's reasoning. First off, he said he and Carter weren't that close. Then he said he was worried for his friend and went out looking for him. Ellis was good at reading people. It was part of the job. But this kid? He was spewing lie after lie and was starting to look guilty as hell. "You're supposed to still be living at the halfway house, but we talked to Rice. He said you haven't been back in days...the days since Carter disappeared. That seems a little coinciden-tal, don't you think?"

Beck's eyes glistened. "I was afraid they'd come after me next."

Kroll slammed his fist on the table. "Who?"

But he'd mistimed his moment of pressure. Beck's face hardened, and he turned stoic. Ellis knew they were losing him again. She leaned back, regarding him a moment longer. "Here's the deal, we're going to book you on suspi-cion of murder unless you give us a reason not to."

Beck gazed down, refusing to answer.

"Who are you afraid of, Tyler?" she pressed. "You'll be safer here than going back to the halfway house."

Kroll leaned in, resting his elbows on the table. "Give me a name," he said evenly, "and I can put you in protective custody so you don't end up like your friend."

"I don't have a name," Beck replied.

"Try again," Ellis said, focusing on him. "If they got to my brother, they will get to you. If you say nothing, you die."

The kid eyed Kroll as he shifted in his seat. "I don't know his name. Carter never mentioned a name."

Ellis had one question left unanswered. "Who offered you the chance to get out of Warren and live at Cochran House with Carter? Someone from the prison?"

His eyes flashed with recognition.

"Was this a quid pro quo situation?" Now his eyes wore confusion. Ellis clarified. "Were you expected to do something in return for such a generous offer?"

Beck regarded each of them before setting his sights on Ellis. "Are you going to keep me here?"

"That depends, Tyler," she said. "If you want us to help keep you alive, we'll keep you here. Otherwise, as far as I'm concerned, they can have you."

12

Night had fallen, and a chill had crept into the air as Ellis pulled into the driveway of her three-bed, two-bath bungalow. McCallister followed behind in his own car, parking along the curb. They climbed the front steps together in silence, the events of the long day weighing heavily on them.

Inside, Ellis flipped on the entryway light and shrugged off her jacket, draping it on the coat rack.

McCallister hovered near the doorway.

"Can I get you something to drink?" Ellis asked, moving toward the kitchen. "You want a beer or something?"

McCallister raised his palms. "I'm all right, thanks."

She nodded, leaning back against the counter with a weary sigh. "I really thought he'd talk."

"Me too."

The vibration of her phone caught her attention. She retrieved it from her pocket, frowning at the name on the screen. "It's Detective Alcott." She answered the call. "Ellis here."

"Good evening, Detective. I hope it's not too late. Figured I'd offer you an update on Mr. Cofield."

"No, not too late at all." Ellis hoped what she'd offered him was enough for the feds to drop their investigation into Andrew. "You had a chance to look at the information?"

"I did. And the first thing I'll say is that I sure as hell don't want to know how you got it. But...I presented it to the bureau investigators."

She waited while he seemed to pause for effect.

"The pending charges against Mr. Cofield have been dropped."

Her shoulders sank in a moment of pure relief. "What about his fiancée, Myra Cook?"

"Her case still stands. But the evidence is clear that Mr. Cofield played no part in his fiancée's schemes."

For a moment, Ellis felt the sting of tears as she closed her eyes. The means by which she'd obtained the information couldn't be revealed unless she wanted charges brought against her and Leo Brown. "Thank you, Detective. I can't tell you how glad I am to hear this."

"I figured you would be. I'm preparing to make the call to Mr. Cofield now...unless you..."

"No, it should come from you," Ellis replied.

"Fair enough. I do hope to never have cause to work with you again, Detective. No offense."

A smile tugged at her lips. "None taken. Thank you again, and goodnight." Ellis ended the call.

"That sounded positive," McCallister said.

Ellis unleashed a deep breath. "Andrew's off the hook. He managed to drum up enough evidence to prove his innocence. That's all that matters."

"Then that's all I'll say about it." McCallister put a hand

on her shoulder. "I know a lot of people depend on you, Becca. But there has to be a line somewhere. You can't fix everything for everyone."

She looked down, smiling a little. "Yeah, well..."

He kissed her cheek. A warmth surged through her body. She missed being close to him. His arms around her felt good. She'd resisted giving in to her feelings for him, angry over what now seemed so trivial. But something held her back. Something that might yet remain insurmountable.

Tonight, though, all the fire in her had extinguished. Running around in circles in search of the truth had taken its toll. Coming to terms with her part in Carter's life, that was still on the horizon. So she offered the part of herself that was too weak to resist him, knowing the fight would return in time. She wouldn't care about that, not at this moment.

As their lips met, anticipation ran down her spine. She leaned into him for the fervent kiss, a soft moan escaping her. His hands roamed her body, cupping her breasts and sending a thrill of desire coursing through her veins.

He moved his attention downward, his mouth tracing a heated path to her neck. His warm breath on her skin made her shiver, the sensation intensifying the ache that had been building.

He unbuttoned her blouse, revealing the delicate bra she wore underneath.

Passion took over as they navigated their way to her bedroom, shedding their clothes in their wake. The memory of Andrew's troubles, of Carter's death, all momentarily forgotten as she lost herself in his touch. The only thing that mattered was the feel of his hands on her body and the pleasure his body offered her.

As their bodies moved together in the rhythm of their shared desire, Ellis reveled in every sensation—every touch and every gasp serving as an affirmation of their connection.

Conflicted about her true emotions, in this moment, she couldn't bear the idea of being without him. But could she stand her ground while being with him?

———

FOR THE PAST SEVERAL YEARS, Bevins had paid little attention to the consequences of his actions. Jack had taken care of things, as always. Even ensuring he'd been hired at Bangor PD. Now, however, something in him had changed. The threat of his actions coming to light now propelled him to face those consequences head-on, whatever that meant.

Sleeves rolled up and the top button on his shirt undone, Bevins sat on the edge of his black sofa. He held his phone, scrolling through all the pictures he'd taken earlier today of his old car he'd thought long gone.

From above, the recessed lights cast shadows down on him. The television was on, but he'd muted the volume. A bag of chips and a bottle of beer, three-quarters full, sat on his glass coffee table. Condensation from the bottle pooled on the surface.

He reached into his computer bag that lay against the sofa and retrieved his laptop. Upon opening it, he searched for the blogger's post. There it was. The man's voice grated on his nerves as he spoke of cover-ups and misdeeds by those who could afford to bury them. He wasn't wrong.

The image appeared. The overturned vehicle, half in and half out of the ditch. At first glance, it looked the same as the one he'd seen in the junkyard. He held the picture on his phone next to the image on his laptop. The model year, the color, the make, that was all the same. But on closer inspection, he saw it now. The interior was a different color. The car Asher Daly had posted had a gray interior. "Mine was beige," he told himself. "And the steering wheel, tan." Bevins glanced back and forth, over and over, to be sure. To be one hundred percent sure. "It's different. It's a different car. That one's not mine." He let his head fall back against the sofa, his mind spinning. "Who gave you that picture? Where did it come from?"

As he sat up again, more important questions presented themselves. Was this even the true scene of the accident? His memory was sketchy, there'd been far too much booze swimming in his brain at the time. Had someone gone to the trouble of re-creating the accident? And if so, then why?

He picked up the phone and called Murph. The hour was late, and he feared his friend wouldn't answer. But after only two rings, he heard:

"Connor, hey, man. What's up?"

"Sorry. I know it's late. Listen, I have to tell you something. Something about the car...I found it. Exactly where you said it would be."

"Holy shit. You went to that yard upstate? Okay. Good."

Bevins took a swig of beer. "Here's the thing...it's not the same car the blogger shows in his post. It's not the same, man. I can't even be sure it's the same location."

The line went quiet a moment. "What the hell does that mean?"

"It means someone gave him that photo, told him the story, and insisted he put it out for all to see. Regardless of whether it was accurate. And I've talked to this guy. I don't think he'll give a shit about the discrepancies."

"Who would do that? Because I gotta tell you, buddy, this won't just hurt you, Jack will be toast."

Bevins slumped back once again. "I know. Somehow, I think that might be the point."

"Okay, so what can I do to help now?"

"I need the report, Murph. I have to see it for myself."

"I already told you, I don't have access to it."

"Then who does?" He waited for a response. "Come on, man. You know I know how to keep my mouth shut. This won't blow back on you."

Murph sighed. "I might know who can get it, but I need time."

"I don't know how long it'll take before this idiot blogger gains traction, but whatever you can do, I'll sit tight."

"I'll be back in touch as soon as I can."

"Thank you, man," Bevins replied. "This means the world to me."

"You might want to hold your thanks—we're not over the line yet."

13

The sunny morning and cool breeze were enough to raise anyone's spirits. As Ellis stepped outside, setting off to see Hank, that cool air brushed against her skin. If she hadn't known better, she might've suspected the world wasn't so bad after all. Then again, she was a cop investigating her brother's murder. Sort of hard to put a positive spin on that.

McCallister had gone home in the late hours of last night. He'd sensed her desire to be alone and hadn't questioned it. Probably fearing to pull on that thread. Regardless, Ellis had to push on with the investigation. Hank deserved closure. This morning, she planned to see him before heading into the station.

Arriving at his house, she entered through the unlocked front door. Ellis had all but given up on reminding him to keep it locked, realizing he was at best sporadic in his efforts. After what had happened to him earlier this year—the stroke, the reason why he'd had it—she thought he would take better precautions. But Hank was who he was, and she wasn't going to change him.

"Dad?" Ellis entered, closing the door behind her. "It's me."

"In the kitchen," he replied.

Ellis made her way through where she spotted Hank at the table, cup of coffee in hand. A newspaper nearby. "Morning."

As he gazed up at her, the pain in his face was evident. It appeared he hadn't slept much, nor eaten breakfast.

"Have you eaten yet?" she asked, making her way to the kitchen cabinets to see if there was any food inside. Upon opening the doors, the answer was clear. "It's looking pretty bare in here."

"I'm fine," he replied, keeping his eyes on the newspaper before him.

Ellis walked around to the table and took a seat. "Dad, you have to eat. You look like you've hardly slept. This isn't good for your health."

He looked at her, wary, grief-stricken. "Listen, Becca, I appreciate your concern, but I've lost my son. I know you understand what loss means. I haven't forgotten what you've suffered. But I need time to grieve. Can you give me that?" Hank went quiet for a moment, taking another sip of his coffee. "He never should've served time. I could've made sure he didn't."

Ellis reached out to touch his hand. "Dad, Carter was dealing. And he was dealing large amounts. He went to jail just like anyone else in his position would have. You helped by getting him transferred to rehab to serve out his sentence."

"And someone got him out ahead of time," he replied, casting a perplexed glance at her. "How the hell was that allowed to happen?"

"That's what I'm working on finding out, Dad. You know that." She took a deep breath. "The DEA's gotten involved now. An Agent Sean Kroll."

Hank pulled back his shoulders, his brow creasing. "Why the hell is the DEA here?"

"Because they think the cartel's infiltrated our city," she replied. "And that Carter might've been working with them."

"No." Hank waved his hand defiantly. "Not a chance."

"Dad, please..."

"I love you, kid, I really do, but you've always believed the worst about your brother. He wasn't involved with the cartel. He wouldn't be that stupid."

"Maybe he wasn't," Ellis replied. "Maybe he didn't have a choice. Look, we think there could be a connection between the prison and Cochran House. I have Gabby looking into the finances, and, well, it's possible the cartel has used their influence with the prison."

"The cartel killed my boy. Is that what you're saying?" Hank asked.

"I don't know yet. It's—a theory. You know I'm going to do everything in my power to get to the truth. I get that from you."

The hint of a smile appeared on his face. "Maybe so."

"I want you to know that I won't stop, okay?" she added.

"Kid, I'm not sure you should go down this path if it leads to the cartel." He fixed his gaze onto her. "If they're involved, they won't care who you are or that you wear a badge. And, frankly, I'm not sure the DEA will care either. They'll do whatever it takes to get their man. Collateral damage doesn't mean a whole hell of a lot to them."

Ellis tilted her head. "You don't know that. And I can handle myself. They have no idea what Hank Ellis's daughter is capable of."

THE WEIGHT of her father's grief rested on Ellis's shoulders. She loved him more than anything, and after having endured so much in the past several months, she wasn't sure if he could take much more.

Now, as she arrived at the station, Ellis headed straight up to CID.

Abbott appeared from the hallway and called out to her, "Becca? Why don't you come back for a minute?"

She glanced right, toward the bullpen, and veered left instead, walking toward Abbott's office. Inside, she was surprised to see Lieutenant Abe Serrano waiting as Abbott returned to his desk. "Good morning, sir."

Serrano was a tall, slim man. His gray hair was thick and full. He and Hank had worked together years ago, with him as Hank's junior partner. Now, he ran the department. "Becca, come and have a seat, would you?"

Hesitant, she sat down, waiting for one of them to speak. "Yes, sir?"

"The DEA's involvement in your brother's murder investigation has directed a great deal of scrutiny onto the department," Serrano began.

Ellis wondered if this was about McCallister or Bevins. "Scrutiny, sir?"

Serrano perched on the edge of Abbott's desk, keeping

his eyes fixed on her. "Let's just say it appears as though they're considering pulling this case out from under us."

Heat rose in her cheeks. "What? They can't do that. It's a homicide in our city. And it's my brother."

"Bingo." Serrano aimed a gun finger at her. "He was your brother. That's what they're taking issue with. But if you ask me, it's got something to do with their ongoing pursuit of the cartel here in Bangor."

"They don't want our fingers in their pie," Abbott cut in.

Ellis leaned back. "So they're not going to let us do our job?"

"So far, they haven't done anything more than suggest this case be headed up by their team. Kroll being the lead," Serrano continued. "So what I'm telling you is that you're out of time. If you want to learn the truth about your brother, you're going to have to jump in with both feet."

Ellis scoffed. "With respect, Lieutenant, I have been." Her mind raced as she considered the implications of the DEA taking over everything. She had been working night and day to find her brother's killer, refusing to let the trail grow cold. There were still leads to follow up on, people to question, evidence to analyze. She wasn't about to hand the reins over to Agent Kroll and allow Carter's murder to get buried under bureaucracy and egos.

She met Serrano's gaze. "There has to be a way I can keep working this case. Carter was my brother. I owe it to him to see this through."

"I understand how you feel, but the fact is, the DEA can pull rank on us if they decide they want exclusive jurisdiction."

"Okay." She looked at Abbott, as though he might offer a solution. "What should I do?"

"Dig deeper," he replied. "Get with the state police and ask for their help with looking into the state prison. If it appears someone on the inside has been compromised, then they'll want to push forward with their own investigation. We need something that gives us an edge over the feds."

Serrano raised a finger. "And you'll need to be careful. Don't go making waves with Kroll. The last thing we need is a turf war."

Ellis stood, ready to press on. "Gabby's been working on ties to the prison. Current Cochran House residents. I'll get an update from her. In the meantime, please do what you can to hold these guys off. Agent Kroll's holding back on us. I'm sure of it. And I need to find out what he knows."

"Then do it fast, Becca," Abbott said. "For Carter and for Hank."

She turned on her heel, walking back out toward the bullpen.

On her arrival, McCallister glanced at her, Kroll at his side. The rest of the team...well, they all looked at her too, their faces masked with concern.

"Sorry I'm late." She thumbed back. "Abbott called me into his office. What's going on? Why are you all looking at me like that?"

McCallister cleared his throat, and everyone seemed to go back to their tasks. "Moss came up here a little while ago."

Sergeant Devin Moss headed up the day shift patrol. Ellis had had the opportunity to work with him recently and had gotten to know Officer Triggs a lot better, too.

"Okay." She wore a puzzled frown. "What did he want?"

Kroll took a step forward. "Beck was found early this morning. Floating in the Penobscot, not far from where your brother was found."

Her heart dropped into her stomach. "No."

"This is on me, Detective," Kroll continued. "I should've ensured his protection. I believed he was safe. They got to him anyway."

Ellis marched to her desk, setting down her things and gathering her thoughts. "He was our only connection to Carter. Where does his death leave our investigation?"

Lewis rounded her desk and approached. "Becca, I did uncover some information regarding Cochran House's finances."

"What'd you come up with?" A flicker of hope surged in her.

"It appears someone inside the prison, likely an accountant or financial officer, approved the transfer of funds into the rehab center's accounts. Money that was coming from undisclosed sources," Lewis added.

"We figure it's cartel money." Kroll jumped in. "If that's the case, then they're working with someone at Cochran House. And I suspect the money was then used to buy off the residents. Get them to sell for the cartel. This is the connection I've been looking for."

"Do we know about these other guys who were transferred to Cochran House yet? Who are they? Where are they?" Ellis shot him a glance. "If you think this was what Carter was into..."

Kroll raised his hand. "It looks like a strong possibility, Detective. Which makes it all the more important to track down these other folks."

"We've been talking about this for days. Why hasn't that happened yet?" Ellis felt rattled that the case was slipping through her fingers.

"It's time to get us on the inside," Kroll said. "Detective

Lewis can send us her report. We'll use that to go back to the people at Cochran House, find out who managed the money. From there, they'll turn over their prison contacts."

"An operation," McCallister added. "We'll run a join operation with Kroll to make it happen."

"The only truth that matters to me is the truth about my brother," Ellis shot back. "This operation—we can run it. Our team. This is still our town."

Kroll shoved his hands into his pockets. "Not anymore, Detective. This town belongs to the Sinaloa cartel. And if you want it back, then you have to play by their rules." He held her gaze. "And I'm the only one here who knows what those rules are."

WHILE ELLIS WAS WORKING to solve her brother's murder, Bevins bided his time, waiting for his friend to get hold of the initial accident report. He'd wanted to be there for Ellis, for all of them, but if he couldn't end this, then it would end him.

A call came in, displaying an unknown number. Bevins snatched his phone from his desk, walking out of the bullpen. "Detective Bevins."

"I've considered your offer."

Bevins stopped in the hallway, recognizing Daly's voice. Maybe this was the answer he needed. Maybe an ending had just presented itself. "And?"

"And I've come to the conclusion that this story—your story—is far more important than any job with a newspaper. So you and your daddy can take the offer and shove it up your rich-boy ass. I'm pushing this whether you like it or not."

Anger balled in Bevins' gut. "You know that photo?" he challenged. "It's not real. It's not even the same car." He waited a moment while the line went silent.

"You're lying."

"The hell I am. My car had beige interior, not gray," Bevins replied. "So whoever gave you that picture told you a story that isn't real. You can go fuck yourself."

"Bullshit." The line clicked. Daly was gone.

Bevins stared at his phone, suddenly regretting his words. What would Daly do now in light of this information? Would it only push him to promote the lie? "Oh Christ, what have I done?"

Defeat weighed him down as he returned to his desk. No amount of money or influence was going to make this go away. He'd lit the match, and Daly would watch him burn.

He pulled up the blog post on his laptop. Son of a bitch was going to destroy him now. That much was certain. He glanced around the bullpen. Everyone else seemed engaged in Ellis's investigation except for Fletch. Something was going on with her, and he didn't know what it was.

She'd been distant for a while. Ever since the Boston situation blew up for McCallister. Everyone knew Fletch wanted to run the department. But it didn't appear as though Abbott was going anywhere anytime soon. She would have to put in her time. That was the way of things.

But then he also knew how much she cared about everyone here. Doing her best to protect them all, it seemed. So Bevins wondered—did she know what was going on with him? Did she know about the blogger? The accident?

Could he go to Fletch? Could he trust her? Yes. That should never have been a question in his mind.

A new comment appeared on the blog post, drawing his attention. "They always get away with this shit," the comment read. "Maybe this time, they'll pay." It was from an anonymous account. Good ol' internet. Never holding anyone accountable for the things they say and do online.

Point was, though, the post was getting noticed. Outrage would grow, maybe even more so now after his lashing out at Daly. That guy didn't care if what he had as "evidence" was fake. He knew the story itself was real. And he knew that because of Bevins' own reaction to it. If Bevins couldn't get Daly to pull the plug, then he had to get out in front of it. And that started with creating his own understanding of the truth about what had happened. A truth that he'd not seen through his intoxicated gaze that night.

Bevins walked around his desk. While the others huddled around Ellis, discussing their investigation, he carried on to go see Fletch. "Hey."

She looked up at him. "Hey, Connor, what's up?"

"Walk with me to the break room?" he asked.

She returned a puzzled stare. "Yeah, sure."

Lori "Fletch" Fletcher was a petite woman. Late twenties. Busted her ass as a beat cop for four years before making detective almost eighteen months ago. Not many people crossed her. Not if they wanted to stay on her good side.

He led them into the break room. They were the only two inside.

"What's this about?" she asked.

"Where to start?" He inhaled a deep breath. Bevins went into the situation—all of it. From the moment he'd gone to see Ellis to this very second. And the look on Fletch's face suggested she'd already been aware of the story. Or at least some of it. "You knew, didn't you?"

"Look, Connor, when the situation with Euan exploded in our faces, I dug deeper. Into everyone. And so, yeah, I knew Abbott brought you on knowing this too."

"You tried to rat me out?" Bevins asked.

She raised her hands. "It wasn't like that. I needed to protect you, Becca, Euan, everyone. Abbott insisted I do nothing, so I didn't. And now, what? What do you want me to do, Con?"

He rubbed the back of his neck. "I need help. I've lived with this secret long enough. Like I said, my MP buddy is trying to uncover the original accident report. I wanted to tell you all this because, well, I guess I already knew you'd be on my side."

Fletch crossed her arms. "But how can I help?"

"I can only get so far without raising red flags."

"Because of your father," she cut in.

"Exactly. But you...you won't have that problem. So, will you help me? I'm trying to get the car brought back here for Seavers to see if he can figure out what happened. I need to see the report." He tried to figure out what she could do. "Maybe you can find something on Asher Daly?"

"The blogger?"

He shrugged a little awkwardly. "Yeah."

The disappointment on her face was unmistakable. "Con, that's not what you want, is it?"

He lowered his gaze. "I don't know. This problem doesn't rest with him. I don't know what I'm saying..."

She reached for his arm. "What if you do get that report? You see all the evidence—and the outcome remains the same? Which is that you were responsible, and your dad tried to cover it up for you. What will you do then?"

He chuckled, no humor in the sound, feeling at his wits' end. "Resign. I won't see this department go through any more than it already has."

Fletch let go of his arm. "Okay, then, I'll help you. But I won't try to take down some innocent blogger. Just remember what you're saying to me now."

"How could I forget?"

14

A call had come into the station. Oliver Rice, the man who ran the halfway house, had asked to speak with Ellis. Turned out, he needed the space and had asked her to come and collect Carter's belongings. She'd been in his room once before, and then she was barely able to keep her emotions in check. The end result had been that McCallister insisted on coming back another time. Well, now that they knew about Beck and how he'd met his end, that time was overdue.

Kroll, with his keen interest in any and all things related to Beck and Carter, had insisted on coming along as they headed out. Ellis held hope that after a first pass, which yielded nothing relevant, Beck's scant possessions might offer a new lead.

Ellis glanced into the rearview at Kroll. "You still haven't heard back from Cochran House about that list?"

"They promised they'd confirm the names today. Once they do, I'll have their files, which will give us a shot at tracking these guys down." He held her gaze in the mirror.

"But to be honest with you, I'm not sure they matter as much as Beck's murder."

She returned her sights to the road ahead. "Seems to me, if all these guys are tied to some scheme with the cartel, they might be in as much danger as Beck was."

An uncomfortable pause ensued before Kroll spoke again. "Just so you know, Detective Ellis, my ASAC approved us working together on Cochran House. That'll open up a lot of resources you folks here don't have."

"Uh-huh." Her hands tightened around the wheel, and she felt McCallister's stare. But this was bullshit. Kroll was either lying to them or spinning lies to his bosses. Whatever he had planned, it didn't involve Bangor PD. Not after what Serrano had told her.

Ellis pulled up to the curb outside the halfway house. The afternoon sun beat down on the hood of her Tahoe, shining in her eyes. She slipped on a pair of sunglasses before stepping out. They walked along the front path that led to the home, McCallister silent at her side.

Kroll lingered a step behind. A nagging sensation pricked the back of her neck where he was concerned. Why he'd wanted to come along, she could only suspect. And what she suspected left her unsettled. She knocked on the door, and a moment later, the middle-aged Rice opened it, standing in shorts and T-shirt once again.

"Mr. Rice," Ellis began, "we're here to collect my brother's belongings."

"Yeah, sure. Come in." He seemed to notice Kroll. "Didn't expect so many of you."

"Yeah, sorry about that," she replied, giving Kroll a sideways glance. "We're all working to uncover the truth about what happened." Ellis peered around, noticing a few other men carrying on with their days. "I don't know if you heard, but Tyler Beck is gone."

"Gone?" Rice asked, his face impassive.

"Murdered, Mr. Rice," she replied.

"Oh." He rubbed his hands through his full head of hair. "I didn't know. Does that mean you'll be boxing up his things too?"

"His mother hasn't come here to claim them?" McCallister asked.

"No, sir. I didn't even know..." Rice headed down the narrow hallway and stopped at the last door on the right. "Here you go, Detectives. I guess...take what you want. I'll throw out the rest."

Ellis walked inside. "We'll be quick." Her gaze swept over the sparse belongings. Nothing had changed since she was last here. She moved through the room, touching the edge of Carter's worn-out mattress, feeling the ghost of his presence. "Let's bag everything up, I guess."

A box of black bags sat on Carter's dresser. Ellis grabbed it. "Rice must've left this here for us." She pulled one out and began to shove her brother's clothes inside.

"Careful, Detective," Kroll said. "You don't know what you might find."

"We've already swept the room. At least, Carter's things." She looked at him. "He didn't leave anything behind."

"Oh, I hadn't realized." Kroll went about examining Beck's side of the room. He pulled down the covers on his bed, patting down the pillow. He raised the mattress and peered underneath.

Ellis watched him, glancing at McCallister, knowing they hadn't been as thorough. Her emotions had gotten the better of her. Once again proving that Abbott was right to be concerned about her working this case.

Mirroring Kroll's actions, she pulled down the covers on Carter's bed and lifted the mattress. "Oh my God."

McCallister walked over to her, seeming to realize their glaring oversight.

"You got to be kidding me." She reached between the mattress and box spring, taking hold of the laptop hidden there. "This belonged to Carter."

"He certainly didn't want anyone to find it," McCallister said. "You think we can get into it?"

She flipped it open, and the screen came to life, prompting for a password. "We'll bring this in, have Brown take a look. Who knows what's on here." Ellis slipped the laptop under her arm, her neglect crashing down around her. But if Brown could access this, the answers to her brother's murder might become clear. "Anything else?" She let her gaze roam around the room once more. "What about Carter's phone? It wasn't on him when he was found."

"My guess...it was tossed into the river," Kroll interjected before turning back to Beck's things. "Oh, hello, what's this?"

Ellis looked over, her gaze drawn to the floor. "Is that a notepad?"

"It was shoved under Beck's nightstand." He flipped through the pages. "Looks like we got names, dates, places. This could be valuable."

Ellis walked toward him, peering at it. Her eyes caught on a single word, isolated on an otherwise blank page, written at the bottom. "Handler."

"Handler?" Kroll echoed, frowning. "As in cartel handler?"

"Or handler inside the prison," McCallister replied.

Kroll set it down. "We'll be taking that with us." He continued his search. "Don't think I'll get as lucky as you finding that laptop. Don't see a phone either."

"Probably ended up in the river too, huh?" she asked, her tone laced with sarcasm. "Let's bag up the rest of this stuff and get out of here." Ellis was anxious to get the laptop to Brown.

Several more minutes passed before they returned to the common area of the halfway house. Ellis caught sight of Rice at the kitchen table.

He promptly jumped up. "That it? You guys get everything?"

"We'll load the bags into my vehicle and be out of your hair," Ellis replied. "Including Beck's things. It'll all be handed over as evidence. Thank you for the call, Mr. Rice. We'll be in touch."

"Yes, ma'am." He opened the door for them. "I hope something in there helps you all figure out what happened to those two kids. They had their problems, but they were good guys, overall."

As they stepped outside, Rice's words echoed in her ears. *Good guys.* She'd never believed Carter was a good person. Now it seemed that someone else had, besides Hank. But it was a little too late. The weight of his death, and now Tyler Beck's, pressed down on her. And along with that burden, the single word "handler" replayed in her mind like an endless taunt.

THEY HAD REACHED the day's end. The setting sun shone through the slats of the window blinds in the bullpen.

Fletch had watched the blogger's video showing the vehicle that had supposedly belonged to Bevins—though he knew better now. She'd listened to Daly rant about how power corrupted and how Jack Bevins, a high-ranking government official, wasn't going to pay the price for covering up a murder—a murder allegedly committed by his own son.

He wasn't wrong. Power corrupted everyone, as far as Fletch was concerned. And when Bevins showed her the image he'd taken at the junkyard in New York, she began to see the problem. "Your friend Murphy. Did he still think he could get his hands on that report today?"

"He didn't know. Said it could take a while, but the thing is, Fletch, I don't have a while."

"No, you're right. This is a time bomb waiting to go off. Regardless of the fact that this guy has a fake photo." She studied the screen again. "Do we know where Daly is based?"

"No. My meeting with him was one he'd set up, but I have to think he's not too far away."

"So he's keeping his mouth shut about who gave him the information," she said.

"Yes, and that's the person we need to find." Bevins tapped on the screen of his laptop. "Whoever provided the image gave him the story as well. Fletch, do you think someone's looking to dismantle our team? I mean, after Euan's deal. Now this? Is Becca next? What happens when whoever this is finds out she murdered her stepfather when she was a kid?"

"Not for nothing, she did have a legit reason. It was self-defense," Fletch replied. "But I get your meaning. I don't want to see her have to relive that horror show through social media." She folded her arms. "Can't figure out why this went to Daly, though. He doesn't have a lot of followers. There are plenty more people just like him who do."

"Maybe others with more traction were savvy enough to see the photo as a fake. Decided not to trust whoever brought it to them." Bevins' phone rang, interrupting his thoughts. "It's him. It's Murphy. I have to take this." He answered. "Hey, Murph."

Unable to hear the other side of the conversation, Fletch watched Bevins's expression. The look on his face suggested they might still catch a break today.

"Yeah, no, I get it," Bevins replied. "Send it to the cloud server, and I'll log in with that password you gave me. No trace of it coming from you. No email or other trail. Got it." His face wore relief. "You have no idea what this means to me, brother. I owe you. More than you know." He nodded. "Will do. Thanks again."

Bevins ended the call and directed his gaze at Fletch. "He got the report. It'd been buried in the archives."

"And?" Fletch asked.

"He's uploading it now to a secure cloud server. I'll print it, delete the file, and there'll be no trace it came from him or that he gave it to me."

"Then let's take a look at this thing," Fletch said.

Bevins waited a moment and then logged into the server. He entered an encrypted key to gain access to the file. "I don't want to download it, so I'm just going to hit print, and then we'll take a look."

Fletch walked over to the printer, waiting for the report to come out. Within moments, she returned with it in her hand. "This is your deal. You look first."

Bevins grabbed it and began to read. Fletch tried to gauge his reaction, but he remained stone-faced.

"Oh my God."

Fletch leaned closer. "What is it?"

Bevins rubbed his cheek, in seeming disbelief.

"Connor, what?" she insisted.

He leaned back, swallowing hard. "There was nothing wrong with the car."

Fletch dropped her shoulders. "Ah, damn. That's what you were told initially, right?"

He nodded. "Yeah, that's right. But there's something else." He handed her the report. "See for yourself."

She skimmed through the first page, seeing exactly what he'd just said, but then on the second page—"What the hell? There was an object in the road?"

"Can you believe that?" He scoffed. "I hit it, going pretty fast, veered off, flipped over into the ditch."

Fletch read on. "The object...it was a knife rest." She looked at him, confused.

"It's a portable frame with barbed wire around it," Bevins began. "The military use them to slow down vehicle movements."

"What?" she asked. "Slow down?"

"As in disable," Bevins added. "Fletch, someone put a knife rest in the road. It was dark. I must not have seen it. When I ran over it, my tires would've blown, causing me to lose control."

"Who the hell would put something like that in the road?"

"I guess," Bevins said, raising his shoulders, pinching his lips, "someone who wanted me dead..."

15

T he discovery of Carter's laptop was the single best argument in favor of Ellis stepping aside from this investigation. The glaring oversight hung above her like a dark cloud. She could point the finger at McCallister, insisting he should've ensured they'd been more thorough that day, but their actions had been a joint decision. And she was the lead detective. What that meant for their partnership now was the real question.

Ellis turned into the stationhouse, parking near the garage bay doors. "I'll see if anyone in Evidence can give us a hand unloading everything."

McCallister unbuckled his seat belt, opening the passenger door. "Kroll and I can handle it. I know you want to catch Brown before he takes off for the day."

"Yeah, I do. Thanks." Ellis grabbed her computer bag from the footwell on the passenger side. Carter's laptop was safely inside. "I'll meet you two upstairs." She stepped down, slinging the bag over her shoulder and heading toward the south entrance. Glancing behind her, she saw McCallister at the back of the Tahoe, raising the hatch. So far, Kroll had said nothing, which was cause for concern. She didn't trust him. And nothing he'd done so far would change that.

Ellis walked in through the patrolmen's entrance, and as she made her way into the corridor, Officer Triggs called out to her.

"Detective Ellis?"

She stopped as he approached. "Afternoon. Shouldn't you be getting ready to clock out?"

"Yes, ma'am." He thumbed back. "I was just about to, but I wanted to ask how things were going. I heard what happened to the guy you tracked down with that BOLO."

"Yeah, well, he wasn't interested in our help; then someone got to him." It hadn't escaped her memory, the notion that Kroll had been the one to suggest he would protect the kid.

"I'm so sorry about that, Detective. I mean, I know this is all tied to your brother's death. I'm sure you were hoping for some answers."

A half-smile pulled at her lips. "It's okay, Triggs. My brother was into something, well, let's just say I don't know that anyone could've gotten him out." She'd said the words enough times now that there was a chance she might start to believe them. "Anyway, I wanted to say thanks."

He shoved his hands in his pockets. "What for?"

"For doing your job. It's all any of us can do. And if you hear of anything or get called out to that rehab facility, you'll let me know?"

"Yeah, of course. Anything you need, Detective."

Ellis nodded. "I appreciate it. I'd better get back to see Brown. Thanks again, Triggs. Good work."

She walked on through the corridor until arriving at the

Forensics department. Harding was at his desk, preparing to leave. "Hey, uh, don't suppose Brown's still here?"

"As far as I know. But you'd better be quick." He eyed the laptop bag. "You got something for us?"

"I do. Hoping you guys can do something with it. It's a laptop. Belonged to my brother."

Harding glanced down. "Right. Well, if anyone can help, it'll be Leo. Goodnight, Detective."

"Goodnight." Ellis walked through the lab, the distinct smell of chemicals and cleaning products lingering. She arrived at Brown's office, enclosed by glass, and knocked on his door.

He waved her inside, and she stepped in. "What you got there, Detective?"

She set down the bag, unzipping it to retrieve the laptop. "Came across this today during a search of my brother's place—"

"I heard what happened. I'm so sorry," he cut in.

"That's kind of you to say." She handed him the laptop. "There could be information on here relevant to his death, but as always, I could use your help."

Brown examined it. "Let me guess, you don't know the password?"

"I do not."

Brown slid a piece of paper and a pen toward her. "We'll start with the obvious. Write down anything you think he might've used as a password."

"Sorry?" she asked.

"Your birthday. Hank's birthday…"

"His mother," she said. "He could've used her birthday or the day she passed away."

"Write it all down. I'll start with that one first and work

my way through. If I strike out, then I'll have to break out the heavy equipment. I'll let you know what I find."

"Please." Her eyes locked onto his. "The sooner, the better."

"I figured."

As Ellis turned to leave, she stopped a moment. "Oh, and you should also know...what you did for my friend?" Their eyes met. She hoped her gratitude was obvious. "It was enough to prove his innocence. Thank you, Leo. It'll never be forgotten."

———

McCallister and Agent Kroll appeared deep in conversation when Ellis returned to the bullpen. He just didn't see it. She was certain McCallister took no notice of Kroll's ambiguous tactics or had simply chosen to ignore them. Tagging along today as he had. What was Kroll's purpose? Unless there was more to Tyler Beck and how he related to Carter than he would admit to. That was beginning to seem a much more likely scenario.

Ahead of her was Bevins's desk. She'd pushed him away, as she had her brother. But there were some things out of her control, and Bevins's past was one of them. Nevertheless, his struggle was evident; even now, his expression revealed uncertainty about his future. "Connor, everything okay? I haven't seen you in a while."

"Yeah." He swatted his hand. "Just dealing with things. Trying to take care of this stuff on my own—like I should be."

A pang of guilt clutched her chest. She searched for

words of comfort and hope, but before she could speak, he stopped her.

"You have enough to deal with right now, Becca. This is my problem, not yours. I will handle it."

What more could she say? Ellis placed her hand on his shoulder. "I know you will." Walking ahead, the absence of Pelletier caught her attention. "Anyone seen Bryce today?"

"He's on a new case Abbott assigned him yesterday," Fletch replied.

Ellis set down her things, glancing at McCallister. "We missed a briefing?"

He walked away from Kroll, returning to his desk. "They had one while we were out. What did Brown say about the laptop?"

"Nothing much. He'll do what he can, as always," she replied.

"Fingers crossed." He thumbed back to Kroll. "We were discussing next steps."

"About?"

Kroll meandered toward her, hands in his pockets. "I got some intel just as we arrived back. I wanted to confirm it before bringing you two up to speed."

"Okay," Ellis replied, dropping onto her chair.

"The information Detective Lewis obtained with that warrant."

"Cochran House's financials," Ellis clarified.

"Right. I ran that up the chain to my ASAC. This was information we didn't already know about, which is great because it gives us a new direction. It points the finger at a prison staffer who's coordinating the money transfer. Our best shot at connecting this information with the cartel is to talk to the employee. He's got his ass in a sling now, and he's about to find out what that will mean unless he cooperates."

"He'll want to save his own skin, no doubt," McCallister replied.

"You sure about that?" Ellis raised her brow. "I wouldn't count on it. He'll be much more afraid of the cartel than he is of us."

"We won't go in empty-handed," Kroll shot back. "I fully intend on sweetening the pot. This isn't my first rodeo, Detective Ellis."

Ellis felt heat rise under her collar. "Forgive me, Agent Kroll, but you believed Beck had information too. Now he's dead. Your intel has led you to Bangor, yet you still don't know who's running their operation here."

"We have theories, Detective Ellis. But you can't make arrests on theories." He spun around the chair next to her desk before dropping into it. "I get why you're pissed at me. I can admit that I should've kept Beck on a short leash. I didn't. But I'm asking you to trust me now. We go talk to this prison accountant...we will get the information that will lead to arrests. That same information, I am certain, will allow us to find the truth about your brother."

"And then what?" She refused to let him off the hook.

"You, McCallister, me, and my team—we put together an operation to bring the cartel member behind the prison scheme out into the open." He checked the time. "Listen, I need to head out. I've got calls to make, bosses to answer to. So I'll plan on seeing you both first thing in the morning? We'll hash this out then." Kroll nodded, making his way through the bullpen before disappearing around the corner.

Ellis kept her gaze on him until he was gone. She turned back to McCallister. "Something doesn't feel right."

"Oh, you made that crystal clear," he replied. "What's going on with you?"

"With me?" She scoffed. "He's hiding something. This handler situation? Notice how that seemed to fall off Kroll's radar? What did he do with that notebook?"

"It was logged into Evidence along with the rest of Beck's things."

"Without a thorough review first?" She looked away. "This guy's making sure we do nothing but run around in circles."

"What do you want to do about that?"

Jumping down McCallister's throat wasn't going to get them anywhere. Ellis needed solutions. "Carter's laptop." She looked straight at him. "It's the only piece of real evidence we've come up with so far. With Beck gone, our leads are too. Money coming and going...Gabby's work on Cochran House. That's all well and good, but it points to a larger problem."

"One that could still be tied to Carter's death," McCallister said.

She nodded, but her attention was diverted at the sight of Pelletier. "There he is. Hey, Bryce. Heard you got a new case. Sorry we missed the briefing." The change in topic would help defuse her anger, she hoped.

Pelletier lumbered to his desk. "Figured you guys would all be gone for the day."

"No such luck. How goes it?" McCallister asked.

"Something I expected to be a slam-dunk...isn't. So there's that." Pelletier dropped onto his chair; the solidity of his full frame slouched low.

"Isn't that always the case." McCallister snickered.

"Yeah, well, turns out the suspect in my B and E lived in a

halfway house. So I went to track him down, but the guy's moved on."

Ellis perked up at the news. "A halfway house? The one in Colonial Pines?"

"The very one. How'd you know?" Pelletier asked.

This was no coincidence. It couldn't be. She got up from her desk. "Who'd you talk to there?"

"Guy's name was Rice, I think. Oliver Rice. He said my perp, Jeremy Burr, had moved on. Did time for drugs. Served out his sentence, then was moved to transitional housing. I put out feelers, but no hits yet."

"We were there today. At Colonial Pines," Ellis said. "When were you there?"

"This morning. I've spent the rest of the day looking for Burr." He creased his brow. "What's going on? Why were you two there?"

Ellis spun around to McCallister. "Why didn't Rice tell us this?"

"I have no idea."

Ellis returned her attention to Pelletier. "We need to find your suspect."

"Join the club. Like I said, that's what I've spent all day doing. You guys mind telling me what this is about?"

"Carter and his friend Tyler Beck—they were residents." She walked to his desk. "Both are now dead. Bryce, if Jeremy Burr has any family or friends around here, we need to know if they've seen him. Maybe one of them is keeping him off the grid. This man is in danger. He might not make it through tonight."

"I've already hit up known family members." Pelletier seemed to consider his options. "Although, he has a sister in

Orono. I ran by but got no answer. We could try again. She might at least know where he went."

With renewed determination, Ellis snatched her keys. "We should go. Now."

As dusk hovered over the city, Ellis led the way to the parking lot, climbing behind the wheel of her SUV. Pressing the ignition, she waited for McCallister and Pelletier to get in. "Kroll can't know about this."

McCallister buckled his seat belt. "Good thing he had other plans."

She pulled out of the parking lot, glancing into the rearview mirror at Pelletier. His cornflower blue eyes never ceased to captivate her. "You have an address?"

He looked at his phone. "Head to the 95 and go north. And then maybe one of you can fill me in on all this."

"Long story short," McCallister began, "we're not sure anyone at that halfway house is safe. Two guys—both dead in the last few days. We think there's a deal with the cartel, the state prison, and the guys getting transferred into the halfway house from a rehab facility."

"Take exit 197," Pelletier said before turning his attention back to McCallister. "That sounds clear as mud. But I'm guessing that's why the DEA is here."

Ellis swerved across two lanes of traffic and barely made the exit.

"Easy!" McCallister braced himself against the door.

She glanced through the rearview. "A little advance warning next time, Bryce?"

"Sorry about that. Make a right in a mile. That'll take us into the neighborhood." She headed in that direction, and then he continued, "Keep going. Should be the fourth house on the left." As Ellis arrived, he nodded. "Yep. That's it. The single-level red house with the sloped roofline."

Ellis cut the engine and peered at the home. "Bryce, why don't you take the lead here?"

"Got it." He jumped out of the back seat, Ellis and McCallister following closely behind. They reached the front porch, and Pelletier knocked on the door.

They only waited a moment or two before a woman opened it. She looked to be in her thirties. Thin with more wrinkles than she should have. Frayed brunette hair and smoker's lips. "Can I help you?"

"Maureen Burr?" Pelletier asked. "I'm Detective Pelletier, Bangor PD. We're looking for your brother, Jeremy. Have you seen or heard from him? Is he here?"

Ellis picked up on a glint in her eye, suggesting this was a visit the woman had expected. "Ma'am, if your brother is here, we need to talk to him."

"This is about saving his life, Ms. Burr," Pelletier added. "Please believe us when we say that if he's here, you're both in danger."

Appearing resigned, she took a step back, opening the door wider. "Come in. Jeremy's in the back bedroom. I'll get him."

The woman headed into the hall and knocked on a door. "Jeremy, come out. The cops are saying we're in danger. I don't know what you did, but you don't get to bring this shit down on me. Now come on. You need to talk to them."

McCallister stood near the front window, glancing out through the blinds. Ellis joined him. The street outside was quiet, just a few parked cars in front of homes and the soft amber glow of streetlights under a dimming sky.

A figure darted across the front yard, heading for the side of the house.

"I'll bet that's him," McCallister said. "We got a runner."

"I see him."

McCallister yanked open the front door and leaped down the porch steps, breaking into a sprint across the lawn.

Ellis turned to Pelletier. "Let's go!"

The man had disappeared around the far side of the house. Ellis scanned the grounds. "Where'd he go?"

McCallister pulled his weapon. "There. I see him."

Once again, he shot away, rounding the corner with Ellis and Pelletier working to catch up.

"Go left," she shouted at him. "I'll go right and catch up with Euan."

"Copy." Pelletier darted away.

She caught up to McCallister and glimpsed the man vaulting over the back fence. "That's him. He's getting away."

"Police, stop!" McCallister shouted, but Burr kept running. He hurdled the fence and charged after him down the back alley, disappearing beyond the trees.

"Damn it." Ellis followed, heart pounding, legs pumping. She grabbed the top of the wood fence, climbing up and leaping over in one swift motion. On the other side, she tumbled to the ground, landing on a narrow dirt pathway between the homes and the tree line several feet away.

She hurried to her feet. McCallister came into view far ahead; she could see he was closing the gap toward Burr. He scrambled over another fence and cut between two houses. Ellis darted away again, working hard to catch up to him. He cleared the fence in a single bound. Now, they were both out of sight.

Ellis searched for a way to the front of the houses again,

running to where they'd disappeared. Between the buildings, a footpath appeared. She ran along it, returning to the street, several houses down from where the chase had started.

She craned left, then right, a smile tugging on her lips. "There you are." Taking off again, Ellis scrambled to catch up to them. Burr was still ahead, but McCallister was only steps behind now. Beads of sweat trickled down her temples, and her heart burned as she watched McCallister grab a fistful of Burr's shirt, slowing him down until they both tumbled to the street. Within moments, she'd reached them.

"Stop running!" McCallister growled, yanking Burr up from the street and slamming him into the nearby lamppost.

Ellis withdrew her weapon. "Stop. Don't move." She caught McCallister's glance, nodding in return.

Burr struggled, panting for breath. McCallister spun him around and cuffed his hands behind his back. Ellis holstered her weapon, helping him get the man under control. She turned at the sound of footfalls. It was Pelletier. "Over here."

"Why are you chasing me?" Burr said, his voice tinged with panic. "I didn't do anything."

"We're trying to help you, Jeremy. Your life is in danger." McCallister held a firm hand on his shoulder. "And if you stay here, so is your sister's."

16

J eremy Burr sat on a chair in his sister's living room, a bottle of water in his hands. Ellis, Pelletier, and McCallister sat across from him on the sofa.

His sister soon returned with more water, handing out one each to the detectives.

The unexpected connection to Pelletier's case suggested the scheme was much larger than Ellis had suspected. But just how to tie the cartel to Carter's murder remained unclear. Kroll had seemed certain of a connection yet had offered nothing concrete. The idea of a partnership with the DEA now felt entirely one-sided.

"You knew Carter Ellis?" she asked.

Burr was a young man, in his mid-twenties, but his long face and slender features made him appear older. It was a look she recognized because Carter once had the very same air about him. Burr was still an addict.

"I knew him. I'd heard he died. Tyler told me." He looked down. "I didn't know Tyler was gone too."

"When did you last see Tyler Beck?" McCallister asked.

Burr picked at the label on his water bottle, avoiding eye contact with any of the detectives. "I saw him day before yesterday."

McCallister nodded. "Did he tell you he was afraid for his life?"

"Bro, we're all afraid for our lives."

"That's why we're here," Pelletier cut in. "Your prints were found at the home that was robbed last night. They had a Ring camera. You were captured on it. So why'd you do it?"

Burr looked at him with a furrowed brow. "Why do you think? I needed the money."

"For a debt or drugs?" Ellis cut in.

Burr's face and manner grew heated. "Look, you said I was in danger. What are you going to do about that, huh? Let me die like Carter and Tyler?"

"Who's your contact?" McCallister asked. "You're selling, aren't you? Same as your friends. Are you doing it for the cartel?"

The corner of Burr's mouth rose. "You think the cartel's going to send someone to deal with us? No, man. You got it wrong. That guy who comes to the halfway house, gives us product and shit, he's not cartel. He's just one of their middlemen. A nobody."

"We need a name if we're going to keep you safe," Ellis insisted. "And I need to know if this is the same person who had interactions with Carter Ellis."

Burr hesitated, glancing between the detectives. "They don't give us names. But you're asking if it's the same dude? Yeah, course it is. He runs all of us."

Ellis glanced away, angry with herself for not knowing any of this had been happening.

McCallister leaned in. "What about exchanges? How do

you get the product from him? Is there an address you can give us?"

Burr chewed his lip. "It ain't a set location. He rotates pickup points."

"Do you know who this guy answers to? You ever see anyone who looks higher up on the food chain?"

"No." Burr set his sights on Ellis. "What I do know is that Carter was meeting with someone else too. Not sure about Tyler, but Carter definitely was."

Ellis felt a surge of anticipation. "Who?"

Burr's mouth turned down in a gesture of indifference. "Can't say for sure, but word has it he was talking to the feds."

"DEA or FBI?" she pressed.

He wiped away the sweat from his brow. "Who knows? Does it matter? I didn't get involved. Tyler and him were tight, but I guess you can't ask him now either." He couldn't quite look at Ellis. "So what's going to happen to me, huh? You gotta put me somewhere they won't find me."

She looked at Pelletier. "You could book him on charges for the break-in. Keep him in custody for a while."

"I'm not going back to prison," Burr said. "Fuck that shit. You said if I helped you, you'd help me."

"And we will," Pelletier shot back. "Detective Ellis is right. The safest place for you is in our custody."

THE MORE ELLIS learned about what her brother had been caught up in, the guiltier she felt. How could she not have known any of this was going on in her city? Surely Moss had had some clue about the scope of the operation. According to Burr, all the people he knew from the halfway house were knee-deep in what seemed like a type of servitude. But what part had Cochran House played in all this? That was where the money had been shifted to. What had been offered to former inmates to participate? Shorter sentences? Money? Maybe it was only the chance to live, to survive.

Under a darkened sky, Ellis and the others returned to the station, with Jeremy Burr now in custody. Pelletier went on to process him while she stood with McCallister, discussing their next steps. "Any chance Moss is still here?"

"Probably. Why?" McCallister asked.

She glanced down the hall, toward Patrol. "Who's he got working Narcotics right now?"

"I have no idea."

She paused to let the idea form. "He has to know something about this. The drugs flowing through some sort of middleman. I'd like to find out if this unnamed middleman is already on Moss's radar."

"Kroll might have a better idea," McCallister said.

Ellis set her hands on her hips, gazing into the corridor toward Patrol. "No. I don't want to alert him to this. Not until we know more. He's keeping us in the dark. He wouldn't be focusing the DEA's efforts in Bangor if he didn't know a lot more than he's been willing to say. We're being used."

McCallister scoffed, as if this was hardly news. "Wouldn't be the first time. That's how these guys operate."

"Yeah, well, not in my city. I'm going to see if I can track down Moss. I want to find out what he knows about the halfway house and Cochran House. Anything that will shine a light on what we're really up against here." Ellis made her way through the Patrol bullpen and straight to the office of Sergeant Devin Moss.

"Good to see I'm not the only one working late," Ellis said, walking inside.

Moss smiled, his lips getting lost under an ample nose. "Detective Ellis, what brings you down here to see us beat cops?"

"Figured since you got promoted to day shift, you would've been long gone," she replied. "But I had to see for myself."

He scratched the back of his head, hardly moving his thick mass of brown hair. "What's on your mind, then? Since I'm here."

Ellis took a seat across from his desk. "We brought in a suspect in Bryce's B and E investigation. A guy named Jeremy Burr."

Moss leaned back. "Should I know that name?"

"He lived at the halfway house where my brother had been staying—Colonial Pines."

"I heard what happened." Moss shook his head. "I'm damn sorry about that."

"Thanks." She quickly moved on. "The reason I ask is that I'm looking to find out more about who you have working narcotics right now. What they have going on."

"A couple guys." He narrowed his gaze. "Sounds like you suspect your brother was tangled up in the trade?"

"Yep. And possibly several of the people who also reside, or resided, in that house. From what I know right now, it seems they'd all been transferred on various dates from Warren to Cochran House Rehab and then on to this halfway house in Colonial Pines."

"That sounds like something that would've made its way through the pipeline, you know?" Moss said.

"I would've thought so." Ellis leaned over. "This guy,

Jeremy Burr? Sounds like he and the others are working with someone connected to the cartel. Which is why the DEA is breathing down my neck right now, insisting on working together. This all came about when my brother died." She leaned back again. "So maybe the dam is about to break. People from that place are turning up dead."

"Well, then...let me see what I can pull up. Do a little digging into our informants. I can send over the files on our active narcotics cases, too, if that would help. Since we assisted McCallister and Bevins in that past investigation, it opened up some significant new leads for us."

"So they're connected?" Ellis asked.

"Don't know. It's possible."

"Might be a good idea to figure out if your informants are also talking to DEA," she continued. "Any chance you could get some answers on that front?"

"If that's happening, we need to know," he demanded. "I'll be damned if the DEA has been coming after my informants and keeping their mouths shut about it."

———

BEVINS STOOD ON HIS BALCONY, his hands pressed against the railing, peering out into the trees. The moon illuminated the lush landscape, and a warm breeze brushed against his skin.

Every word of that report haunted him as he relived those hazy moments when his entire world had collapsed. But Daddy had seen to it that he never paid the price. He'd asked Fletch for help, but after seeing the report, what could she do? Someone had intended for him to run over that barbed-wire obstruction, causing the accident. The only solace was in knowing he hadn't been the cause of the crash, regardless of the fact he'd been intoxicated.

He'd left the office tonight feeling confused, distant from the team, hopeless. And as he cast his gaze out over the tree line, he considered how best to handle this new development.

Frustrated, Bevins returned inside, dropping onto his sofa and opening his laptop. The passenger in the accident, Lance Curry, had been a close friend. A West Point cadet. He was the one Bevins had left alone to die inside that car. But as he searched the name of his friend, the only thing that turned up was that he'd died in a car wreck. No when or where or how. It was as though Lance had been practically erased from existence.

"Goddam it." Bevins slammed the lid. This was getting him nowhere. He walked to the kitchen, yanked open a cupboard, and grabbed a bottle of whiskey. He felt his eyes sting with tears before deciding to open the bottle. The fiery smell of rye and oak burned his nostrils. He poured it down his throat, feeling the burn with each swig, then set down the bottle hard enough to splash its caramel-colored liquid onto the granite countertop.

Bevins grabbed his phone from his pocket and dialed Fletch. She answered on the third ring. "It's me." He felt out of breath, like the panic in him was about to burst its dam. "Can we meet? I—I need—"

"I'll come to you," she cut in. "You home?"

"Yeah."

"Give me twenty minutes."

Bevins ended the call. He paced his apartment, meandering into his bedroom, wondering how many women had been there and why. He thought back to all the arrogant remarks he'd made to the people on his team. Boasting about how great a detective he thought he was. What a joke.

He leaned against the doorframe, wondering why the hell Ellis ever defended him. He hadn't deserved it. It was as if he'd been this person who'd only cared about himself for so long that now, to feel something else—regret, shame, fear of losing everything—it terrified him.

A knock sounded on the door. Bevins walked toward it, pulling it open.

Fletch looked him up and down. "For God's sake, Connor, are you drunk?" She stepped inside without waiting for an invitation.

His chin quivered as he closed the door behind her. "I needed something to take the edge off."

Fletch sighed, gentle but firm as she guided him to the couch. "Come on, sit down; talk to me. I want to help, but you've got to keep your shit together."

Bevins sank onto the couch, the fight draining from him. "I don't know what to do, Fletch. I let him die and, what's worse, I let my dad cover it up for me. And now..."

She settled next to him on the couch. "Hey, look at me. We're going to figure this out. But getting drunk and losing control isn't going to help. You've got me in your corner no matter what."

He turned toward her, his eyes searching her face. In his drunken, emotionally charged state, he found himself leaning in, overcome with gratitude for her unwavering support. Their lips met, and he kissed her.

Fletch gently pulled back after a moment, placing a hand on his chest. "Connor, wait."

Bevins blinked, emerging from his stupor. "I'm sorry." He

ran a hand over his face. "I shouldn't have done that. I don't know what I was thinking."

Fletch offered a sympathetic gaze. "It's okay. We've all been there. Done things in moments of weakness we regret later. But this isn't you, it's the alcohol and everything you're dealing with."

He nodded, his expression still strained. "You're right. I'm sorry, I'm not myself right now." He leaned back, staring at the ceiling.

"Tell me about your friend Lance."

Bevins pulled up again, some clarity returning to his eyes. "He was a good guy. One of the best at the academy. Better than me by far. His classroom scores, tactical scores, everything."

She sighed and appeared hesitant. "Maybe that was the problem."

He narrowed his gaze. "What do you mean?"

"Maybe he was better than he was supposed to be." Fletch reached for Connor's hand. "Is it possible that you weren't the target that night, and Lance was?"

He paused, glancing down at his hands, her fingers around his. "To think about it now...it feels like it was a dream. The car swerved; tires squealed. I never saw anything in the road. I just remember us laughing and listening to music." He stopped, feeling the pain filling his chest. "When I came to, the car was totaled and Lance..." His face crumpled.

"You don't have to say it," she said.

Bevins took a shaky breath. "My dad showed up before the cops. He pulled me out of there, told me not to say a word to anyone. And I didn't. The next day, the whole thing disappeared." He snapped his fingers. "Like nothing ever happened, except now my friend was dead. No way he was the target. I'm the one whose dad was a high-ranking official. Lance...Lance didn't have any enemies."

"I don't know, Con," she replied, raising her brow. "Maybe he did and didn't know it."

ELLIS EMERGED from Moss's office, hopeful the files he was about to send would shed light on what his team had been covering regarding the narcotics trade. Moss had suggested the case he'd worked with McCallister and Bevins wasn't tied to this. Maybe he was right, but in some ways, they were all connected. It was unavoidable.

They'd brought down a large operation. Could this situation have been the cartel's answer? Going a different route? Anything was possible. As she began her trek to the lobby, she heard her name and stopped to turn back. "Leo?"

He hurried to catch up to her.

"What are you still doing here?" she asked.

He paused to catch his breath. "You were right. He used his mother's birthday as a passcode."

"You got into Carter's laptop?" Her eyes lit up. "What'd you find?"

"Come on and I'll show you." Brown turned around, leading the way back.

Ellis trailed closely behind. This was the best news she'd heard all day. While they now had a possible witness in custody, thanks to Pelletier, this could be what they truly needed. Maybe it would even reveal whom Carter had been meeting with.

"Your brother kept a schedule." Brown sat at his desk and began to type at a feverish pace.

"That doesn't seem like him," she replied.

"Come take a look."

Ellis walked around, peering at the screen over Brown's shoulder. "Okay. There's a calendar here." She read on. "Appointments but no names. What about emails?"

"Nothing that stood out, but it might be best for you to see for yourself and make that determination." He pointed at the screen. "First, take a look at the dates here."

Ellis examined the calendar again. "That last one...he was found two days later in the river." She scanned dates and times, but saw nothing to suggest who Carter had been meeting with. Most of the entries were vague—"Meet J at the spot," "Pickup at 11." But two days before Carter's body had been found, the entry simply read, "9 p.m. appt."

"Anything else about that nine p.m. meeting?" Ellis asked. "No location or initials to identify the person?"

Brown shook his head. "No. It's all pretty cryptic."

Ellis quickly pulled out her notebook, jotting down the three meetings, which were all scheduled for 9 p.m. "That's something. Three meetings with potentially the same person." She tapped her pen on the notepad. "I need to figure out where these meetings took place. Can you pull his phone records and see if there are any calls or texts around those times that might indicate a location?"

"Already on it," Brown replied.

"Thanks." She patted his arm. "You're a miracle worker, Leo. Thanks for this. I'll work on what we have until you find more."

"Glad I could help."

17

J eremy Burr was safe in Bangor police custody, but for how long? His association with her brother and Tyler Beck put him squarely in the middle of this investigation. To what end, Ellis couldn't yet be certain. The laptop, now in Leo Brown's capable hands, would yield answers in time. The question was, how much time did they have?

Returning to the bullpen, Ellis found that only McCallister remained there. "Where's Agent Kroll?"

"Gone," he replied. "Said he had to check in with his team."

She set down the notepad on her desk. "Brown retrieved a calendar from Carter's laptop. Several dates were marked with appointments at the same time, so I asked him to pull phone records to cross-reference those appointments with any calls he made at the time."

"That could open doors for us," McCallister said. "Who do you think he was meeting?"

"I'm betting on a cartel connection, which makes Burr's

presence all the more important." She checked the time. "Listen, it's getting late. I think I'll head out. I'll see you tomorrow?"

"Same time as always." He grinned, though she sensed an underlying disappointment in his tone. "Goodnight, Becca."

"Goodnight." Walking out, she felt his eyes on her, as though he knew she had no intention of going home. Not yet. She wanted to go back to where it had happened. Try to retrace what she believed had been her brother's final moments before going into the water.

Kroll's single-minded focus on cartel activity left her investigation without forward momentum. Except for the laptop, a critical piece of evidence that she had previously overlooked. Brown and his infinite talents held the key, but was there more she could do? Going back to see Hank, only to reveal she'd had no news, would salt the wound. Failure was never an easy thing to come to terms with, so Ellis would not accept such an outcome.

Under the summer night sky, she returned to the river-walk. The city was alive with visitors and residents enjoying the warmth of the season. Ellis passed several people taking evening strolls after dinner at one of the many restaurants in the area. The river sparkled under a clear sky and full moon. Music from the bars sounded in the distance.

She was reminded of Piper, her dearest friend since high school. They would often come out here after a few drinks. Laughing and talking, complaining about Andrew before the divorce. So much had happened in the past few days, she hadn't even called to tell Piper about Carter. She'd be angry about that, and retribution would come in the form of a full embrace followed by tears, followed by an apology. The two never could stay mad with one another. How she missed her friend right now.

The sound of the current filled her ears as she stood near the handrail. Climbing over, she approached the river's edge, near to the bridge. Cars rushed overhead. Waves pushed against the rocks around the pylon. "I'm so sorry I wasn't here to help you. You didn't deserve this." Tears spilled down her cheeks. She imagined Carter's last moments as the smell of the surging river filled her senses. "Who brought you here? Who did you meet with?"

The questions lingering in the air, Ellis opened her eyes and her gaze swept across the street, away from the water. They locked onto a solitary ATM enclosed in a small vestibule inside the larger bank building. "The camera."

She returned her sights to the river, then back to the camera on the machine. Was it possible it could have picked up movement from so far away? The location was farther upstream from where he'd been found, away from any public parking. A location she'd dismissed on first arriving at the scene, before even a hint of a suggestion that Carter had been murdered. And again, Abbott was proven right. Her bias against Carter, her own brother, had refused to allow her to consider alternatives.

The vestibule was unlocked, but the bank was, of course, closed. Retrieving any potential footage would have to wait, along with the hope this would not be another dead end. Yet the reality was—it was Carter's laptop that would change the trajectory of her investigation. This new idea was little more than a grasp at straws, but waiting, letting Kroll direct the orchestra, was getting her nowhere.

Amid the lively atmosphere of the riverwalk, Ellis returned to the parking lot. Walking to her Tahoe, a soft click echoed. Her head snapped toward the sound, her instincts flaring.

A car parked in the shadows flickered to life, its headlights slicing through the darkness.

She placed her hand instinctively on her sidearm, attempting to make out the type of vehicle, though distance and darkness hindered her. But before she took a single step toward it, the vehicle roared to life, retreating toward the other exit. This was no tourist or resident. Ellis knew someone had followed her. The taillights faded from view. "And who might you be?"

Her senses heightened, her mind projected an image—a fleeting memory of a dark vehicle of similar design. Ellis straightened up, still peering out at the lights of the shops and restaurants. "Kroll." There was one way to know for sure that this wasn't her bias showing through once again. Kroll had mentioned where he'd been staying—the Charles Inn. Right down the street.

She drove on and within two minutes had pulled around the back to the hotel's parking lot. She cut the lights and coasted to a stop.

There, under the faint amber hue of a streetlamp, was the black Lexus. Dark. Similar style.

Ellis got out, eyes peeled, and walked toward the vehicle. Placing her hand on the hood of the car, it was warm to the touch. "Kroll, why the hell are you following me?"

THE MORNING SUN crept over the horizon, shining through Ellis's windshield. Here she was, early Monday, idling in the station's parking lot. She tapped her fingers on the steering wheel, keeping her gaze fixed on the entrance. It was all she could do over the weekend to keep from confronting Kroll at his hotel. But doing so would risk blowing up her investigation, losing it completely to the DEA.

McCallister's black Ford pulled up next to her. He must've seen that she was still inside. Good, because she'd been waiting for him. Ellis stepped out to meet him as he emerged. "Morning."

"What's going on? Why are you out here?" He leaned back inside and retrieved two cups of coffee. "Here. Figured you could use it."

"You have no idea how much. Thanks." Ellis took a sip, shifting her gaze to the station's entrance. "The other night... after I left here, I drove down to where we found Carter."

"Can I ask why?"

"I haven't been myself on this case, Euan. I've let my feelings about my brother get in the way of my objectivity." She took another sip as he glanced away for a moment, seemingly holding his tongue. "We should've found that laptop days ago. Anyway, I went back. There's an ATM machine farther upstream. I'd like to request the footage from it, if for nothing else than to cover our bases."

He held the paper cup with both hands. "We can do that. But you didn't answer my question. Why were you sitting out here?"

"Kroll. He hasn't arrived yet," she replied.

"How does that matter?"

Ellis kept her gaze on the entrance. "He was following me the other night." She raised a preemptive hand. "It's fine. I didn't do anything stupid. I tracked down the vehicle, not knowing for sure it was him, until I arrived at his hotel. It was his car I saw. That's why I've been sitting out here. I'm trying to figure out what to do about it."

"Let's go in." McCallister placed his hand on her back to usher her ahead. "We'll talk to Abbott. Get his take."

As they walked through the lobby and toward the stairs, Ellis stopped at the bottom step to see Pelletier on the landing. "Morning, Bryce. We still have Burr in custody?"

"Morning, guys." He nodded. "For now. I'm going to file charges today, so we'll see when the judge schedules the arraignment and go from there. He'll probably get bail, but I'll do my best to keep him from posting it. Make sure he sees the danger."

McCallister nudged Ellis, tossing a nod to the lobby. "Look who's here."

She turned back to Pelletier as he stepped down to join them. "Listen, I'm expecting Brown to send over Carter's phone records. Can you do me a favor and follow up with him on that?"

"Yeah, of course." He picked up on the bristling tension. "Something going on with that DEA agent?"

Ellis grinned. "I'm about to find out."

THE POUNDING IN BEVINS' head drowned out the chatter as he arrived in the bullpen. No sleep and too much booze over the weekend had left him exhausted. He felt Fletch's eyes on him, following his every step as he reached his desk. He was grateful she'd been there for him the other night, but now felt embarrassed for having made a clumsy move on her.

She walked over to him, sympathy masking her face. "How you feeling?"

"I've been better." He chuckled awkwardly. "You? Did you get any sleep?"

She tilted her head. "Some. So what's the plan?"

Bevins opened his laptop. "I'm going to see what I can find on Lance, like you said. Then I've arranged to get the car back here. I have to follow up on where it's at right now." He set his gaze on her. "Thanks for coming over, Fletch. It meant a lot to me. And I'm sorry I, you know…"

"Yeah, no. Don't worry about it." Fletch swatted away his words of apology. "Just remember, if the accident was buried deep, that means your friend was buried too. Don't expect to find much in the public domain. You might stand a better shot making some calls to the family."

"Christ, I can't talk to them." He looked away. "They blame me. They're right to blame me for what happened."

She reached for his hand. "What happened wasn't your fault. Not entirely. We read the report. We know what was put out in the road. That's what caused the accident."

"Yeah, you're right." Bevins nodded. "I'll consider contacting Lance's folks."

18

Ellis was about to charge forward, demanding answers as to why Kroll had been following her. It was up to McCallister to get her to see reason. Assuming she was right, giving away her hand by confronting him with accusations was the wrong way to go about it. Kroll knew the players. They still needed him in this game if they hoped to win.

McCallister stepped in front of her as she rounded her desk. "Becca, wait." In a low tone, he continued, "We need to let this play out. If you tell him that you know what he did, we'll be shut out of whatever remains of this investigation."

"Are you kidding me?" She shot Kroll a sideways glance. "He's not our friend."

"We don't need friends. We need answers." He leaned closer. "And that man has them. Right now, we tell him we have Burr. That it happened after he left, and the guy was wanted on Bryce's B and E investigation. We had nothing to do with it, not until we learned about the connection to the halfway house. The guy's smart," McCallister added. "He knows how to talk his way out of trouble. But we'll be better armed. And we can start putting two and two together."

At this, Ellis nodded. "Fine. I can get on board with that."

"Come on." He looked back. "We need to do this now while our people gather the phone records and the ATM footage. Kroll isn't off the hook. We're just trying to figure out whether he's an ally."

After a few moments, he'd talked her into it. Ellis spun around, walking toward Kroll's desk. "We have an update. You got some time?"

"Of course." He rolled back in his chair. "What's going on?"

Appearing reluctant, Ellis launched into it. "We tracked down a B and E suspect named Jeremy Burr. His name is also in connection with a narcotics investigation headed up by Sergeant Moss. Detective Pelletier brought Burr in for questioning on his case, but also to assess whether he had any information related to Carter's murder. Turned out, he was living in the same halfway house."

"Sounds like an odd coincidence." Kroll's expression remained neutral. "And did he have anything useful to share?"

"Not much. But after we made the connection to our investigation, we thought we'd take a run at him. Care to join us?"

"Absolutely." He stood, with a gesture of readiness. "I'm set when you are, Detectives."

McCallister felt relieved Ellis had gone along with the plan. He'd seen the way she'd looked at him earlier, talking about her brother's laptop. She blamed him, as well as herself, for not finding it the first time. Or at the very least, she had been angry they hadn't conducted a more thorough search. But he'd seen how she was in that moment. Despite all her anger at Carter, she loved him. And that meant her emotions were getting in the way. He'd done what he thought needed to be done, and that was to hold off for another time. Maybe he had made the wrong call, but he'd do it again if necessary.

They headed downstairs to the holding cells, with Kroll following.

When they arrived, Ellis caught up to the officer on duty. "We'd like to have Jeremy Burr brought to an interview room."

"Yes, ma'am." The officer headed away.

McCallister eyed room two. "Looks empty. Shall we?" He opened the door, gesturing inside. After Ellis and Kroll entered, he let the door close and joined them at the table. Ellis still seemed on edge, simmering anger just visible under the surface. What bothered him was why. Why would Kroll follow her to begin with? She knew so little about her own brother's death, let alone a larger criminal enterprise involving the Mexican cartel. What was Kroll afraid of?

The door opened, and Burr shuffled in, looking annoyed at being pulled out of his cell. His eyes darted between the detectives, lingering for a moment on Kroll before his gaze slid away.

"Have a seat, Jeremy," McCallister said, motioning to the chair across the table.

Burr sat down, his face and body language betraying his apprehension.

"We just have a few more questions for you," McCallister continued. "You were living in the halfway house with Carter Ellis and Tyler Beck. We believe their deaths are connected to large-scale drug operations here in Bangor."

Burr shifted in his seat but didn't respond.

"Here's the thing," McCallister said, leaning forward. "Your name has come up multiple times during our ongoing investigations into drug distribution networks operating in Bangor." That was a lie, but he needed something to pierce through the armor.

Burr shrugged. "You got me on the B and E. Fine. But I got nothing to do with any drug deals."

For a split second, McCallister noticed Burr's eyes shift once more to Kroll. It seemed Ellis picked up on it too. "Forgive my manners. I should introduce you to DEA Agent Kroll. Agent Kroll, do you have any questions for Jeremy?"

Kroll leaned forward, meeting Burr's gaze. "It's clear that the detectives sitting next to me think that you know the victims in our investigation, possibly owing to the larger issue of your involvement in trafficking operations. Can't argue their logic; you did live in the same house with them. Now, something tells me a low-level trafficker like yourself doesn't operate in a vacuum. In fact, I'd bet you have connections."

There it was again. Something in Burr's eyes changed. McCallister was certain now—these two knew each other.

"I don't know what you're talking about, man. I don't know anything about the cartel or anything else," Burr said. "I know Carter and Tyler were a couple of dudes who lived with me at the halfway house for a while. Don't know who killed them or why."

"See, I don't think that's entirely true." Kroll raised his finger. "I think you know exactly who's bringing the drugs in. And that those same people might be the ones who wanted your buddies dead."

Burr licked his lips, darting his gaze as if looking for an

escape. He looked back at Kroll. "I don't have to say shit to you. I want a lawyer."

EVEN AFTER FLETCH'S insistence that he contact Lance's family, Bevins tried again to find something—anything about his dead friend. Using the police database, he'd dredged up a death certificate. But his West Point Academy records were sealed. It should have come as no surprise: Jack had covered his ass and his son's. Yet, years later, someone had uncovered just enough to reignite the flame.

Bevins wasn't going to get this information on his own. He needed someone with security clearance to pull Lance's files out from under lock and key at West Point. Should he go to Jack? His father had buried all of this, but in light of this new information, the obvious intentional sabotage, why would he still have chosen to cover it up?

Bevins picked up his phone and pressed Murphy's contact. The line rang for a moment, and then he answered. "Hey, can you talk?"

Murph was quiet for a moment. "Hang on."

Bevins heard movement, as though Murph was walking somewhere. He waited.

"Okay, yeah, what's going on? Everything all right?" Murph asked.

"I'm at a standstill, man. I don't know where to go from here."

"Look, Con, I can only do so much. I already put my ass on the line to get you what I did."

He rubbed his temple. "Yeah, I know that, and I appreciate the hell out of it. I won't ask for anything else except for maybe someone you could point me to."

"What do you mean?" Murph asked.

"I need someone who can pull Lance Curry's academy files. I tried. I can't access shit. Just his death certificate. And after what I read in the report, going to Jack would be a big mistake." Bevins listened while it seemed Murph was considering the request.

"I might know a guy. But look, it might cost you. Money or a favor or something like that. Don't know, but he won't do this out of the kindness of his heart."

Bevins nodded. "I hear you."

"Then let me make a call. Give me till the end of the day, and I'll have an answer for you."

Relief swelled in his chest. "Thank you, man. I know what I'm asking, and I know you're sticking your neck out for me. It won't be forgotten."

"Yeah, well, going down this road is dangerous, all right? We get caught, both of us will go to prison."

There was nothing to say after that, so the call ended. Bevins set down his phone, hating himself for asking Murph to stick his neck out again, praying it wouldn't get chopped off. He rubbed his face, feeling tired and frustrated. And when his phone rang again, he thought for a moment it was Murph backing out, but instead it was a number he didn't recognize. The area code—he did.

"Detective Bevins," he answered.

"Detective, now, huh?" A gravelly voice sounded. "That car you wanted moved..."

It was then he realized the caller was the old guy from the junkyard. "Yes, sir. I understand it's in transit now."

"Not anymore, son. It's been returned."

Bevins drew in his breath. "Returned? To you? Why?"

"You got me. All's they said was that it had something to do with some sort of military investigation. Said whoever bought it had no claim to it."

"No claim?" He pulled back in his chair. "It was in your yard, and I bought it."

"I'm aware of that. What I'm telling you now is that they ain't gonna let you take it, son. Now, as far as the money goes..."

"Keep it. For your troubles. Thank you for the call." Bevins set down his phone, hard. "What the hell?"

———

THEY'D HAD no choice but to end the interview with Jeremy Burr. The man wanted his lawyer. That was that.

Ellis had agreed to McCallister's plan. As far as she was concerned, this was another strike against the DEA agent. He and Burr seemed to have known each other. But what did that mean? And could it lead to answers about Carter's death? Now was the time for her to play along. The three walked through the corridor, back toward the lobby. "I think we know now that Burr was into the same deal we think Carter and Beck were into." She captured Kroll's attention. "The size of this operation seems to be growing."

"I agree," he replied. "Our information from the border crossing has led us here. The cartel is making its presence known. So if we can find out who's calling the shots, then I can take that to the rest of my team and find a way to bring it all crashing down."

Ellis now had no choice but to assume Kroll had been a handler, and these guys were his informants. Beck, Burr, and maybe Carter too. It explained why Beck had written "handler" in his notebook. Could've been what got Carter killed. How long were she and McCallister supposed to hide the fact that they knew all this? McCallister had wanted to use this opportunity to buy time. Was it enough? She was about to find out.

Pelletier was at his desk when they returned to the bullpen. He was exactly who Ellis had hoped to see in this moment. She set down her files and walked over to him while McCallister kept his attention on Kroll. "Did they give you the footage?"

"It took some persuasion," he began. "They wanted a warrant, but I told him we were only interested in identifying a potential murder suspect, so they handed it over."

"And have you seen it?" Ellis asked.

Pelletier shifted his gaze beyond her to McCallister and Kroll. "You might want to look at it first before sharing anything with the DEA."

A roiling sense of dread balled in her gut. "Abbott's office? I need to update him anyway."

Pelletier nodded, snatching the flash drive from his desk. "Let's go."

She left McCallister to keep Kroll occupied while she and Pelletier headed toward Abbott's office. Standing outside, Ellis caught his attention. "Sarge, mind if we come in?"

Abbott nodded as he closed the file on his desk. "I've been waiting for you. Tell me what you have."

Ellis closed the door as they entered. "Bryce has ATM surveillance footage upstream from where we found Carter. He wanted me to see it privately first. Figured you should be in on it too."

"Privately? Why?"

She glanced away. "Sir, I'm not sure what to make of Kroll. Something about his involvement in our investigation makes me think he's only looking to learn what we know."

Abbott reached out for the flash drive as Pelletier handed it over. "We'll discuss that in a minute. Let me take a look first. Have you seen it?"

"No, sir." She walked around to watch over his shoulder.

Abbott inserted the flash drive into his laptop and opened up the video files. The first file loaded, and he hit play.

On the screen, the riverwalk path appeared empty at first. Then a lanky figure with familiar dirty blond hair walked into frame.

"Oh my God. It's Carter. When was this?" Ellis asked, her voice trembling despite herself.

"I flagged the first video you're looking at now," Pelletier said. "It was nine p.m., two days before you found him."

"Nine o'clock." Ellis nodded. "Matches the appointment in his calendar."

They continued to watch as Carter paced back and forth, glancing around as though nervous. After a couple of minutes, another man approached him.

"You gotta be kidding me." She pointed at the screen. "That's Kroll. Tell me that's him."

"Looks like him to me," Abbott replied. "Same height, hair, similar build."

The two exchanged what appeared to be heated words, though the video had no sound. Carter was waving his hands in apparent frustration or maybe fear, while Kroll stood firm.

"There's our proof," Ellis said. "He was there. Agent Kroll was with Carter before he died."

They continued watching as Carter grew more agitated. Finally, he turned and stormed off down the sidewalk. Kroll watched him go, then pulled out his phone. Within moments, Carter had disappeared from view; then Kroll was gone.

Ellis stared at the screen. "That's it. That's all there is?"

"No one else comes into frame until daylight," Pelletier replied. "But it's there in black and white—Carter was there."

"With the DEA agent," she added. "But he left, meaning whatever happened during that conversation set Carter on a path that ultimately led to his death."

Abbott raised his hand. "Hold on, Becca. You don't know what was said. All you know is that when Kroll left, Carter was still alive. Someone else got to him."

"There's no way to know that based on this video alone." She searched for meaning in the evidence presented. "Kroll thinks we don't know about his contact with Carter. Why would he keep this from us and our investigation into his death? Why not admit to meeting with my brother two days before he died?"

Abbott rubbed his temple. "I can only imagine he's keeping it hush-hush so that he can learn for himself who murdered Carter. If he lets you in on the fact Carter was an informant, which I assume is where you're going with this, that could derail your investigation and his."

"I don't get how that's possible." Ellis walked around the desk again to face Abbott. "Unless...What if Kroll was the one who signed him out of the facility? Put him in the halfway house? And he did so without permission from

Hank, who had guardianship." Ellis shot a glance at the door. "I have to talk to Kroll. He needs to know we know what he's done. If we don't do this, Sarge, then Carter died for no reason." Ellis marched out of Abbott's office.

Pelletier hurried to catch up with her. "You sure about this, Becca?" he asked, chasing her down the hall.

She turned to him but kept up a brisk pace. "We're not getting anywhere, and it's because of Kroll. He wanted this joint operation, yet he's the one who's been holding back. I have to know why."

They arrived at the bullpen, and Ellis headed straight to Kroll's desk, bypassing McCallister along the way. "Agent Kroll." She slammed down the flash drive onto his desk. "I need you to tell me why you were talking with my brother two days before he was found murdered."

Kroll's face grew taut. "What's that now?"

Ellis heard McCallister's footfalls approach, but she wasn't going to stop now. "This is footage from the ATM across the street, upstream from where we found my brother. You met with Carter. Had what looked like a heated conversation, and then he left. And you left. Why?" She took in a breath to steady her anger. "Why were you there?"

19

The sweeping views of the Potomac with the Washington Monument farther afield offered a stunning backdrop to Jack Bevins' Pentagon office, where he served at the pleasure of the Secretary of Defense.

A knock on his door drew him away from the view. "Come in."

A young man in a crisp blue uniform delivered a steaming cup of black coffee and placed it on the desk.

"Thank you."

"Yes, sir." He saluted sharply before exiting the office.

As he took his first sip, the familiar chime of his secure cell phone had him frowning as he glanced at the display. He answered. "Bevins here."

"Jack, it's been a while. How are you?"

A crease appeared as he furrowed his brow still more. "Charles, it has been a while." Jack immediately realized something was up. This wasn't going to be a casual conversation. "What can I do for you?"

"It's more what I'm about to do for you, Jack." He paused

a moment. "Looks like someone's been digging around your family's garden recently."

Jack adjusted his tie, pulling back his shoulders. "In what way, may I ask?"

"The report. The original report. It's been accessed. Copied to a cloud server."

Now he raised his chin in defiance. "You know this for certain?"

"Is that a real question?"

Jack sighed. "All right. Do you have a name?"

"No. Whoever accessed the file did so anonymously and through a secure VPN. The server was also secure. I only know that it was accessed. Figured you'd want to know too."

Jack ran his finger around the rim of the steaming coffee cup. "And the car?"

"Still in the junkyard. But someone was there recently. Tried to have it moved. The old guy who owns the place filed a transport ticket, which got flagged in the transportation department. I was duly notified. That's how I found out about the report too."

"Has anyone else been made aware?" Jack rubbed his forehead.

"Not to my knowledge. This is cause for concern, my friend. What do you plan to do?"

"I have some ideas. Do me a favor? Keep me posted if anything else relating to that file turns up. Anyone else looking into things."

"You know I will. Jack, this isn't something you want getting out."

"I am aware of that, Charles. It won't. I'll put a stop to it. Thank you for the call." Jack set down his phone, taking hold of the coffee cup for a sip. The implications of this news would demand his full attention.

Someone was looking into the MP report about his son's car accident. Even went so far as to find the vehicle. He had thought that was all in the past, but clearly someone was still interested in digging up dirt on the Bevins family. Someone likely beyond the pissant blogger who'd posted those absurd lies.

Jack contemplated calling his son but decided against it. No need to worry him unnecessarily, plus the boy could sometimes be reckless in how he handled things. Better for Jack to investigate this himself first. The timing of this blogger and now the file? No coincidence.

He slid open a desk drawer and riffled through a stack of business cards until he found the one he was looking for— an old buddy from intelligence circles.

Jack picked up his phone. "Rich, it's Jack Bevins."

"Jack, how the hell are you?" Rich replied.

"I've been better. Listen, I need a favor."

"Name it."

Jack turned his chair around to the window once again. "I need to find out who's been looking into Connor's old files. One in particular. I suspect you already know to what I am referring."

"I have a solid idea."

"Good. It's been accessed and uploaded to a cloud server. I need to know by whom," Jack said. "How long will it take for you to get that information?"

"Depends, but I'd say in the next twenty-four to thirty-six hours, I should have it narrowed down," Rich replied. "That too long?"

"No. No, that should be fine. I'm also looking for someone, if you'd be so good as to help with that endeavor as well."

"Give me a name."

Jack grabbed his coffee again, bringing it to his lips. "Someone on the internet who thinks people give a shit about what he has to say." He took a sip, swallowing the warm brew. "He's sticking his nose where it doesn't belong. I'll send you the details. I need a location."

"I'll get on it right now. That, I can probably get to you by the end of today. Soon enough?"

Jack smiled. "Perfect. Appreciate the help, as always. Talk soon, my friend."

ELLIS WASN'T ABOUT to budge until Kroll confessed to keeping the truth from them. McCallister was at her side. Pelletier had returned to his desk, seemingly unsure of how much he should be involved in this.

With her eyes fixed on his, she continued, "Did you kill him?"

"No. For God's sake. Of course not," Kroll shot back. "Look, I couldn't tell you any of this for fear of jeopardizing your investigation."

"My investigation?" Ellis rocked back on her heels. "How the hell would knowing you were Carter's handler have jeopardized anything? Did you sign him out of Cochran House and oversee his transfer into the halfway house too?"

Kroll appeared resigned, rubbing his neck. "I couldn't risk exposing my informants, including the ones inside the cartel. Which, if you would've known the truth, you would've uncovered as well, ensuring they ended up just like Carter."

Ellis paced a tight circle. "I can't believe this."

McCallister reached out for her. "Becca..."

"No." She shrugged him off. "Who ordered his murder? Was it the cartel? And who else are you working with, because I suspect Tyler Beck was also one of your informants. What about Jeremy Burr? Is he?"

Kroll waited for her rant to end. "You want me to answer, or are you just going to keep lobbing questions at me?"

Ellis felt her phone buzzing in her pocket. She retrieved it. "I have to take this." Moving away several steps, she answered. "Dad, what's up?"

"Detective Rebecca Ellis, I take it," the voice replied.

She stopped cold, a chill climbing up her spine. "Who is this? Where's Hank?"

"Retired detective Hank Ellis?" the man asked. "He's here. He's fine. And he'll remain that way—as long as you give me what I want."

She looked at McCallister, knowing her face must've been stark with worry.

His expression, she was sure, mirrored her own.

"What's going on?" Ellis walked back to her desk, placing the call on speaker. She waved Kroll over as well. "What is it that you want? You still haven't given me a name."

"Your brother owes me a lot of money, Detective. I need to know where he is. Your father doesn't seem to know."

She looked at Kroll. "I haven't seen Carter in a long time. If you know him, then you know he and I don't get along." Ellis's mind raced as she tried to keep the caller on the line, hoping to learn what the hell was happening. "If you know my brother, then you know how unreliable he can be. When was the last time you spoke with him?"

The man snickered. "Don't play games, Detective. Carter took something from me and then disappeared. I know you know where he is."

Fear gripped her chest as she considered Hank's health. "Look, my brother and I aren't close. But he's still family. If he owes you money, I can help square things. Just tell me how much."

"This isn't about money anymore. This is about respect. Your brother disrespected me and my organization. There are consequences for that."

Organization. Ellis latched onto the word and changed tactics. "I want proof my father is alive and unharmed. Let me talk to him."

There was a pause, then the sound of movement and muffled voices on the other end of the line.

After a few tense moments, Hank's familiar raspy voice came through. "Hey, kid."

Relief flooded through her. "Dad, are you okay? Are you hurt?"

"I'm fine," Hank said, though his voice sounded shaky. "I was just having a nice conversation with my new guest."

So they were at Hank's house. Before Ellis could respond, the phone shuffled again, and the man was back. "There's your proof. Now, where is Carter?"

Ellis hesitated. "How do I know you won't hurt my father once you find out?"

"You don't," he said. "But if I don't get to Carter, your old man might find himself in urgent need of a hospital."

"Carter's in rehab," she sputtered.

"Wrong answer, Detective." The line clicked.

Ellis stared at her phone. "No!"

McCallister took her by the shoulder. "We have to get to his house. Now. Who the hell is this guy, and how the hell did he know where Hank lives?"

"It's Carter's supplier. The one I've been after." Kroll dropped onto the edge of Ellis's desk. "He doesn't know what's happened, meaning he wasn't the one who took your brother's life."

"Screw that, Kroll. My dad's in trouble. We need to get there right now." Ellis checked her gun. "Whoever this is, I'll talk to him. Tell him the truth about Carter, and we'll work out a deal."

Kroll jumped up. "That's not how these people operate. I'm going to need you to take a breath, Detective. This man isn't going to hurt your father."

"How do you know?"

Kroll grabbed his things. "Because they won't want the blood of a cop, retired or not, on their hands. We go there together, and we'll end this."

"I'm going, too," McCallister said.

"He'll expect us to bring plenty of backup, having plenty of his own," Kroll continued. "We don't want that. So here's what I expect to happen. He'll call back. Insist on meeting someplace else. Someplace unfamiliar. I'll go with you, and we'll tell him about Carter and make sure your dad is safe."

Her phone rang again. She viewed the caller ID. "It's him."

"Answer," Kroll said.

"Ellis here."

"So, Detective, are you ready to work this out, or am I going to have to take care of this problem myself?"

"Let him go, and I'll tell you what you want to know," she replied.

"How about this? How about you and I meet somewhere. We'll talk. You tell me what I want to hear, and I'll make sure my people take their leave from your dad's house. Deal?"

She closed her eyes, feeling anger rise in her chest. "Where?" Ellis grabbed a pen, writing down the location. "It'll take me at least twenty minutes to get there."

"I'm feeling generous. I'll give you thirty." The line ended again.

"Thirty minutes." Her attention was drawn to the hallway. "Sarge?" He stood beside Bevins, who must've left to get him.

"What's going on? What's happening with Hank?"

Ellis filled him in on the situation. "I was thinking if we send some of the team to Hank's to keep watch, I can go meet with this man and bring Kroll with me."

"Then go. Now."

"Best you stay out of sight," Kroll said. "I guarantee you he'll have greater numbers."

Ellis marched through the bullpen, Kroll rushing to keep up with her. They hurried into the parking lot, Ellis saying nothing along the way.

Kroll grabbed his keys from his pocket. "I'll drive. You're in no state."

She eyed him, steadying her nerves. "Fine." When they arrived at his car, she stopped cold, wanting to confront him about the other night. But right now, she needed him. He knew these people, so there was no choice but to trust him. Ellis stepped into the passenger seat of his black Lexus. He slipped behind the wheel and started the engine. Within moments, they were on the road.

Kroll glanced at her. "Look, Ellis, I get how this must be for you..."

"I don't think you do. Respectfully, you should've come clean about your relationship with my brother. And now he's dead." Her eyes stayed fixed on him. "Because of you."

Kroll glanced away for a moment. "Carter was in trouble, okay? I had to get him out of there before the cartel got to him. Look, you might not want to hear this, but Carter was pushing product for them. They all were. Unfortunately, he sampled a little too much of it before it reached his customers. They quickly figured out he was short-changing them. Carter came to me for help."

Ellis considered his words, unsure of whether to trust them. "And Tyler Beck?"

"I think they were looking for Carter, too, and Beck was in the wrong place at the wrong time. That halfway house?" Kroll said. "I got Carter out of there that night. Met him at the riverwalk, which is why I appear on that security camera. I was trying to convince him to let me put him into protective custody. He said no."

"Why would he refuse?"

"I have no idea. Maybe he thought he could talk his way out of trouble. They chose your brother because of you, Ellis. Because they knew you were a detective here. They were trying to get him to push you for information. He promised he could. But, apparently, he'd made a promise he couldn't keep."

"But the man with my father now, he didn't kill Carter?"

Kroll kept his gaze on the road ahead. "No, he's a middle-man; he's operating at the direction of the real bad guys. Those were the people I was trying to get."

"So what happens when this middleman finds out Carter

is dead? That has to mean the cartel didn't kill him, if he doesn't already know."

Kroll looked through the windshield for a moment, as if considering his next words. "Could've been a rival. The cartel has been up against the local trade, quietly stamping them out. Someone likely got to Carter before they could get to them."

Ellis glanced at the road signs. "We're almost there." She called McCallister. "We're pulling up to the meeting spot now. Are you all in place?"

"We're here and in position."

"Can you see him inside?" she asked, her voice faltering. "Is my dad okay?"

"I don't know, Becca. The curtains are closed. We can't see anything."

She glanced down a moment. "Okay. Just be ready. I'll keep you posted." Ellis ended the call.

"This is it, here." Kroll turned into the park north of downtown.

"Why did he choose this spot?"

"Hard to say." Kroll cut the engine. "Maybe to get us as far away from your dad as possible."

"He has to know we'd send people there," she added.

"Probably. Let's just see what he has to say." Kroll stepped out. Ellis joined him, and they walked toward the rendezvous point.

"I don't even know what this guy looks like," she continued.

"Oh, you'll know him when you see him. Besides, I know him very well. I've studied him. I'll recognize his face."

A gazebo lay several feet ahead. Two men stood at attention behind another man who was seated at the table inside.

"That must be him," she replied.

Kroll kept his gaze ahead. "You got it. I need you to stay clear-headed. I know this involves your dad, but these people, they don't fuck around, Ellis, you understand me?"

"I might not be DEA, but I know what the hell I'm doing."

They approached the gazebo shading the table where the man sat. One of his guards held out his hand to stop them.

"Detective Ellis, I assume?" the man asked.

"Yes."

"And you must be Agent Kroll," he added. "I've heard a lot about you."

"All good, I hope."

"Sure." He set his sights on Ellis once again. "So, where is your brother, Detective?"

She swallowed the lump in her throat, hoping he didn't pick up on her hesitation. "Sorry to disappoint you, but he's dead."

The man swatted away the notion, laughing. "Shut the fuck up. He's not dead."

Ellis grabbed her phone and held up the image on the screen of Carter's bloated body on the banks of the river. "I assure you, he's dead."

The man peered at it, getting to his feet. "Well, that does present a problem, then, wouldn't you say?"

"Not for me," Ellis replied.

He laughed. "I like you, Detective." His gaze shifted between them. "So I wonder who's going to pay me back, then?"

"Let my dad go, and we can talk," Ellis said.

"I don't think you're in any position to be making

demands, Detective." He nodded to one of his men, who pulled out a phone and showed Ellis a live video feed of her father bound to a chair in his living room. Hank's face was bruised and bloodied, but he was conscious.

Ellis struggled to keep her emotions in check. She had to stay calm and controlled if she wanted to get her father back safely.

"As you can see, Hank is still alive...for now," the man said. "But his fate depends on you. I want the money your brother owed. Fifty thousand dollars. And I want it tonight."

There was no way the department would authorize paying off a dealer, or a cartel member, whoever the hell this guy was. She'd have to come up with the money herself, and that would be next to impossible. She stole a glance at Kroll. His expression was unreadable. Was he going along with this charade, or did he have his own plan? There was no way to tell.

"I'll get you the—" she began.

"Hang on," Kroll jumped in. "How about something in trade?"

"Trade?" The man looked at Kroll. "What do you have that would interest me?"

Kroll appeared hesitant for a moment. "I'll call off the raid."

He glanced back at his men. "What raid?"

"We know when and where the next shipment is coming. You let Hank Ellis go, never to harm him again, and I'll make sure my team is sent off in another direction."

Was Kroll really doing this? Was he going to throw away his shot at making arrests to save Hank?

"I'm supposed to believe you'll follow through?" the man asked.

Kroll raised a shoulder. "What can I say? You're going to have to trust me."

"And how do I know you have the information you say you do?" the man said.

Kroll retrieved something on his phone and showed it to him. Ellis couldn't see, but the look on the man's face suggested Kroll knew exactly where this raid was going down.

The man raised his phone to his ear, making the call. "Leave the old man."

Ellis felt the pressure in her chest release.

"Go on and leave. No one's going to stop you." He looked at Ellis. "Isn't that right, Detective?"

She grabbed her phone, preparing to text McCallister. "That's right."

"I imagine your partner will contact you in about two minutes, saying my team is leaving."

They stood in silence for what felt like forever. Then the call came. "Euan?"

"He's safe, Becca. They left."

She ended the call, closing her eyes.

"So, now that's settled, we'll be on our way." He walked toward Kroll, squaring up to him. "I see you, Agent Kroll." He leaned to whisper in his ear, "I see everything."

Kroll smiled. "Right back at you."

20

The only thing that mattered to Ellis was her father. He'd been put in the crosshairs because of Carter. This shouldn't have come as a surprise. What did come as a surprise was Kroll's negotiation with the cartel. Giving up a raid on a delivery wasn't going to go down well with his superiors. But Hank was safe. And Ellis had just arrived at his home to confirm that.

McCallister stood outside on the front porch. The afternoon skies still shone brightly, forcing him to shield his eyes as Ellis pulled into the driveway. She jumped out, running toward him. "Is he okay?"

"He's fine, Becca." He opened the door for her. "Go see for yourself."

She darted in without another word. "Dad? Dad, where are..." Hank was in the living room, sitting in his favorite recliner. She rushed to his side. "Dad, are you okay?"

He donned a half-grin through his bruised features, aiming to hide the extent to which he'd been rattled. The hardened retired detective was rarely shaken. "I'm okay, kid. I'm okay. Did you arrest the guy?"

She glanced down, shaking her head. "Agent Kroll made a deal."

"Ah, damn it, Becca." He sighed. "You had the cartel in your sights, and you let them go?"

"I couldn't be sure what they would do. I wasn't going to put your life at risk because your son was caught up in something dangerous." Ellis immediately regretted laying blame on Carter. "I-I didn't mean..."

"I know what you meant, kid. What did Kroll bargain for in exchange?"

"It doesn't matter."

"It does to me," he insisted.

Ellis closed her eyes for a moment, having no intention of making him feel bad over this, but knowing Hank wouldn't let it go. "He gave up an operation. They'd planned a raid at a drop-off point. Said he'd call it off in exchange." She could see the disappointment in the old man's gaze. "Look, Dad, we're getting closer to learning what happened to Carter. I think it's clear now that his ties to the cartel were what got him killed. I just need to know who did it." She glanced back to see if Kroll was within earshot. "One other thing. Kroll said he'd pulled Carter out of the halfway house for his own protection. Carter was his informant. He glossed over an answer when I asked if he'd signed him out of Cochran House, so I suspect he did."

"Only the DEA could've done that without my authority." Hank tried to stand, but Ellis stopped him.

"Dad, relax. Carter promised those people he could give them intel on our department. Information on busts, our informants. He used his connection to me, insisting he could deliver. And when he couldn't, Kroll got him out to save him."

"So he claims," Hank shot back.

She couldn't argue his point. Especially considering Kroll kept that little detail a secret. "I'm not finished with this, okay? I'm going to find out who's responsible for Carter's murder."

"No. That's enough now, Becca. You hear me? These people—they aren't to be trifled with. Look what happened to Euan only a few months ago. And as far as you know, that wasn't related to the cartel. But I'm starting to think otherwise. The DEA doesn't come to town without reason." He pressed lightly on the bruise under his eye. "Once these people come in, all bets are off, you understand? They operate with complete disregard for human life. I won't have you brushing up against them again."

"So you're telling me not to do my job? In fact, you're telling the entire team, hell, the entire department, not to do our jobs. No. I won't let them take over our city. None of us will. Carter was murdered. I will do what I have to do to arrest the person responsible, whoever it is."

HER NERVES STILL FRAYED, Ellis had insisted on keeping a patrol unit in front of Hank's house. Hank wasn't happy about it, but deep down, Ellis was sure she saw a little relief in his gaze.

Now, having returned to the station, determination fueled her. "We have Burr in custody," she began, pacing in front of her desk. "He's already seen his lawyer. So now's the time to see if we can work out a deal. The name of a cartel leader in exchange for dropping the B and E charges."

"We already know the players," Kroll said. "You met one of them."

"He didn't kill my brother," she replied.

"Well, he had something to do with it." McCallister stepped in. "Or why make a run at your dad?"

Ellis glanced at the board where they'd laid out the case as it currently stood. The gruesome image of Carter's body on the shoreline. The man who ran the halfway house. Cochran House. It was all spelled out before her, yet she still couldn't see the words. "Then it had to be someone under him. Either way, we need Burr to talk, and as far as I'm concerned, we do that by offering him a way out."

Kroll moved in next to her, folding his arms. "He's not going to give us any more than he already has. If he does, he's as good as dead. And he knows it."

"What, then?" Ellis threw her hands in the air. "I won't back down from these people. I will find out who murdered my brother. So either come up with something, or I run with my own plan."

McCallister stood next to her. "I know you're fired up about this, but we need to be smart."

She shrugged him off. "Why am I the only one who has any interest in getting to the bottom of Carter's murder? Now, they come after Hank, and still no one seems alarmed?"

"I get what you're saying," McCallister said. "But we won't get anywhere by rushing in blindly. Burr isn't going to talk. The cartel has him too scared. We need to find another angle."

Ellis turned away, her frustration building. She knew

McCallister was right, but it didn't make it any easier to accept. Her attention turned to Lewis, who'd just entered. The look on her face offered a glimmer of hope of new information.

She wore a knowing smile. "While you were dealing with the Hank situation, I finished going through your brother's phone records."

"Thank you so much, Gabby." Ellis left the others to stare at the board while she and Lewis headed back to her desk. "Did you find something?"

"Most of the calls were to burners. Dead ends." Lewis raised her index finger. "But there was one number that stood out. Carter called it several times over the past month or so. It's registered to a prepaid cellphone, so there was no name attached. But I was able to retrieve the IMEI. That's the identity number used to track a device on a cellular provider's infrastructure," she explained. "I got a location. An apartment building, not far from Cochran House."

Ellis waved over McCallister. When he approached, she continued, "Gabby found something. An address based on Carter's phone records. We can check out this place, talk to management and get any security video they have. We'll find out when Carter was last seen there."

"And who he might've met with," McCallister added.

Kroll stepped up. "I might be able to help on that end."

"How so?" Ellis asked.

"We have a list of possible locations of cartel members. I can see if this apartment building is one of them."

"You have a list?" Ellis shook her head. "Why not go after them with surveillance, then? Try to arrest them. I mean, what's the point in knowing where these people are if you can't do something about it?"

"Because they'll only find replacements," Kroll replied. "We start arresting people who don't hold value, they'll only be replaced by more who don't hold value. We keep track, Detective, in hopes of finding those who do matter."

"Fine. Okay." Ellis was never so glad to not be a DEA agent, or any federal agent for that matter. It was a wonder they accomplished anything. Either that, or Kroll had reverted to giving her the runaround. His purpose, unclear. She turned her attention to McCallister. "I only care about finding who killed Carter. Euan, you and I can go there now. Kroll can tell us if someone who doesn't matter lives there."

———

BEVINS HAD REMAINED on the outside, watching the rest of his team work on an increasingly important investigation. But until his own problems could be resolved, he wasn't going to be helpful to anyone. Abbott had given him leeway to resolve this. Just how much slack he would be allowed remained to be seen.

Inside the bullpen, he peered through the window at the late afternoon sun, waiting for the story from the blogger to spread like a disease, consuming his life and the lives of those around him. Never mind the car situation. How could anyone else have known about it? "It's the Army. Of course they knew." The idea terrified him, the recognition that their reach was seemingly endless.

He'd bided his time while Murph worked to uncover more details about his friend Lance Curry. A man he'd left to die. Murph would see a swift end to his career if discovered, and that wouldn't be all that would end. He'd already risked so much to get Bevins the original accident

report. Now he'd asked him to risk it all. To put everything on the line. Was it fair? No, but what choice was
there?

Military files were impossible to access except to those
on the inside. So in this case even a computer expert like
Detective Lewis wouldn't be able to work her magic, as she
had for Ellis earlier.

Fletch must've noticed his turmoil as she walked over,
drawing his attention. "Listen, Connor, you gotta chill out,
okay? You've done everything you can do. Now, it's a waiting
game."

His elbows on his desk, he turned his gaze up at her. "I
can't sit here and do nothing. I've asked people to risk everything for me, yet I sit back and wait? No. That's not how this
is going to work."

"Then what? What are you going to do?"

With a sigh, Bevins turned to his laptop, logging into his
email. "I'm going to tell Murph to stop digging. It's not worth
the risk. I'll figure out something else." He typed the
message, his finger hovering over the send button. "I have to
pull the plug, Fletch. I can't let Murph do this."

"Then what's the answer?"

He looked at her, feeling the sting behind his eyes.
"Resign. I can't hurt the department if I resign. Murph will
be in the clear if he stops now. Nothing will change for
anyone else but me."

"And what if you go to prison, huh?" Fletch shot back.
"No, I'm not going to let that happen. We now have evidence
that the accident wasn't your fault."

"I was still drinking…"

She raised a hand. "Never mind that part for now.
Someone wanted you to crash. Whether you were the target

or your friend was, we don't know. But don't you think it's worth finding out before you give up?"

Bevins stared at the unsent email on his computer screen, Fletch's words ringing in his ears. There was more to this accident than he had originally thought. Someone had intended him to crash that night. Giving up now would mean never learning the truth. With a defeated sigh, he deleted the email. "You're right. I can't give up yet. I have to know what really happened that night."

Fletch gave him an approving nod. "Okay. Good. So what's our next move?"

Bevins leaned back in his chair. "Lance is the key to all of this. I'll have to wait for Murph to see what he can find. And then, like you said...maybe it's time to talk to the family."

"Why the change of heart?"

"Because I need to do this. I can find his parents." He glanced out into the hallway. "But it's going to take time, so I'll need to ask the sarge for a leave of absence."

"I can come along if you want," she said. "I've got some vacation time squirreled away, and I'm not working any active cases right now."

"I appreciate the offer, but I think I have to see them on my own."

THE APARTMENT COMPLEX, with its Tudor-style roofs and gray vinyl siding, marked the approximate location where Carter's phone calls had been answered.

Ellis drove into the parking lot, taking note of the several buildings laid out in a square. They surrounded a large, enclosed pool. "This is the place. Anything yet from Kroll?"

McCallister checked his phone. "No, but let me make a call before we go in. I'll see if he has any updates." With his phone at his ear, he waited for it to be answered. "Hey, it's McCallister. We're here. You have a name for us yet?"

Ellis watched his face as though she might be able to read his response.

"Okay, yeah. Get back to us as soon as you have anything." He ended the call.

"Nothing yet, huh?" she asked.

"No. He says he's got a call into his ASAC, so we'll have to wait. In the meantime, if Carter was here, we'll find out. Let's go talk with the manager of this place and see if he's willing to share information." McCallister opened the door. "Let's move."

Ellis joined him as they made their way along the sidewalk leading to what appeared to be a clubhouse. A sign was posted on the door. "Office."

"Must be the place." McCallister held open the door for her.

Ellis walked in to find a long front desk, the name of the apartments hanging on a backlit sign on the wall behind it. Her gaze was drawn to a man who appeared polished. Crisp white shirt. Blue tie. Not older than thirty. He seemed focused on his computer, offering no acknowledgment of their arrival. "Excuse me?" she asked. "We're with Bangor PD."

At this, he shifted his sights to them.

"I'm Detective Ellis. This is my partner, Detective McCallister."

"Sorry." He straightened his back and put on a wide smile. "What can I do for you?"

"We're looking for someone who we suspect visited one

of your residents over the past month or so. We don't have a name of this resident, but we'd like to take a look at your security video. I have a few dates in particular I'm interested in checking out."

The young man let his gaze roam over them, as if assessing whether they were who they said they were. "What'd this person do—the one you're looking for?"

"He was murdered," Ellis replied flatly. "We're interested in who he came here to see."

With a resigned sigh, he got up from the chair. "Yeah, okay. Guess it won't matter 'cause he's dead. Come on back. You can look for yourself."

Setting aside the man's obvious lack of compassion, Ellis followed him, determined to learn whether Carter had met with a member of the cartel.

They entered a small office cluttered with file boxes and supplies. A desk lay in the center with two monitors on top. The man took a seat and began entering commands. "What do you want to see?"

"We need to take a look at the past several days," Ellis replied.

"All right. How about we start with Monday?" He typed in the date, then clicked enter. Several small video boxes populated the screens, each one showing a different camera view of the apartment complex. "You can scan through here if you want, forwarding as necessary, or I can copy it to a USB for you."

"We'll take a look first," Ellis replied.

The manager got up and left them to it, closing the office door behind him.

She and McCallister pulled two chairs over to the desk and sat down to pore over the footage. For the next several minutes, they watched the timestamped video, looking for any sign of Carter coming or going. They saw plenty of residents but no sign of her brother.

After reviewing the footage without success, Ellis quickly figured out how to forward it to the dates that Carter's phone had pinged a tower near the apartments. Again, they scanned through residents coming and going, deliveries being made, and occasional guests arriving, but still no Carter. Ellis rubbed the back of her neck, frustrated.

"Keep going," McCallister said. "If he was here, we'll find him."

She queued up another batch of files. More of the same parade of people flowing across the screens. Until..."There! The parking lot camera. Is that him?"

McCallister leaned in, squinting. "Can't tell for sure. Try to get a better angle from a different camera."

After flipping between a few different views, they spotted him again, this time on the sidewalk leading around the back of one of the buildings. A tall, slender figure in jeans and a graphic T-shirt.

"It looks like him." Ellis felt her phone buzz in her pocket. She quickly retrieved it, relieved to see it was Kroll. "Ellis here."

"We got a name—Miguel Slayton," Kroll said. "Mid-level player who handles distribution inside the city. I'm sending you his photo now."

Ellis felt a rush of renewed hope. "Do you have a unit number? We're still here, and we just saw my brother in some of the surveillance footage."

"We're working on it. My guys are tracking down his known aliases and properties as we speak, looking to confirm the location."

"Keep us posted. As soon as you have a unit number, call me. We'll get eyes on it right away." She ended the call and looked at McCallister. "Miguel Slayton. Waiting on confirmation that he lives here."

"Kroll needs to work fast. We could bring Slayton in right now if he's home."

Her phone rang, and on noticing the caller ID, she held it up for McCallister. "Fast enough for you?" Ellis answered the line. "That was quick."

"Slayton leased a unit registered under the name 'Esteban Cruz.' Apartment number two-one-eight. But listen, you can't go after this guy. Not yet."

"What? Why not?" She glanced at McCallister, raising her palm. "We have Carter on video here. And now we know there's a cartel contact. We have to bring this guy in."

"Listen to me," Kroll insisted. "You can't go there. You can't get shit without a warrant, in any case. Come back. Now that we have a name and know for certain Carter was there during the timeframe in question, we can work the case. That's how it has to be. Otherwise, you spook this guy by running up there, guns blazing, he'll be in the wind, or worse, he'll inform his higher-ups we're on the hunt."

Ellis squeezed her eyes shut. "Yeah, okay. We'll wrap things up here, bring back a copy of the footage and talk when we return." She ended the call, stunned.

"He pulled the plug, didn't he?" McCallister asked. "Can't do much without a warrant."

"We have probable cause." She pointed at the monitor. "My brother was here."

"But we don't see him meeting with anyone. We could bring Slayton in for questioning, sure. But we can't search his apartment."

Ellis rose from the desk and walked into the hallway, craning left, then right. There had to be something she could do. Walking away from this man who could well be the one who killed Carter—it didn't sit right. She returned inside. "I have an idea. We'll go back, but not yet."

McCallister narrowed his gaze. "Becca, come on. No unnecessary risks. Not where these people are concerned. We need to keep this by the book."

"I intend to. I'm thinking there's a shot we can collect DNA from Slayton, or Cruz, or whatever the hell he wants to be called. We still don't have Rivera's full report back yet. He might've discovered foreign DNA on Carter's body."

"He was in the river for at least twenty-four hours," he replied. "Any DNA left would've been long gone."

"Not necessarily. Not if he tried to fend off the attack. Listen to me, Euan. We can work on getting the warrant for this guy—fine, I can accept that. But what if we have a chance to firm this thing up?"

"A one-in-a-million chance. You want to stick it out here in the hope we see Slayton coming out of his apartment?"

"I can't go back just to sit on my thoughts." Ellis tilted her head. "Besides, I don't have any other place to be. Do you?"

21

The television was on, but Bevins paid no attention to it. Sitting on his couch, he tossed back a swig of beer. The sarge had authorized his request for time off, though he'd seemed hesitant about Bevins' plan. But how else could progress be made on this situation?

A knock on his apartment door came unexpectedly. He pushed off the couch and muted the television before heading toward the small foyer. Peering through the door's security lens, he quickly pulled back. "The hell?" Bevins opened the door. "Dude, what are you doing here? Did you drive? Bro, that's, like, eight hours."

"I know." Chris Murphy darted his gaze as though fearful of something. "They know it was me."

"Who knows what?" Bevins stepped aside. "Come in. I'll get you a beer." He secured the door behind Murph and padded in bare feet to his kitchen.

Murph set down his keys on the counter, pulling out a stool to sit. "This is bad, man. I don't know how they found out it was me, but they did."

Bevins popped open the bottle tops and offered one to his friend. "You're going to have to start at the beginning. Just take a breath, man. Tell me what happened."

Murph downed his beer, wiping his mouth with the back of his hand. His fear was palpable. "So, I get this call late this afternoon from someone at the Department of Defense."

Bevins set down his beer. "Oh, shit."

"Right? Anyway, they tell me a secured file was accessed and uploaded to an unsecured server."

"That cloud server you used?" Bevins asked.

"No, I mean, shit, it was secure. Encrypted." He shook his head in disbelief. "And you know, I was also trying to check out what the deal was with Lance Curry. Maybe that was the real problem."

"Then what happened?"

Murphy shrugged in despair. "They said they were revoking my security clearance and that I need to attend a preliminary hearing."

"What? For this? You had clearance. You did nothing wrong."

"Yeah, well, tell that to them. So I don't know. I figured someone high up on the food chain got wind of what I was doing, and now they're going to bring down the hammer." He eyed Bevins. "So I came here for help. My wife's terrified. I told her that if they come to see her, she knows nothing. You gotta call your dad, man. See if he can clear all this up for me. I mean, he'll do that, right? I was only trying to help you find out what happened in that accident."

Bevins lowered his gaze, defeat weighing down his shoulders. His father had gone to great lengths to cover up what really happened that night. And now that Bevins knew someone had intentionally caused the accident, he didn't know whom he could trust, including his own father. "I don't know. My old man has pulled a lot of strings over the years, but I'm not sure we want his help on this one. I'm not sure we can trust him."

Murph dropped his head into his hands. "Oh my God. What have I done?"

"The thing is, Murph." Bevin's chest tightened. "What if this is actually Jack's doing?"

"Then we have an even bigger problem." Murph stared at the bottle of beer. "Because that would mean you think your own father is behind this. And that's why the DOD called." He looked at his friend. "Jesus, Con, do you think he's behind the accident, too?"

"Maybe, and I'm not sure I want to know why he would've been." He paused a moment. "Did you find out anything at all about Lance before all this went down?"

"Nah, man. I didn't get very far before they shut me down. Although..." His eyes lit up for a moment. "Right before they kicked me out, I saw a reference to a file on Curry. Looked like it might've been disciplinary records. But I didn't get a chance to access it."

"Disciplinary records?" Bevins said.

"Possibly. Like I said, I didn't see it." Murph took another swig of beer. "Look, all this shit came up because of this dumbass blogger, right? So who the hell turned him on to this whole thing?"

"Someone who wanted to bring trouble for me," Bevins replied.

"I don't think so, man." Murph picked at the label on the bottle. "I think it's someone who wanted to bring trouble for your dad."

THE SKIES HAD TURNED to dusk while Ellis and McCallister waited in the parking lot. Waited for a miracle, it now seemed.

"No sign of Slayton anywhere, Becca," McCallister said. "It's been two hours. How long are we staying out here?"

She kept her gaze fixed on the building that housed unit 218. "I don't know. I just know that someone came after my dad today." She turned back to him. "My dad, Euan."

"I'm so sorry that happened. We all love Hank. And after his stroke...I know how you've been keeping a closer watch over him. I get that. But this wasn't because of you, Becca. This was Carter's doing. He brought this onto you and your dad."

"Once you're under these guys' thumbs..." Ellis shook her head. "It's impossible to break free."

McCallister rested his elbow on the passenger door. "Maybe Kroll was right. Let him work on getting the warrant for Slayton's apartment. He'll be able to do it a hell of a lot quicker than we will. Then we can come back here and do this right."

"What if Slayton's gone by then?" she asked.

"He could be gone already. And we're sitting here hoping for a miracle."

Ellis traced her fingers over the steering wheel. "You know, when all this started, when we found Carter...Sarge said I shouldn't be the one to work the case. That I was too close. I knew he was right, but rather than agree with him, I guilted him into letting me run it."

"He's your brother. I would've done the same thing," McCallister replied.

Ellis dabbed her eyes, clearing them of the tears that threatened to spill. "I've made mistakes…" She trailed off before clearing her throat. "Let's head back." She pressed the ignition. "Kroll will probably have the warrant by morning."

The highway strained under the heavy rush-hour traffic. A tense silence hovered around Ellis and McCallister. She thought about Hank and what he would say to her now. That her mind was clouded by grief and guilt, even if she refused to admit it to herself. And that her thought processes and her actions had been filtered by those emotions. Sitting in a parking lot, hoping a suspected cartel member might take out his trash. Really?

In hindsight, it had been a foolish endeavor. McCallister had seen it yet allowed her to take the lead. He loved her, and that was part of the problem. She needed a partner to help her snap out of it. To help her see that she was making her decisions under the influence of a personal attachment to this investigation. There were no checks and balances between them, and that reality could jeopardize the case or, worse, get one of them killed.

Arriving back at the station, the sun had dipped behind the building. Ellis parked, seeing no sign of Kroll's vehicle. He remained a hindrance as far as she was concerned. A man with unknown ulterior motives, who had opted to follow her for reasons she could only guess. Nevertheless, they'd returned empty-handed. As empty-handed as when they had left.

Entering the lobby, Ellis stopped a moment. Minor activity surrounded her. Officers walked with purpose. Visitors meandered in the seating area. She turned to McCallister. "Jeremy Burr is still in our custody."

"From what I gather, yes." He regarded her. "And? I

thought we discussed with Kroll that Burr wasn't going to open up."

She peered at him. "Come on, Euan. We both saw how Burr looked at Kroll. They know each other, and Burr was too afraid and unsure to say a word about it."

He shoved his hands in his pockets. "What are you saying?"

"I'm going to talk to him now. Kroll's gone." She glanced into the hall. "This is our chance to figure out what Kroll is really doing here, because it sure as hell isn't for the reasons he's told us."

"You said Kroll offered to back off an impending DEA raid to keep Hank safe," McCallister said. "Doesn't that speak to his intentions?"

"True." Ellis sighed. "But I need you to back me up on this. I'm going to talk to Burr. If he opens up, great. If not, then at least I tried. I don't see a downside here."

McCallister stepped back, raising his hands in surrender. "Do what you have to do. This is still your investigation. Not mine. Not Kroll's."

Feeling emboldened, Ellis nodded. "Yes, it is." As she reached the front desk, she eyed the officer. "I need someone to bring up Jeremy Burr to one of the interview rooms."

"Now?" he asked.

She slapped the top of the desk. "Now."

"Yes, ma'am." He went to work, making the calls for the interview.

Ellis picked up her phone and called Pelletier. "Bryce, hey, it's me. Sorry to bother you at home."

"Don't be. What's going on?"

"Your B and E suspect?"

"Jeremy Burr," he replied. "What about him?"

"I'm going to talk to him again. Bryce, I think he knows Agent Kroll, and maybe he'll open up if Kroll's not there."

The line fell quiet for a moment. "Without his lawyer present, whatever he does tell you won't be admissible. His lawyer will have it tossed out so fast your head will spin."

"I know. And I'm okay with that," she replied. "I just need answers about Carter. Burr didn't kill him, but he might know who did. I'll take care of it from there. I won't do anything if you don't want me to. He's your suspect, on your investigation. I don't want to screw that up for you."

Pelletier went quiet again, but only for a moment. "Talk to him. See what you can get. I've got him on the B and E. So if there's a deal to be made first, let me in on that before you agree to anything."

Relief swept through her. "I will. And thank you, Bryce."

"No need. I just hope Burr has something useful to say. I'm so sorry about what happened with Hank, Becca. You should know that."

"I do. Thanks again, and I'll be in touch if something comes out of this." She ended the call.

"Detective Ellis?" the officer at the desk called out.

"Yes?"

"They're taking him to room one. He'll be there in a minute."

"Thanks." She looked back, realizing McCallister was gone. She glanced at the stairs in time to see him at the top. He was walking back to the bullpen. He didn't understand why she needed to do this. He didn't seem to think Kroll was doing anything more or less than his job. But something about Kroll had raised her hackles. He had given up the raid to save Hank, but had he done so to win her over? To get her to fall in line with what he wanted?

For now, she turned her thoughts to Burr, walking down the hall and into the interview room. Her eyes were drawn to the camera above. No red light meant it wasn't on. And no one was in the observation room next door. She was alone with Burr, a situation that might end up biting her in the ass down the road.

"What am I doing here, Detective?" Burr asked.

Ellis pulled out a chair, taking a seat. "Hope I didn't interrupt your dinner. This won't take long."

"You already know I can't say anything to you without my lawyer."

"I understand. And I'll be honest with you, Jeremy, I'm not here to talk about your B and E charge. I'm here to discuss Agent Kroll."

His expression tightened. "What about him?"

"I need to know if you were working with him in some capacity. Now, when he was here and we all questioned you, it seemed as though you were hesitant to speak."

"Because I don't know anything." He slouched in the chair. "I don't know anything more about Carter than I already told you."

"Okay." She nodded. "I can buy that. But I think you do know Kroll. And now that I know he was running Carter, I'm thinking maybe he was running you too? And Tyler Beck?"

Ellis leaned forward, studying Burr. He shifted in his seat, avoiding her gaze.

"I only know him from what Carter and Tyler said."

"Come on, Jeremy." She leaned back in the chair. "I know you're not being straight with me. Kroll had his claws in my brother, and he had them in you too, didn't he? What did he offer in exchange for your help?"

Burr fidgeted with his hands, and she noticed how torn

and ragged his nails were. "I ain't saying nothing against him. He finds out I talked, I'm a dead man. Probably already am."

"Not if you cooperate with us," Ellis said. "We can protect you. But you need to tell me everything you know about Agent Kroll. Why was he getting people out of Cochran House and putting them into the halfway house? Just for cartel information? Seems like a lot of effort."

Burr glanced around the room as if expecting Kroll to materialize from the shadows. "Kroll's dirty. He works for them—the cartel. Tells us we need to move product that comes over, makes sure we do it, or we get our asses shipped back to Warren."

A sense of vindication came over her. Stunned vindication. This was beyond anything she'd expected. Far more than a handler, Kroll was cartel. Unless Burr was lying, but why would he lie about something like this? Something that could get him killed. Ellis leaned in. "Tell me more."

With one last cagey look around, Burr began to talk. "It started with small stuff at first. Kroll would get us to pick up packages from certain locations and drop them somewhere else. Pay was good, so we didn't ask questions."

"We?" Ellis interrupted. "Who was helping Kroll besides you?"

Burr hesitated before answering, "Me, Carter, Tyler, a few other guys from Cochran House who got moved to the halfway house. Things escalated. The cartel started using us to pick up larger loads from points near the border. Serious weight." He set his sights on Ellis. "Carter wanted out. He'd promised things...things he couldn't deliver."

She'd already figured out what it was Carter must've promised. It started to make sense now. Why Carter was seen on that ATM footage with Kroll. It had looked like an argument. Kroll had insisted he'd been trying to help Carter. That didn't seem to be the case now. "Do you believe Agent Kroll was capable of killing Carter?"

"Capable?" He scoffed. "No doubt about it. He would've killed any one of us if we'd pushed back hard enough."

"Thank you, Jeremy." Ellis got up. "You can go back to your cell now."

"Wait. What about making sure I'm protected? If Kroll finds out I talked..."

"He won't. I'll keep my word to you. I'll talk to Detective Pelletier, who brought you in. We'll sit down with the DA. Figure a way to get you out of here within the next twenty-four hours. You have my word."

Ellis left the room, then stood in the corridor, her head spinning. That day at the halfway house, when they'd seen Kroll...he'd come off as wanting what they'd wanted—to arrest whoever killed Carter. But now it had begun to make more sense. He knew she'd figure things out, so he'd played this game, pretending to want a joint operation. Really, he was just keeping eyes on them, figuring out how much they knew.

She walked through the hall, patrolmen and women passing her by, offering pleasantries. But all she could think about was Kroll. It seemed more likely than ever that he'd murdered her brother. Beck too. He was one hell of a good liar; she'd give him that. Spinning tales of his meeting with Carter. Pretending he was only there to help him.

Climbing the stairs, she walked into the bullpen. McCallister was the only one there.

He regarded her with a wary gaze. "How'd it go?"

Ellis walked to her desk, slumping into her chair. "Burr

says Kroll is dirty. That he's working for the cartels and was getting the guys out of rehab and into the halfway house to help him move product."

McCallister rubbed his temple. "Holy shit. You believe him?"

"He offered some pretty convincing information," she replied. "Which means we'll never get that warrant. Kroll will find a way to make sure it doesn't happen, coming up with some excuse as to why." She sat up, tilting her head. "Don't you think it's strange that we've only ever talked with Kroll? No one on his team. No one from his department. Just him."

"I guess so." McCallister shrugged, but his eyes glinted in recognition of the point she was making. "I didn't think much of it. Although Abbott got a call from his ASAC about the joint operation."

"A man who said he was the ASAC," she said. "Do we know if Abbott ever questioned it?"

"I doubt he felt he had a reason to." McCallister looked out into the empty bullpen, seeming to come to the same realization as she had. "And when we started to get close, someone went after Hank."

Ellis nodded slowly. "Yes, they did."

He turned back to her. "What now? What's the plan to expose Kroll for who he is without getting ourselves killed in the process?"

"First, get Burr out of here. Get him someplace far away where he can stay safe. He's our only witness. I'll let Bryce know what's transpired. He can work with the DA to drop the B and E charges in exchange for his information and his safety."

"We still don't know if Kroll murdered Carter," McCallister reminded her.

Ellis chewed on her lip, pondering the question. "I don't know about you, but if Carter wanted out, which Burr said was the truth, then he has an argument with Kroll, right? I gotta think he figured out how to get Carter out of the way before he had a chance to come to me or Hank."

"Just so I'm clear," McCallister pressed her, "you're saying it was Kroll who killed your brother?"

"I am." Ellis got to her feet. "And we're closer than ever to finding that out."

22

Twilight had blanketed the city. Stars shone. The moon, only three-quarters full, still illuminated the roads and landscape as Ellis arrived to see her father. She stepped out of her car, nodding to the patrolman, whose presence offered assurance.

Ellis made her way to the front door and checked the handle. It was locked. She inserted her key, opening the door to step inside. The house was dark except for the television. And as she walked into the living room, she found Hank asleep on his recliner. Approaching him, she gently took his arm. "Dad?"

He jumped up, raising his hand that clutched a gun. Ellis blocked it. "Dad! It's me. It's Becca."

"Oh, Christ." He lowered the weapon. "Kid, you scared the bejesus out of me. What are you doing sneaking up like that?"

"I'm sorry. I was trying to wake you as gently as I could." She eyed the gun. "What are you doing with that?"

He sat up. "If you think I'm going to let someone else get

into this house and hold me hostage, then you don't know me very well."

"I know you well enough," she exclaimed. "Jeez, Dad, we have a unit outside, for God's sake. No one's coming back for you." She kneeled in front of his chair, taking his hand. "I'm so sorry that happened to you today."

"It wasn't your fault, kid, all right? I know you think I wore blinders where Carter was concerned, but I knew who he was. I knew the kind of stuff he'd gotten himself into. Although, to be honest, I didn't think the cartel would have been one of them."

"Dad, listen to me. I found out something tonight. The agent working with us? Kroll?"

"What about him?"

"He's in on it. He works for the cartel."

Hank drew back his shoulders. "You know this for a fact?"

"I have a witness. He's not the most reliable, but it's all I have to go on."

"Good Lord." He took a deep breath. "What are you going to do?"

"Talk to Abbott and Lieutenant Serrano, I suppose. I know when I'm out of my depth."

"It won't be easy. You understand that, right?" he asked, squeezing her hand. "I won't lose you too, kid, you hear me? My heart can't take it."

Ellis donned a gentle smile. "Nothing's going to happen to me, I promise. Now that I know what we're dealing with, we'll figure this out. I'll talk to Abbott and Serrano first thing, before Kroll arrives. I'll tell them what I know, and we'll put our heads together."

She rubbed his arm. "As far as you go, I'm going to keep a

unit here twenty-four hours a day until this is over. I won't take any argument."

"Trust me, kid. You won't get one from me." He kissed her cheek. "Now go on. Get out of here and do what you need to do. I love you, Becca."

"I love you too, Dad. Now go to bed. You'll end up with a sore neck if you sleep out here."

ABBOTT'S OFFICE smelled of freshly brewed coffee. The sun had just peeked above the horizon. Ellis and McCallister had arrived only moments ago, requesting an urgent meeting with their sergeant and Lieutenant Serrano.

They'd waited for the lieutenant to arrive. Ellis turned at the sound of footsteps behind her.

"Sorry I'm late." Serrano walked into the office. "I talked to Hank a few minutes ago. He seems better than when I talked to him last night."

Ellis nodded. "He's doing all right. I appreciate you keeping the unit out there."

"Listen, Becca." Serrano turned serious, folding his arms over his slim chest. "We have ourselves a real problem. One I'm not sure we, as a department, can handle on our own."

She glanced at McCallister. "Sir, we don't know who we can trust at Kroll's office in Buffalo. We start telling them we have a witness saying he knows Kroll is rotten, word will get back to him."

"She's right." McCallister took a seat next to her. "As far as we know, his ASAC could be involved. He was the one who talked to you, Sarge, about the joint investigation."

"He did," Abbott replied. "You could be right. But that makes this all the more difficult."

Ellis crossed her legs. "So what do we do? We can't just sit on this information. If Kroll is on the wrong side of this and had something to do with Carter's death, we have to expose him."

Serrano eyed his sergeant, who remained at his desk. "We need to gather more evidence first. Something we can use to build a case against him, besides a drug-dealing ex-con looking to get charges against him dropped."

"I don't want those two ruffling DEA feathers." Abbott nodded at his detectives. "I'll reach out to some other DEA contacts I have. See if Kroll's name comes up in relation to any internal investigations. Might be able to shake something loose there."

"In the meantime," Serrano continued, "we act normal when Kroll arrives. And get that kid, Jeremy Burr, transferred the hell out of here. Keep Kroll in the dark about it. That'll buy us some time."

Abbott laced his fingers on his desk, fixing his gaze on Ellis. "This goes sideways, we need to get all of you away from this city, including Hank. No telling what could happen if Kroll gets a whiff that we know."

"Yes, sir," she replied. "We'll keep the status quo. Let Kroll run on this warrant situation. Pretend we don't know anything."

THE SIX-HOUR DRIVE FROM BANGOR, south to upstate New York, had begun. The sun was just barely over the horizon. Bevins rolled along the highway in his black Mustang with

Chris Murphy, his friend who now faced serious charges of disclosing classified information, in the seat beside him.

The files should never have been classified in the first place. And even though Murph had clearance, he was on the hook—thanks to Bevins. Now was Bevins's chance to make it right.

As the highway stretched ahead, he glanced over at his friend. "Hey, Murph, I've been thinking more about the accident. I know you saw the report detailing what someone left in the road."

Murph looked at him. "Yeah. Which is why we're in this situation now. Someone knows what I saw, and they're coming for me."

He nodded. "I don't know what to ask them—Lance's family. How to approach them. I mean, they aren't going to want to talk to me. They blame me."

"Then make them see otherwise," Murph said.

"How do I do that without acknowledging that I think someone else tried to kill him or me, or both of us?"

Murph ran a hand through his hair. "Look, I think the objective here is to find out if Lance had any suspicions before his death. Maybe he talked to his family, his mom and dad, or whatever, about what was going on at the academy at the time. Lance was a good guy. If he had concerns, he must've told someone."

"I was his best friend." Bevins shot him a glance. "Why not tell me?"

"That's the real question."

The remainder of the journey was filled with hit songs playing on the radio and little conversation. They finally arrived at Lance's family home by midday. The quaint suburban neighborhood was filled with the sounds of laughter from children playing in the warm summer sun. Dogs barking. Lawnmowers mowing.

They stood under the front porch. Bevins hesitated, shame and regret consuming him.

"You gotta do this, man," Murph said.

"Yeah." He cleared his throat and knocked on the door. When it opened, it was the first time in years that he'd seen Mrs. Curry. She looked much older than he remembered. It seemed she recognized him as well.

"Connor?"

He forced a smile. "Yes, ma'am. It's me. Connor Bevins."

She looked at Murph, then beyond him as though in search of their purpose. "What are you doing here? And who's this with you?"

"This is my friend Chris Murphy. I was wondering if we could talk for a minute, Mrs. Curry. About Lance?"

The mention of her son's name made her eyes glisten. She studied him for a long moment, the wrinkles around her soft brown eyes deepening. Finally, she gestured inside. "Come in, both of you. Connor, I think it's well past time we talked."

He stepped inside, instantly recalling the smell of the home. Like springtime and chocolate chip cookies.

"Come and have a seat in the living room. I'll bring some iced tea."

He didn't argue, and they both walked into the living room, taking a seat on the edge of the overstuffed brown sofa. Bevins jingled his keys, a nervous response to being in this home again. He waited for Mrs. Curry's return with tea he didn't want.

She entered, a tray with glasses balanced in her hands. She set it down on the light oak coffee table before taking a seat across from them. Silence persisted for an uncomfortable length of time before she broke it. "I won't pretend I wasn't angry with you, Connor. For a long time, I blamed you for what happened to Lance. But staying angry won't bring back my boy." Her voice caught on the last word.

Bevins felt tears well but fought back his emotions. "I'm so sorry."

Mrs. Curry clasped her hands in her lap. "I know you are, son. Lance cared for you deeply. He wouldn't want me to hold a grudge."

"I cared for him too. He was the best friend I ever had..." He was unable to continue as tears suddenly streamed down his face.

Mrs. Curry looked at him kindly. "I know you loved him. And he loved you too. That's why I can't stay angry. But I do think it's time you told the truth about what really happened."

She knew? Of course she did. Jack had probably made sure to issue the appropriate threat should she or her husband have come forward at the time. Along with plenty of money. But Bevins doubted any amount of money would've silenced Mrs. Curry. She would've done whatever it took to protect her son's memory, so what had stopped her?

"Yes, ma'am. I should have come forward sooner. I want to rectify my mistake. That night, I'd been drinking. Lance tried to get me to pull over, but I insisted I was fine." He swallowed hard. "When I woke up in the hospital, my dad was there. He told me he had taken care of everything."

"And he did." Mrs. Curry nodded. "The official story never made sense to me. Lance's father told me not to question it. But he's gone now too, so there's nothing left for me to lose."

Murph leaned forward now, his elbows on his knees. "Mrs. Curry, we wanted to ask if Lance ever confided in you about anything troubling him before the accident. Anything at the academy or with his other friends?"

She appeared to think about the question, and then something changed in her expression, and she peered directly at Bevins. "I have no proof of what I'm about to say. But Lance did tell us a few things. Things that...let's just say they would've shone an uncomfortable spotlight on your father."

Bevins leaned back, struggling to contain a rising tide of emotion. "What did Lance tell you?"

Mrs. Curry stared off into the distance for a moment, seeming to consider how to relay what she knew. She finally looked at Bevins again. "As you may have known, Lance worked in the recruitment office at the academy."

"I was aware, yes," Bevins replied.

"Unfortunately, he happened to overhear a conversation with your father one day, not long after you were admitted, from what Lance told me." She took a sip from the glass of iced tea. "Son, he'd overheard that your dad, well, please accept what I'm about to say, not as a slight on you...but your dad ensured you were accepted through...donations to certain people with political aspirations at the time."

Bevins closed his eyes, an embarrassed snicker escaping his lips. "Why am I not surprised? I never wanted to go to West Point. He insisted."

"It was then Lance got curious," she continued. "Eventually, he found proof of what your father had done. Now, I don't know what he did with that proof, but he told me about it."

Murph looked at him. "Connor, what the hell does this mean?"

He returned his friend's gaze as anger caught in his throat. "I think it means someone wanted Lance to keep quiet about what he knew."

"But you were in the car, too," Murph said.

Mrs. Curry looked at him. "I don't want to believe this is true, but maybe the accident happened with the intention of murdering my son, knowing that Connor would ultimately survive."

"How would it be possible to know for sure?" Murph pressed.

Bevins glanced at him. "Maybe whoever put the device in the road didn't care whether or not I survived."

23

Getting Jeremy Burr safely out of Bangor police custody had to be done in a way so as not to alert Agent Kroll. It was going to take Detective Pelletier's help. Ellis had tracked him down in the kitchen, pouring himself a cup of coffee. "There you are. Good morning."

"Becca." He turned around with the carafe in his hand. "You want a cup?"

"No, I'm good, thanks." She walked toward him. "Listen, I need to tell you something."

"About Burr? How did it go with him? I just got in, haven't had a chance to check in on him yet."

Ellis glanced around, ensuring no one had eyes or ears on them. She leaned in closer. "He said Kroll's crooked."

"What?" Pelletier almost spilled the coffee. "Crooked how?"

"He's been getting these guys, including my brother, out of Cochran House to work for the cartels, taking his cut along the way and ensuring the DEA knows nothing about it. That's what we suspect, anyway."

"Oh my God. Are you sure about this? Burr isn't just blowing smoke to get himself a deal?"

"I don't think so. We didn't have a chance to ask Beck. He was killed, so was my brother. For now, I need your help."

He took a sip from his mug. "Of course. What do you need me to do?"

"We have to get Burr out of here. Out of our custody and it has to happen before Kroll arrives."

Pelletier eyed the clock on the wall. "When might that be?"

"About an hour. Maybe less. It's not much time, I know. Can you do it?"

He nodded. "I'll have to. I'll make it happen."

Ellis could always count on him. She missed how close they used to be. Laying a hand on his shoulder, she smiled. "Thank you. And you don't know anything about this, okay?"

He quirked an eyebrow. "About what?"

"Exactly. Thanks, Bryce." Ellis headed back to the bullpen. On her return, Lewis called out to her.

"Hey, Becca, I got a little more information on those Cochran House bank records." She grabbed the file, walking over to join her.

"Great. What did you find?"

Lewis opened it, pointing to the documents in question. "Look—SARs were issued on those large deposits."

"Suspicious activity reports." Ellis nodded. "Did anyone look into them?"

"I made a call to FinCen first thing. They flagged the account, and as we continued our discussion, I let them in on why I was looking into Cochran House. Apparently, we aren't the only ones. They suspect someone inside Warren has been taking a little off the top before making the deposits. Small amounts. Hardly noticeable until now."

"Someone from the prison was skimming?" she asked.

"Looks that way. Best guess? It's a signatory. Someone with authority."

Ellis considered the implications. "I wonder if that someone was working with Kroll. Offering him a slice of the pie to keep the DEA off their backs? This whole thing is looking increasingly like a massive operation with several moving parts."

It all fit with what Burr had told her about Kroll's corruption. He was clearly abusing his position to line his own pockets. This gave her even more motivation to get Burr to safety. "Great stuff, Gabby. Keep digging into those records. I want to know exactly how much Kroll benefited. We'll need proof against him."

Lewis nodded. "I'm all over it."

Ellis returned to her desk, where McCallister waited. "Bryce is going to get Burr out of here this morning. Hopefully before Kroll..." Her attention was drawn to the corridor.

"Morning." Kroll appeared, heading over to his desk. "Ellis, McCallister, I would've been here sooner, but I got called into a meeting with my ASAC."

"Everything all right?" she asked.

"Just our weekly updates." He set down his things and dropped onto his chair. "So, our plan was to get the warrant to search Slayton's apartment, right?"

"That's the plan." Concern for Bryce formed a tight ball in her gut. "How long do you think it'll take to get it?"

"Not long. I'll work on it this morning."

Ellis nodded, trying to appear casual even as her mind raced. "Sounds good. But before we get the warrant, Euan and I should follow up on a couple of other leads. We got a tip about a possible witness who was near the river around the time of Carter's murder." She glanced at her partner, hoping he'd play along.

McCallister gave her a subtle nod.

Kroll frowned, looking between them. "Who's the witness? Did someone call into the station?"

"Someone who works in the area. I guess they caught wind of the story on the news and recalled something. Anyway, we'd better follow through on it to cover our bases."

Kroll eyed them. "Right now?"

"I can't think of a better time. Once that warrant comes through, we'll be slammed." She stood, grabbing her keys. McCallister joined her. "Let us know when you get that warrant signed."

The two headed downstairs to see Pelletier, not giving Kroll a chance to voice further objections. He stood at the front desk, phone at his ear. He waved them over, noticing their hasty approach.

"That's great; thanks for the update," Pelletier said before hanging up. He turned to them. "That was the prison transport team. They'll be here to pick up Burr in about thirty minutes."

"Good, because Kroll's here." Ellis glanced upstairs. "Our time is up."

LIEUTENANT ABE SERRANO and former detective Hank Ellis had worked side by side for a number of years. Serrano was junior to Hank, and when Hank retired about six years ago, Serrano continued to move up in the ranks. But the two were still close. Abbott had known Hank as well, but it was the lieutenant who had remained Hank's confidant. It was the reason they'd gone to see him this morning.

The man had been through a lot in a short amount of time. He'd been a recent target with an attempt on his life, thanks to an old case he and Serrano had worked twenty-odd years ago. And after suffering a stroke as a result of that attempt, he'd struggled to fully recover. Now that he had, a member of the Sinaloa cartel had taken him hostage. Serrano felt responsible. But he needed one more thing from his old friend.

They pulled up to Hank's home. As they walked up the short driveway, Serrano saw him through the front window, sitting in his usual spot—an old recliner. Serrano knocked on the door. After a few moments, he heard slow footfalls, and then the door finally opened.

"Well, look who's here." Hank opened the door wider for them. "Like I said on the phone, Abe, I'm doing fine. No reason for you both to leave your posts."

The two men stepped inside.

Hank moved slower these days, thanks to the stroke. "Can I get you some coffee?" he asked as he walked into the kitchen. "Still got some left in the pot."

It pained Serrano to see his former partner this way. "No, thanks. This isn't exactly a social call, Hank." Serrano took a seat at the table while Abbott joined him. "We're here for another reason, unfortunately."

Hank's lips downturned. "I'm guessing that reason goes by the name of DEA Agent Kroll. The kid came over to see me last night. Told me her suspicions."

Serrano rested his arm on the table, crossing his long slim legs. "Your contact—any chance he's still there?"

Hank lowered himself onto a chair at the end. "Probably. But he works out of the New York office. From what I gather, Kroll's out of Buffalo."

"Yeah." Abbott nodded. "Which could be exactly the reason to reach out to someone in a different office. He has no connection to Buffalo."

Hank sipped on the coffee he'd poured for himself. "What do you want to know?"

Abbott glanced at Serrano before continuing. "We need Kroll out of the picture ASAP. Our witness is being transferred out of Bangor police custody as we speak. If he gets wind of what Becca and the team are up to, he might inform the cartel. That happens..."

Hank raised his hand. "Enough said. What about some of the folks you know, Jim?"

"I reached out to an old friend in New Jersey. He's looking into things for us. But you might be the best one to move this forward, Hank, and quickly."

Hank considered their request. "All right. Let me see what I can uncover. He still owes me a favor or two." He leaned forward toward the counter, grimacing as he stretched for the phone that lay on top of it.

Abbott stood up to get it, handing it over.

"Appreciate it." Hank took the phone, slipping on his reading glasses and opening his contacts list. It took a few moments, but then he found the number and made the call.

"Hey, Marty, it's Hank Ellis...Yeah, been a while, hasn't it? Listen, I need a favor..." Hank explained the situation with Kroll, nodding while he listened.

Serrano and Abbott weren't privy to the other end of the conversation, but Serrano thought it appeared positive.

"Think you can find something we can use as leverage?

Enough to get him pulled off this case and out of Becca's way?" Hank asked. "I appreciate it, I really do. Let me know as soon as you come up with something."

Hank ended the call and removed his glasses, returning his attention to Abbott and Serrano. "Might take a while, but he'll see what turns up. For the time being, you both need to do whatever it takes to keep my kid safe. I already lost one of them. I won't lose another."

ELLIS HAD MADE up the story about a potential witness. So what could she and McCallister do now to help drive the case against Kroll while Pelletier worked to transport Burr? Even Lewis was in on the action...and that was when it occurred to her. Still inside the station's lobby, she turned to McCallister. "The halfway house. We should talk to Rice."

"To what end?"

"Gabby said she found SARs in Cochran House's banking records. That tracks, considering we've seen how many inmates have been moved to Cochran House..."

"Then on to the halfway house," he interrupted.

"Exactly. So let's see what we can do to get him to talk." Ellis peered up the stairs again. "At least until Bryce takes care of his end of things. By then, we'll see if Kroll actually comes up with a warrant on the apartment."

"You don't seem to have much hope of that happening."

Ellis started toward the exit, McCallister at her side. "Nope. I sure don't."

They stepped outside. Clouds blocked the morning sun, cooling the air a little. Ellis unlocked her Tahoe, and they jumped in. With her grip on the wheel, she pulled away, heading toward Colonial Pines once again.

"I have a feeling Gabby will uncover a money trail to Rice, too. Not just Cochran House," she said. "Once we tell him Burr's in custody, he might be willing to open up if he thinks it'll save his own skin."

McCallister had gone quiet, which wasn't like him. "You don't think I'm on the right track with Kroll, do you?" she asked.

He gave a deep sigh. "Burr said he was in bed with the cartel. What reason does he have to lie except to get himself a deal?"

"Look, I know we're a long way from actual evidence to prove it, but, Euan, I'm right about this. Kroll isn't who we think he is. I really need you to back me up."

He held her gaze for a long moment. "I always do."

This wasn't the time to argue. They handled things differently. That was just the way of things. For partners, it was how it should be. Yet it seemed, since this case started, he'd refused to push back against her theories.

Ellis drove on, thinking of nothing else but Kroll and how he fit into her brother's murder. She rolled up to the halfway house. "Let me call Bryce before we go in. I want confirmation Burr is out." Ellis pressed his contact, and the call rang through on her speaker.

"Becca, where are you guys?" Pelletier asked.

"Sitting in front of the halfway house. Did you get Burr out of there?"

"I did. He's on his way to Augusta as we speak. Then he'll be moved to Portland, where a few old coworkers of mine will look after him till we can work out a deal with the DA."

"Good." She smiled at McCallister. "We'll keep him

moving around so Kroll doesn't figure it out. Has Kroll said anything to you?"

"No. Not a peep. Then again, I've been hustling to make this happen. Haven't even been upstairs," Pelletier replied. "I do know that Abbott and Serrano took off. Didn't say where they were going."

"I have a feeling I know where they went. Listen, we'll be here for a little while; then we'll head back to the station."

"Watch out for yourselves."

"Will do. Thanks, Bryce. See you soon." Ellis ended the call and opened her door. "Let's see how cooperative Mr. Rice wants to be this morning." Walking up to the house again, a pang of guilt struck her hard in the chest. She tried to conceal her emotions, wondering how long it would be before the dam burst.

McCallister knocked on the door.

Rice opened it. "Didn't expect you two. What can I do for you both?"

"We'd like to talk to you about DEA Agent Sean Kroll," Ellis replied. "Do you have a minute?"

Rice's face paled at the mention of Kroll's name. He glanced around before stepping back and gesturing for them to come inside. "All right then." He wiped down his brow with a handkerchief, walking to the kitchen table. "It's a warm one already today. Damn AC is on the fritz again. What do you want to know about Kroll?"

"We've learned a lot about the operations between the prison, Cochran House rehab, and your halfway house here." Ellis took a seat.

"What's that got to do with some DEA agent?"

"That's what we're here to find out." Ellis waited a moment while McCallister sat down too. "This is your chance, Oliver, to tell us what you know about Kroll's deal with the cartel."

"What's that now?" He recoiled slightly, his eyebrows raised. "Cartel? Yeah, I don't know anything about that."

"No?" McCallister asked. "So the guys who come here... all transferred from Cochran House...you don't know anything about Kroll's involvement with them?"

"No, sir."

"Kroll's home base is in Buffalo," Ellis began. "It's possible he has similar operations in other locations. But I suspect he might've been made aware, through his own sources, what's been going on between the state prison and all the rest. Figured he had a shot at getting in on it and took full advantage of the guys who came here, including my brother."

Rice darted his nervous gaze between them. "Like I said, I don't know. Suppose you should ask the man yourselves."

"And he probably offered you a fair amount of cash to let him do what he wanted. Running these guys. Getting them to do the cartel's dirty work," McCallister added. "But you know, if Kroll killed my partner's brother, well, that was a serious miscalculation on his part."

For the first time in a while, Ellis felt McCallister had her back, even if he still didn't believe she was on the right side of the equation. Kroll's connection to the prison and Cochran House was something Lewis would likely uncover. But the real case, as far as she was concerned, was what Kroll was doing to the guys here. What he'd done to her brother.

"Look, I had no idea what Kroll was really up to," Rice said, darting his gaze as if making a decision. Then, at last, he spoke. "He approached me months ago about redirecting some of the funds. Said it would help grease the wheels with getting more guys placed here after their release. I just...I just looked the other way. I never wanted to get mixed up in anything illegal."

"Well, you did," McCallister said. "And now we need your help taking Kroll down."

"How?"

Ellis leaned in, locking her steely gaze onto Rice; the man was sweating profusely by now. "We need everything you have on Kroll and his operation. Names, meeting places, transactions—everything."

Rice got to his feet and walked into the kitchen. Near the washer and dryer that were tucked into a back corner, he opened one of the cabinets. Soon, he returned with a file. "I've been keeping notes. Names of some of the guys he was working with, a few locations." He handed it to Ellis. "I figured this day would come and that I might need insurance."

24

I t was Hank Ellis who would have the connections to run this new information up the ladder. Ellis had called Abbott with the news, learning that her bosses had already gone to see her dad. Now it was her turn to help bring this to an end.

By midmorning, she and McCallister arrived at his home. As they reached his door, Ellis knocked and turned the handle. "Dad, it's me. I brought Euan along."

They walked inside. Hank's voice sounded in the distance. "In the kitchen."

She led the way inside. Hank smiled as he made himself a snack of peanut butter and celery. It was a good sign he was beginning to better handle his grief. No doubt, the request for his help aided in his sense of value and purpose. "Glad to see you're eating."

He held up the plate. "Gonna take more than a gun to my head for me to lose my appetite." He nodded at Euan. "Good to see you, son."

"And you, sir," McCallister replied.

"So, tell me what you two uncovered."

Ellis walked toward the kitchen table and set down a file. "We paid a visit to the manager of the halfway house. Oliver Rice. Turned out, he figured the path Kroll was going down might blow back on him, so he took precautions."

"Such as?" Hank walked around the kitchen island with his snack.

They hovered over the table while Ellis pointed at the documents. "Money—skimmed from the account used to pay for the transfers from the prison to the rehab, then to the halfway house. And access." She flipped the pages of notes. "Kroll used every one of those guys to work for the cartel."

"Including Carter," Hank said.

"Yes." Her eyes locked with Hank's, both seeming to understand that maybe Carter hadn't been to blame for this turn of events. "Gabby found several SARs, and FinCen was already looking into some of this. We believe Kroll was working with someone inside the prison too. We don't have a name yet. And I know Sarge and the lieutenant came to see you."

"They did. I made some calls, but with this...I have more for them to look at."

"How long, sir?" McCallister asked. "How long before we can alert the higher-ups at the DEA about their man?"

Hank examined the documents while he crunched on a bite of celery. "Well, this is compelling. I'll get it over to them ASAP. I'd say we should hear something by the end of the day, if not sooner."

"We have to keep Kroll occupied in the meantime," Ellis said. "He claims to be working on a warrant for Miguel Slayton, aka Esteban Cruz, who I now believe may have been given the order to kill Carter. Probably Tyler Beck, too. Kroll was Carter's handler, so I suspect ultimately, it was Kroll's doing—issuing kill orders."

"Somehow, I doubt that warrant will come through," Hank said.

"Me neither," she replied. "That means we'll have to find a way to keep Kroll from figuring out what we know."

Hank reached out for his daughter's arm. "Listen to me, kid. It'll only take this halfway house manager to feel a tiny bit of pressure for him to talk. So if Kroll suspects anything... that you two have been going behind his back...none of us will be safe."

ELLIS HADN'T WANTED to leave Hank, but the plan was set in motion. They had to get back to the station. But they kept the patrolman outside his house. She prayed he would keep her father safe. Things were coming to a head, fast. And when that happened, when dangerous people were backed into a corner, all bets were off.

Now, they'd returned to the station to find Kroll at his desk.

Ellis approached him. "No luck with that probable witness. Just another dead end."

He peered at her, a curious look in his eyes. Did he know what they suspected? If so, why was he still here? "It happens sometimes." Kroll slapped down a document onto his desk.

Ellis glanced at it. "You got the warrant on Slayton?" This was an unexpected development. Why was he prepared to go after someone he had most likely directed to kill her brother?

"I did." He shot a glance between them. "So, you two ready to go serve this? I think we've all wasted enough time today."

She looked back at McCallister, who mirrored her expression. "Of course. We're ready when you are."

They trailed behind Kroll downstairs and into the lobby. Neither of them had the chance to inform Abbott of this development.

Outside, under a clearing sky, an insurmountable tension built as though Kroll already knew what they'd done. Ellis climbed into the passenger seat of Kroll's Lexus. The very car she'd spotted following her only days ago. Probably should've acted then, but as always, she'd wanted more. She'd wanted this man to pay, certain of his involvement in Carter's death.

Kroll pressed the ignition. "I have no doubt Slayton played a part in the murder of your brother, Detective Ellis. He's a suspected hitman for the cartel. We get him on murder, there's a hell of a good chance he'll turn on some of his people." He glanced at her with a smile. "We're one step closer to exposing the operation on our side of the northern border."

"I hope you're right, Agent Kroll." Ellis peered through the sideview mirror, McCallister capturing her gaze from the back seat. It seemed neither of them had a clue as to how this day would end.

The drive to the apartment was a nerve-racking game of chess. Ellis's mind raced, strategizing ways to delay Kroll from potentially eliminating Slayton—a key piece on this complex board. Could they feign confusion over the address or apartment number, buying precious minutes? Or assert the need for additional backup before proceeding? She just needed to stave off Kroll long enough for Hank to present their damning evidence to the DEA.

The apartment building loomed in the distance. Kroll parked in front of it. "Here we are. Check your weapons, and let's go get this guy." He climbed out.

Ellis turned back to McCallister as Kroll headed to the sidewalk. He shook his head, preempting any words she might utter. It seemed he knew, just as she did, this wasn't going as planned. "Son of a bitch." She opened her door, stepping out to join them. "Do we know for sure he's here?"

Kroll pointed to his right. "That's his car there. He's here."

"Can I take a look at the warrant?" Ellis held out her hand. "What are we authorized to take?"

Kroll hesitated, then finally offered it to her. "The usual stuff, Detective. But by all means, let's stand out in the open while you look it over."

Moments ticked by as she reviewed the document, her brow furrowing in feigned concentration.

"You done?" Kroll asked. "We need to do this now. I figured you'd be happy about this, Detective. Instead, you seem hesitant. Why is that?"

She held out the document. "Wouldn't want to let him off on a technicality, Agent Kroll. You should know how easily that can happen."

He snatched it from her. "Sure." Without another word, Kroll climbed the stairs to the second-floor breezeway.

When Ellis and McCallister caught up to him, he pounded on the door of unit 218. "DEA. Miguel Slayton, we know you're here. Open the door."

There was no response from inside the apartment.

Kroll pounded on the door again. "Slayton, open up, or we're coming in anyway. We have a warrant."

Still nothing.

Kroll tried the doorknob and found it unlocked. "The hell?" He drew his gun and nodded to Ellis and McCallister. Both brandished their sidearms in response. He slowly pushed open the door, light spilling inside the otherwise shadowy apartment.

The living room was sparsely furnished with just a sofa, a coffee table, and a small TV. Fast-food wrappers and empty beer cans littered the floor. The air was stale and humid.

Kroll moved in, waving the detectives on. He walked into the hallway. Ellis aimed her weapon, scanning the living room and kitchen. McCallister stayed close to her. Neither certain what would happen next. Slayton was supposed to be here. Kroll had pointed out his car when they arrived. This wasn't looking good.

Ellis kept an eye on him. Trusting this man would be a mistake, one that could be fatal. Kroll continued into the hall, heading toward one of the doors. She glanced at McCallister. He nodded.

Just as Kroll wrapped his hand around the door handle, a crash rang out from the back of the apartment.

"He's bolting out the window!" Kroll yelled, sprinting into the room.

Ellis hurried through the bedroom and into a small bathroom, where Kroll now stood. "Goddam it."

Inside, the bathroom window had been shattered, shards of glass scattering in the tub. The shower curtain fluttered in the breeze.

Glass cracked under Kroll's feet as he craned out the

window, scanning the ground below. "I see him. Let's go." Kroll darted away.

"He's going to kill Slayton," Ellis said as McCallister entered. "We have to stop him." She sprinted through the living room and ran outside to where Kroll was seen jogging down the stairs. She looked back. McCallister was only steps behind. "Hurry. We can't lose him." Ellis reached the stairs and leaped down, two at a time. She felt McCallister closing in on her. "There he is. But I don't see Slayton."

"Keep going. Run," McCallister said, sounding breathless.

In the distance, a figure sprinted between the buildings.

"That's him." Her legs pumped hard as she and McCallister closed in on Kroll.

"There!" Kroll looked back at them. "Come on, goddam it. Hurry."

Ellis felt her heart pounding as she raced after Kroll. Why was he insisting they keep up with him? She was sure he'd wanted to shoot Slayton so he wouldn't talk.

As they rounded the corner of the next building, Kroll suddenly stopped short, raising his hand for them to halt. Peering around the edge of the building, they spotted a man's foot visible behind a dumpster. "That's him." Kroll signaled for Ellis and McCallister to circle around the other side while he approached from the front.

Drawing their weapons, they slowly closed in on the dumpster. As Kroll neared, Slayton leaped from his hiding spot, clutching something in his hands.

"Drop it!" Kroll commanded.

Slayton turned to face Kroll. His eyes were black with fear, and in his hands he held a small pistol.

"Drop the gun, Slayton," Kroll ordered again.

His gaze darted around, looking for an escape.

Ellis could see the desperation mounting in the man. She wanted him to say something, anything that would prove their theory about Kroll. But he wouldn't. No one with a gun aimed at their head would say a damn word.

Slowly, Slayton lowered the pistol to the ground. As he straightened back up, his eyes met Kroll's. In that brief moment, a look of understanding seemed to pass between them.

Ellis witnessed the exchange. "What the...?" But before she could process this further, Slayton bolted again, running toward the chain-link fence at the edge of the parking lot.

Kroll swiftly raised his weapon and fired. The crack of the gunshot reverberated painfully in her ears. Everything seemed to move in slow motion as Ellis watched the man tumble to the ground, a blossom of red spreading across his back.

"No!" Ellis cried out. She rushed to Slayton's side, kneeling next to him as he lay dying. The man's eyes were open but glazed over, blood dripping from his parted lips. "You know what he did," she whispered. "Tell me."

But no words came. He was gone.

Rage and despair swirled in her chest as she returned to her feet, eyes fixed on Kroll. His gun was still raised, eyes empty. "What the hell did you do?"

"He was going for the fence," Kroll replied matter-of-factly. "I did what needed to be done."

"You mind lowering that gun?" McCallister asked, holstering his own. He walked toward Kroll, grabbing his shoulder. "We needed him alive."

"He was armed. Get off me! He was a cartel thug. What the hell's wrong with you people?"

Ellis secured her gun. "Don't pretend you didn't do this to save your own ass."

LIGHTS from three patrol units flashed in the late afternoon sky. An ambulance waited with its doors open.

Sergeant Abbott pulled up to the scene and approached his detectives. "What the hell happened here?" He took in the sight of Slayton's body sprawled on the pavement. "You were serving a goddam search warrant."

"I'm well aware." Ellis glanced at Kroll, who was several steps away, talking on his phone.

McCallister rested his hand on her shoulder. "We didn't get the chance, Sarge. Slayton was there, slipped out of the apartment. Kroll gave chase—took him out."

"Before we could question him," Ellis cut in. "He claimed Slayton was going for the fence, even though he'd already dropped his weapon."

Abbott set his hands on his thick waist. "So he was armed?"

"Yes, sir," she replied. "But like I said, he wasn't when he took off for the fence."

Abbott's mouth tightened into a thin line. He turned to McCallister as if searching for agreement.

McCallister nodded. "The choice to bring him in was removed from our hands. Kroll shot an unarmed man."

Abbott shook his head, taking in the scene. "This doesn't look good. Kroll overstepped his authority on this one, and our department will suffer for it."

The agent walked toward them, dropping his phone into his pocket. "Sergeant Abbott, your people fill—"

Abbott's eyes blazed with anger. "You'd better have a damn good explanation for this, Agent Kroll."

Kroll appeared just as calm as the moment he shot the man. "Slayton was a cartel operative. He was armed. When I got him to lay down his weapon, he bolted. I neutralized the threat."

"Threat? That wasn't your call to make," Abbott shot back. "He was our suspect—we were bringing him in."

"Excuse me, Sergeant Abbott, but I obtained the warrant. This was DEA territory," he replied. "You have a problem with it, take it up with my ASAC."

Abbott stepped away in a huff. Ellis and McCallister joined him.

Ellis kept an eye on Kroll. "He wanted Slayton's mouth shut, so he shut it for him."

"We still have him, Becca," McCallister said. "The documents Rice handed over...Gabby's FinCen intel. Hank's contacts...Kroll's going to be behind bars in a matter of days, maybe less."

"Doesn't help me figure out who murdered my brother." Ellis shifted her gaze to the coroner's van as they loaded the body. The evidence technician marked the locations of the shell casings and any other evidence. "I have to know if Kroll directed Slayton to kill Carter. How the hell am I going to find that out now?"

McCallister glanced up to the apartment. "We go inside his place and pull DNA. Pull prints. Anything we can find."

Ellis looked at Abbott, hoping for his approval.

"You have a warrant," Abbott replied. "Go."

They climbed the steps to Slayton's apartment. Inside, the living room blinds were still closed, and shadows clung to the walls.

"I'll start out here," Ellis said, moving through the kitchenette. Dirty dishes were stacked in the sink and on the counter. It seemed like Slayton lived alone and didn't care much for cleaning.

McCallister headed for the bedroom while she continued her search. Opening cabinets and drawers, she sought out any documents or personal effects that could prove her theory about Kroll. She opened the bottom right-hand kitchen drawer, riffling through the junk until she stumbled on a photo. "Holy shit." With a gloved hand, Ellis picked it up. "Euan, come take a look."

He emerged from the back. "What'd you find?"

She held up the image of Slayton and Kroll together. "It doesn't look like Kroll was aware this photo was being taken. Maybe a private meeting of some kind."

"Could be one of Slayton's associates who took it. They needed something that proved Kroll's connection to Slayton. He's being handed a file."

"Then the only reason Slayton would still have it is in case he needed to blackmail Kroll, or to use it to ensure Kroll could get him out of a bind if necessary."

"Blackmail sounds about right. Hide it. Now. That stays between us for the moment." McCallister peered around the room. "Look for a phone or laptop. It'll help us to confirm what that photo shows."

They moved swiftly through the apartment, knowing that at any moment, Kroll would realize what they were up to and join them. They knew now that he would stop at nothing to protect himself.

"Any more luck?" Ellis called out to him.

"Not yet," McCallister responded from the bedroom.

Ellis checked the living room again, shifting the furniture

and peering behind the TV stand. As she moved a stack of old takeout containers, a laptop appeared, tucked away in the corner. "I've got something."

McCallister hurried over as she picked it up.

"It'll be password protected," Ellis said. "We'll need to get it to Brown ASAP."

"I haven't come across a cell phone," McCallister said. "If it was on him, who knows if Kroll's got his hands on it now."

Ellis glanced at the front door, which had remained open. "Come on. We've been up here long enough. We have the laptop and a photo. That'll have to do."

25

The long, monotonous drive to upstate New York and back again sapped every ounce of energy Bevins had. With his passenger and friend, Murph, beside him, the sun slowly descended behind the horizon, painting the sky in shades of pink and orange.

Mental and physical exhaustion seeped into every bone and muscle. Uncertainty about what all of this meant cast a heavy fog over his mind. He knew now that Lance had information that had most likely led to his death. And while it didn't help Mrs. Curry, the woman offered forgiveness to him, and that, alone, had made the trip worthwhile.

Darkness enveloped the car as it rolled along the highway, headlights shining in the light that remained. "Someone made sure the accident would kill Lance," Bevins said, his hands gripping the steering wheel of his Mustang.

Murph glanced at him, and Bevins felt he was holding his tongue. "What is it?"

"I don't know, man. I'm in over my head. My ass is on the line, and I won't get out of this one."

"You will. I promise I won't let you go down because of me."

"That's the problem," he replied. "Don't you see? Con, you can't be that blind, can you?"

Bevins shot him a look. "What are you talking about?"

"Jesus." Murph threw his hands in the air. "Lance had something on your dad. He died not long after. Hello? Two and two, brother."

Bevins peered out over the road again. "A fact not lost on me, if that's what you're implying."

"So what are you going to do about it?"

It all made sense now. Why Jack had gone to the lengths he had—supposedly to protect his son. He wasn't protecting his son. He was protecting himself. "He made sure the accident would kill Lance. And I'm not entirely sure he cared whether it killed me in the process. So now this blogger, Asher Daly, knows. Someone told him. Someone who doesn't like Jack very much and who knew this dark little secret of his."

Murph let out a long breath. "Yeah, man, I think so. It's the only thing that ties everything together."

"I'll have to tread carefully," Bevins added. "This shit is deeper than I thought. This is the DOD. The Army. Maybe even members of the goddam presidential cabinet. Someone wants this out in the open. And we need to find who that someone is."

Bevins pulled into the stationhouse. "Come on. Let's go inside. I have some things to discuss with the sarge." He opened the door to find Ellis and McCallister in what appeared to be a heated conversation with the DEA agent. Bevins looked back at his friend as they stood in the lobby. "Wait here a second."

Murph folded his arms across his chest. "Sure."

Bevins listened in on their conversation as he approached.

"We have reason to believe Slayton was connected to the attack on my brother," Ellis said. "We're taking his laptop as evidence."

"On whose authority?" Kroll demanded.

"Mine. This is my case, Agent Kroll. You have no jurisdiction."

Kroll smiled. "Is that right? Because last I checked, anything linked to the cartel is DEA jurisdiction. And Slayton was part of their operation. It was my warrant, don't forget, Detective Ellis."

McCallister stepped forward. "We're going to run it to Evidence to find out who killed Carter Ellis. Stay out of our way, Kroll."

"Everything all right here?" Bevins cut in.

Ellis looked at him. "Connor, where have you been? Everything okay?"

"Yeah, fine. I took some time off to fix something."

She gave him a look he easily recognized. "And did you?"

"I got answers. Maybe not the ones I wanted." He thumbed over to Kroll. "What's the deal here?"

Ellis eyed the agent. "Nothing Lieutenant Serrano can't help with."

"Okay. Listen, I gotta run some stuff by Abbott. I'll catch up with you two later." He returned to his friend, feeling uncertain about leaving his team. But now, the look on Murph's face left him feeling even more doubtful. "What is it? What's wrong?"

Murph held out his phone. "I just got Lance's file."

"How the hell?" Bevins grabbed the phone. "You said they kicked you out, took your clearance."

"I called in a favor," Murph said. "So if you want to look at it, know that I'm already in this up to my ass. You will be too."

"If it contains what I hope it will, there's someone else who should be more worried than us. Come on. We'll go to my desk upstairs." He led the way, passing by Ellis, McCallister, and the DEA agent. On their arrival, he gestured to a chair. "Take a seat. Show me what you got."

Murph opened the file, handing his phone to Bevins.

"Cadet Lance Curry," Bevins said as he read. He scanned through the file, his mouth open as he absorbed the details. Some of which he'd learned from Mrs. Curry. "It's all here. How I was admitted. The recommendations against it. Jesus, why didn't Lance tell me this?"

"Because he was your friend," Murph replied. "And this was your dad."

"This is proof. Lance filed a report that got buried." Bevins leaned back in his chair. "My father was using his position, as always. And he silenced Lance when he tried to speak up."

"What are you going to do, man?" Murph asked. "We are so screwed right now."

Bevins ran a hand through his hair. "I don't know yet. Someone out there knows this too. That's how all this started." He thought for a moment and then eyed Fletch as she walked in.

She must've picked up on his distress. "First of all, what are you doing here?" she demanded as she walked over. "You were supposed to take a few days off. Secondly, what's wrong?"

Bevins filled her in on the new information. "What do we do now? Murph is busted. I'll be busted after this."

"No." She raised her hand. "Not if this comes to light. You and your friend won't be touched. But let's think for a second. Someone else already knows this information, right?"

Bevins nodded.

"Right, so who would've done that? You figure out that part, and you can take it up the chain. I wouldn't do that until you're damn sure."

"Yeah, you're right. Thanks, Fletch." Bevins went back to the report, carefully reviewing it. "The guy Lance reported this to? Who was he?" He read on until he got the name. "Lieutenant Colonel Gregory Huff."

Murph leaned back. "Holy shit. I know that name."

"How?"

"New joint chiefs are being appointed." Murph eyed him. "Connor, man, he's up for your dad's job."

A STANDOFF HAD ENSUED. Ellis had refused to hand over Slayton's laptop, instead insisting their forensics team review it. Kroll then demanded to talk to Abbott.

This was where she hoped Abbott, along with her father and Lieutenant Serrano, had been given enough time to bring the DEA up to speed on their seemingly corrupt agent. "He's in his office." Ellis gestured to the stairs. "Have at it."

McCallister had remained at her side; neither of them was inclined to give in. She sensed Kroll's rising anger, feeling his gaze bore into her.

"You're out of your depth, Detectives," Kroll replied. "You

have no idea the lengths the cartel will go to get what they want."

"I have some idea," Ellis added. "If you want this laptop, I have no problem handing it over after our people have looked into it."

Kroll's lips curled into a smile. "Okay." He brushed past them, climbing the stairs before turning toward Abbott's office.

"Jesus." Ellis let out a breath. "I need to get this to Brown right now."

"Go." McCallister peered up to the second floor. "I'll run interference with Kroll and Abbott. Tell Brown he'll have to be quick."

"I have no idea if he'll be able to access it. Certainly not within minutes. This rests on our bosses' shoulders now. We've given them everything, and it's going to have to be enough to persuade someone at the DEA to take notice."

McCallister grabbed the handrail. "You have to try. Do what you can."

She headed into the hallway, toward Forensics. Putting Brown under this kind of pressure wasn't ideal, and it might end in failure, but she had no choice. Entering the lab, she eyed Harding at his desk. "I need to see Brown."

Harding immediately picked up on the urgency in her tone. He thumbed back. "In his office. Go ahead."

"Thanks." Ellis carried on through the short corridor before arriving at Brown's office. His door was open. "Hey, you busy?"

He peered at her, scratching his beard. "Is that a joke?"

Ellis walked in, setting down the laptop on his desk.

"Who does that belong to?" Brown asked.

"Miguel Slayton, suspected member of the Sinaloa

cartel. He was gunned down by the DEA agent working with us. This was found in his apartment."

Brown nodded. "Leave it. I'll get to it as soon as I can."

Ellis placed her hand on his shoulder, the gravity of the situation weighing her thoughts. "There's no time, Leo. Look, I don't know if you'll be able to access this or not, but please, I'm desperate."

He resigned, opening the laptop. "Without a password, you know I can't get into this thing. I'll have to send it off. And even then, there's no guarantee. What do you think I can do with this?"

It was then Ellis heard muted voices. She looked at Brown. "You hear that?"

His brow creased. "Yeah. What the hell's going on?"

"Stay here." Ellis marched through to the main part of the lab, where Harding and others remained. "Don't anyone leave, all right?"

"What's going on, Detective?" Harding asked.

"I don't know, but I'm about to find out." She opened the door, her hand on her sidearm, and looked out. The hallway was empty, but the noise grew louder. Firm, loud voices and heavy footfalls. She marched ahead, making her way toward the lobby. A group of DEA agents had arrived, their jackets emblazoned with the initials on the back. "Oh my God. They did it."

Abbott and Serrano had come through. These guys were here for Kroll. She looked up at the second-floor landing, her bosses meeting with the team that had reached the top. Ellis searched for McCallister. "Where are you?" He was supposed to be with them. And where was Kroll? Ellis started up the steps, capturing Abbott's gaze.

He offered a nod and a closed-lip grin.

As she reached the top, she caught up to him. "Where's Euan?"

"In my office, holding Kroll until these guys take him." He regarded her. "Becca, what you and the rest of the team uncovered...the DEA Chief of Operations was keenly interested in. And it was Hank who used his contact to take it to the top and get this noticed."

A moment later, Kroll emerged in cuffs, being led by his own department.

Behind them, McCallister emerged. Their eyes met. He returned a nod.

The lead agent stepped forward to meet Abbott. "Sergeant Abbott, we'll need the files, evidence, everything you have on this investigation."

He shot a glance at Ellis before returning his focus to the man. "We still have a murder to solve. Two, actually."

"I understand that, sir, but we'll be taking over from here." He looked at Ellis. "Are you one of his?"

Ellis nodded. "And the murder victim is my brother. I need to see this to its end."

The agent appeared to consider her request. "Then I promise to keep you in the loop, Detective..."

"Ellis. Rebecca Ellis," she replied.

"I have a feeling it won't take much for Kroll to open up. And the evidence your department has already presented leads me to believe Kroll will want to work out a deal."

"Thank you, sir." She waited while the DEA took Kroll away. The entire team had emerged on the landing, watching the remarkable scene unfold. Kroll locked eyes with her, a crooked smile pulling at his lips. The look unnerved her, like he knew he wouldn't pay for what he'd done. How many agents, she wondered, were in the cartel's pockets? All of this drama and activity, yet still no answers about her brother's murder.

Abbott rested his hand on her shoulder. "You still need answers, I see that. And they will come. I promise you."

While this was the outcome she'd hoped for, it offered little relief. "Then they'll have to come from me, sir."

AFTER THE SITUATION with the DEA had settled, Bevins knew the time had come to present Abbott with the information about his father. He and Murph were in the break room when Bevins turned to his friend. "I need to bring this to my boss. I'll get with him now, and then we'll get out of here, hopefully with an idea of how I can keep you out of the fallout from all this."

Murph nodded. "Yeah, okay, man. I'll stick it out here. Good luck."

"I'm going to need it." Bevins headed out into the hall, passing by the bullpen, making his way to Abbott's office. "Hey, Sarge. Can I talk to you? I have information on that thing I've been working on."

Abbott raised an eyebrow, then nodded. "Close the door. Take a seat."

"First of all, the information I have...some of it was classified. And the person who offered it to me did so because he's a friend." Bevins shook his head. "I can't let him pay the price for accessing it."

"Tell me what you have, son," Abbott said. "Then we can worry about the rest."

"Yes, sir." He handed over the original accident report.

"My buddy did some digging. Uncovered this. It's the accident report. The original one."

Abbott thumbed through it. "I see."

"Yeah, so it looks like someone wanted me to get into that wreck. And I think I know who. Long story short, my friend who died, Lance Curry, he—uh—he had information on Jack. Damning information. And as you can see, an object had been placed in the road. I hit it, flipped the car, and that was that."

"Go on."

Bevins felt the weight, the horror of it all. "I think Jack wanted my friend out of the way. Not sure if he cared whether it took me down too, but point being, my friend had told someone else about what my father had done, using his influence, bribing people to get me into West Point. Lieutenant Colonel Gregory Huff. My friend tells him; then he's killed in the accident I thought I'd caused. It's covered up. I'm confident Huff then realized the timing of Lance's death and the implications of it. Finds the original report and learns the truth. He held onto it until it suited him to use it. At that time, he then sent it to the blogger."

"So your friend had damning information on Jack. Jack, by all accounts, caused the accident that took that young man's life. And this Lieutenant Huff has a grudge and decides now's the time to come forward?"

"No, not a grudge exactly," Bevins replied. "Huff wants my father's job. New staff is being selected soon."

Abbott set down the report, his forefinger and thumb rubbing the bridge of his nose. "Well, that changes things."

"What do I do, sir?" He gestured outward. "Murph is here. Scared shitless. Everything I thought I knew turned out to be a lie."

"Huff was smart to send the information to a no-name blogger. Any self-respecting reporter would've confirmed sources, shedding light on why Huff held onto the truth for so long. And eventually, even with this no-name guy, it'll gain traction, leaving Jack with everything to lose. Huff's hands are clean."

"Do I tell Jack I have a pretty good idea who blew the whistle to the blogger?"

Abbott fixed his gaze on him. The look in his eyes was like nothing he'd ever seen from the hardened old guy. "I can't advise you on this one, son. Dirty politics are outside my wheelhouse. I'm damn sorry your father got you into this. When Jack came to me, a reference from a friend of a friend, he was upfront. Told me about the accident—but clearly not everything about it. Said you deserved a second chance. I agreed, which is why you're here." He unleashed a heavy sigh. "If the public picks up on this, Jack will most certainly lose everything. But I'm afraid you will too."

"I was complicit. I let him cover it up." Bevins felt the sting of tears in his eyes. "I was stupid and scared and young. I know that's no excuse. I'm not afraid of retaliation, but Murph—I have to protect him."

"This is your decision to make, Connor. But whatever happens, I will stand by you. So will your team."

He got up from the chair. "Thanks, Sarge." This was something he had to face on his own. The time had come to confront Jack about what he knew and what he suspected.

What this meant for his future remained unknown. But his conscience would be clear. He had allowed Jack to cover all of this up, pushing it to the back of his mind, stamping down on it, never to be brought up again. And he'd been okay with that—for a while. Until he realized he couldn't be that person anymore. That guy who didn't give a shit about anyone but himself.

Training with McCallister and learning from Ellis...it had changed him—for the better.

He returned to the break room to find Murph sitting at one of the tables. A can of soda in his hands, his knee bouncing underneath. Bevins hesitated. "Hey, man. Thanks for sticking around."

Murph spun toward him. "I got nowhere else to go. What did your boss say?"

"He said this was on me." Bevins joined his friend at the table. "I decided it's best if I go see Jack again. Tell him what I learned. I'll keep you out of it. I swear."

"They already know it was me who pulled the file," Murph said. "You can't help me any more than you can help yourself."

26

The day of Carter's funeral, the sun shone, and the fresh breeze cooled the skin. Ellis and her father stood over the coffin as it hovered above its final destination. It was all she could do to keep Hank from collapsing under the weight of his grief.

As Ellis glanced around, her heart warmed at the sight of nearly the entire police department in attendance. If ever she doubted where she belonged, she only needed to look at the faces that surrounded her. And Piper, who'd always been there for her, stood only steps away, ready to catch her if she fell.

Ellis kept her arm wrapped around Hank's shoulders, holding his hand as the casket was lowered. His agony must be unbearable. No one should have to bury their child.

Regret lingered as she reexamined her relationship with Carter. Never close, partly due to the age difference, partly due to the fact they had different mothers. Even when Carter's mother died from cancer, Ellis had kept her walls high, never fully overcoming her own mother's loss to comfort her brother.

As the first clumps of dirt hit the polished wooden coffin, her thoughts drifted back over the years. Ellis saw a gap-toothed Carter at five years old, grinning up at her after she pushed him on the swing set. She saw a gangly, pimple-faced teenager sneaking out his bedroom window to meet up with shady friends. She saw the track marks on Carter's arms and the desperation in his bloodshot eyes when he came to her, time and again, for money.

Ellis had pitied Carter, but she'd also held him at arm's length, wary of enabling his addictions. In the end, she realized, they had both failed each other. Family was family, after all.

She studied her father's face etched with grief. Hank had tried so hard to steer Carter right, getting him into rehab again and again, refusing to give up hope even when it was clear his son was lost. Ellis both admired Hank's devotion and was mystified by it. She had written Carter off long ago, frustrated by his lies and betrayals, his self-centeredness. Hank was a better person than her, still seeing the good in Carter even when he stole from him.

Ellis felt a pang of sadness, realizing her half-brother's wasted life. He had been murdered, and the culprit remained unknown.

The minister ended the service. Piper walked toward her, taking Hank's hand in her own. "Let me help."

Ellis nodded, a tender smile on her face. "Thanks, Pipes."

The two ushered Hank away. McCallister looked on, ready to aid in any way he could. And when Ellis and Piper helped Hank inside her Tahoe, he approached.

Ellis reached out for Piper's arm. "Go ahead. I'll be just a minute."

Piper held her gaze a moment, as if to ensure she was leaving her friend in good hands. "Okay."

And when she carried on, Ellis turned back to McCallister. Hands in his pockets. Gaze downcast.

"Listen, I know this probably isn't the best time to discuss this, but Brown emailed me with some new files he found on Carter's laptop."

"He emailed you?"

"He didn't think it was appropriate to email you today, of all days."

"Right." She nodded. "What he found...does it help with the DEA's prosecution of Agent Kroll?"

"Uh, no. No, this was something more personal, Becca."

She checked Hank was inside and closed the car door. "Personal?"

"Brown wanted to know if you planned on going back to the station today. I told him absolutely not..."

"Yeah, I was."

"Becca, you don't..."

"I want to. Just for a little while. Hank's going to need some time to himself to grieve because he won't do it in front of me. Then I'll stay with him at his house tonight."

McCallister nodded. "Okay. Then you should see Brown when you get there."

"Aren't you coming?" she asked.

"You want me to?"

"Of course I do." Ellis walked around to the driver's side and stepped in. "Dad, I'm going to take you home; then I have to go back to the station for just a little while. I'll pick up some dinner and head back over this evening."

Hank peered through the passenger window. "Okay, kid. Whatever you need to do."

She pressed the ignition. "I also thought I'd crash on the couch tonight. If that's okay with you."

Hank turned to her, his eyes red, his lips quivering. "Yeah, sure. Maybe we can catch the game."

The sun had warmed the day as they arrived at Hank's. She stepped out, a mugginess hanging in the air. Walking around to the passenger side, Ellis opened the door. "Come on, Dad. Let's get you inside."

Hank made a beeline for his recliner as they entered. "I just need to sit down for a while."

"Sure. I'll get you a glass of water." Ellis headed toward the kitchen and grasped the edge of the sink. Her head sank, and tears spilled. After a few moments, she gathered herself, wiping away the remnants of grief from her cheeks, and filled a glass with tap water.

While Hank rested on his recliner, Ellis returned with the water. "So, like I said..."

"Go on, kid. I'll see you when I see you." Hank took a long drink.

"Yeah, okay, Dad." She bent and kissed his cheek, gently. "I love you."

FROM THE MOMENT Ellis walked into the station, the faces of those around her appeared somber. Most had been at the funeral. But such was the life of cops, there was no time for hosting a wake. Instead, they'd all returned to work, as she had.

Ellis nodded and smiled as condolences were offered,

feeling too numb to hear them. The funeral had been more difficult to get through than she'd expected.

She walked past the patrol unit's bullpen and waved at Triggs. He returned the gesture, his face appearing saddened. Ellis reached the lab and entered to find Brown at his desk.

"Becca, I didn't think…"

"Euan said you found something else on Carter's laptop?"

"I did." He reached for the computer. "Since the case is still active, I wanted to keep working on it, hoping to find something that will point you in the right direction."

"I appreciate that. What'd you find?"

"Uh, well, I saved the files to this flash drive." He handed it to her.

"Great. I'll take a look." Ellis dropped it in her pocket. "Thanks, Leo. Thank you for all you've done."

"Yeah, sure. I only wish we could've come up with more on Slayton's computer before the DEA took it."

"Me too." She offered a polite grin and headed back upstairs to CID. The team were at their desks. She noticed Bevins, who had kept quiet about dealing with the blogger who'd posted that image. She was glad; right now, she didn't have the bandwidth to deal with that.

McCallister stared at his computer, finally noticing her arrival and offering a warm smile. "How's Hank doing?"

She shrugged, taking a seat at her desk. "All right. I got the files from Brown."

"Good. Good."

He didn't know what to say or do, and that was fine. Neither did she.

Ellis inserted the flash drive into her laptop and retrieved the files. The one marked "Becca" was the one she opened first. It contained a Word document. A letter addressed to her. Ellis began to read it.

If you're reading this, Becca, then I really fucked up, and I'm probably dead. That shouldn't come as a big surprise to you, though, huh? A guy here at the halfway house helped me figure out how to hide this file well enough to be overlooked, but not so well that a good computer guy couldn't find it. Just FYI...he served time in Warren for cybercrimes. Go figure. So I hope he was right.

I've had ample time to consider the impact of my actions over the past several months. Both on you and on Dad. I know what he did to get me transferred into Cochran House. I also know what it cost him to do it. He's always been a better father than I deserved. But what he couldn't have known was that there were forces behind his efforts that led me down a path I now realize I can't escape.

Her eyes stung as she continued to read.

Dad suffered a lot because of me. Both financially and emotionally. I blamed him for my mother's death, as unfair as that was. But deep down, I know he loved June with all his heart, and she died because she got sick. That's all.

But this brings me to you, my half-sister and pain in my ass. My life's choices were in stark contrast to yours. The civil-minded, do-gooder cop that you are. Just like Dad. I say that with all appreciation for the life you chose to lead.

Becca, I'm sorry. Sorry for what I've put you through. Sorry for making you ashamed and embarrassed of me. No point in denying it. You were. And that's okay. I deserved it.

Ellis felt the lump rise in her throat.

I decided to write this, knowing the position I've allowed myself to be in, once again. And knowing that I might not make it out this time, no matter how many strings Dad tries to pull. And I figured you'd be the one to break my top-secret passcode. Mom's birthday. What can I say?

So I hope you are reading this because it's the only way I know of that I can express my true feelings for you. Of course, if you are reading this, well, I'm long gone, but I'll get to that in a minute. I hope Dad's okay. Please make sure he knows none of this was his fault.

I love you, Becca. I admire you. And I always have, even though I have never shown it or given you cause to believe it. I wanted to be like you and like Dad. Doing good things for people, but it wasn't my path.

I hope, one day, you'll be able to forgive me for all that I've done to cause our family harm. I would understand if you didn't. Regarding how I ended up writing this letter now...I should say that I am in fear for my life. I have a meeting soon, and I intend to bring my phone and record the conversation because I'm not sure I'll be coming back here. I've been working as an informant for the DEA. Yeah, can you believe that? To be honest, I didn't have much choice. I was caught selling again from the rehab facility, and this guy, Agent Kroll, he said if I helped him, he'd make sure I wasn't charged. He got me out of there and into this house.

The meeting is in an hour. I'm going to Flour Mill Dam. You remember that place, right? Dad used to take us there for picnics. I don't feel good about this meeting, but like I said, I wasn't given a choice. So if I don't make it, you know where to look, haha.

Take care, sis. I wish you all the happiness in the world. Dad too.

Love,
Carter

Ellis closed the lid of her laptop. Tears streamed down her cheeks. "Flour Mill Dam."

McCallister turned to her. "What's that?"

She stood up, snatching her keys from her desk. "That's where we need to go. Right now."

THE PARKING LOT was surrounded by trees that obscured the waterway. Behind the tree line were benches and tables for people to enjoy a picnic while the rapids continued downstream, eventually dumping into the Penobscot.

Ellis cut the engine. "This is where Carter said he had a meeting."

"But he didn't mention who with?" McCallister asked.

"No, which makes this all the more confusing. Maybe he left something here for me to find? I don't know, but I have to go look."

"All right."

The two stepped out and walked down through the trees, the stream revealing itself. Ellis looked on. "There must be something here. There won't be any security cameras."

"All we can do is have a look around," McCallister replied.

"Yep." Ellis walked on, checking every table, every bench. Looking for anything that appeared out of place. "Come on, Carter. What did you want me to find?" She set her hands on her hips, peering out over the ground.

"Becca?" McCallister called out. "Over here."

He stood near the display feature that explained the history of the dam, the wildlife and its impact on the Kenduskeag stream. She jogged toward him. "What is it?"

McCallister squatted near the display, pulling away dirt and leafy debris.

"Oh my God." Ellis joined him, peering down at what had been wedged in the soft soil. "You think that's Carter's phone? We never found it."

"I don't know. It's smashed all to hell, but we should see if Brown can do something with it."

"Yeah." She returned upright, patting her pockets. "I don't have any gloves."

McCallister retrieved a handkerchief. "I'll get it." He reached down and picked up the phone. "You have any luck over there?"

"No. Who could he have been meeting?" She scanned the ground around them and then walked toward the shoreline. She was several feet away when a piece of plastic just under the water's surface caught her eye. It appeared to be stuck under a rock waves lapped against. "What is this?" Ellis pulled out a credit card from her wallet and squatted once again. With her card, she flipped over the piece of plastic. It bobbed up and down on the water. "Jesus. Euan, look at this."

He headed toward her, steadying himself on the uneven terrain covered in tree roots, rocks, and wet earth, soon catching sight of what she'd uncovered. "You gotta be kidding me."

Ellis lost her breath for a moment, her chest pounding. "Maine State Prison. Associate Warden William Fenton. It was him. Carter met with this man, and something happened." She stood and peered out over the water. "They got into a fight maybe. Carter dropped his phone. This guy lost his ID badge, and it floated downstream. I don't know..." Ellis continued walking along the shoreline. McCallister followed. "Maybe the guy put a bag over Carter's head."

"That would cause hypoxia," he said.

"Yes." Ellis steadied her nerves. "Fenton then pushed him into the water, and the current carried him down to the Penobscot."

"Until he was stopped by the rocky shoreline at the pylon," he added. "Becca, this is what your brother wanted you to see."

She shook her head. "The associate warden killed him. But why?"

They returned to her Tahoe and headed away. She pressed her foot down on the gas.

It was McCallister who offered a calming word. "Becca, you've been through a lot today. This can wait until tomorrow."

"No, it can't." She hardened her gaze. "That letter, Euan... The things Carter said. He was in trouble and believed he was in danger. Yet he didn't call me or Hank. I did that. I made him think we didn't care, that he had no one to turn to."

"Well, it wasn't like he didn't give you cause."

"I know, but now he's gone. If I'd known—"

He placed his hand on her thigh. "This isn't on you, Becca. Your brother was in deep. That's painfully obvious now. He signed his death certificate the moment he agreed to work for the cartel. Nothing you could've done about that."

She focused on the road again. "And I was so certain Kroll did it. Or Slayton. And now it turns out the goddam prison warden did it."

McCallister raised his hand. "Let's not jump the gun yet. But why don't I text Gabby and ask her to cross-reference Carter's phone records with numbers pinged at the prison and around Warren itself?" He reached for his phone and typed the message.

"Yeah, that would be great. It could be the evidence we need. I should call the sarge. Tell him what's going on." She pressed his contact number.

Abbott answered. "Becca, where are you? Back at Hank's?"

She glanced at McCallister. "No, sir. I'm with Euan. We're heading to Warren. To the prison."

"Why?"

"I'll explain more fully later, but right now, we're going to see the associate warden. We think he killed Carter."

Abbott groaned. "What?"

"I know how this sounds, Sarge, but we found an ID badge belonging to Associate Warden William Fenton, and what we think is Carter's broken phone."

"Where the hell did you find those things?"

"At Flour Mill Dam," she replied. "Brown retrieved a file Carter left for me. It seemed he figured we'd find it eventually. He said he was meeting someone at the dam but didn't give a name. I don't know why. We came here, and...Sarge, this was where he was murdered. Shoved into the stream that carried him to the river."

"I can't believe this." Abbott's usually gruff voice was shot through with incredulity. "So Kroll didn't kill him? Neither did Slayton or any other cartel member?"

"It doesn't look that way, Sarge. But Kroll was a bad actor, regardless."

"No, I see that. Look, this is the last thing you need to be doing today, but I get why you are. Keep me posted."

"Will do, Sarge."

27

The sun was low in the sky by the time they reached the prison. Ellis parked her car, grimacing at the sight of the entrance. "How are we going to play this?"

"Our best bet is to go straight to the warden," McCallister said. "Present the evidence. The ID badge is pretty convincing."

"Right. And then we ask to bring Fenton back with us. Take him into custody."

He eyed the building. "We don't have enough evidence yet, and the warden may want to get the local authorities involved. If he does, we won't have much choice but to agree."

"If we could pinpoint the day of this meeting," Ellis began, "then we can confirm whether Fenton was here."

"The phone records will probably lead us to a date," McCallister said. "What I don't get is how or why Fenton was involved with your brother. Assuming he's part of the money kickback scheme, he'd have had nothing to do with the inmates."

She opened her door. "The only way we'll find out is to ask him."

They entered the Maine State Prison and approached the front desk. The officer on duty looked up as they displayed their badges.

"Detectives Ellis and McCallister to see Warden Baker," Ellis said.

"Let me see if he has a moment. I assume you don't have an appointment?"

"No, sir. But it's regarding former inmate Carter Ellis. We've been here before on the matter."

"One moment."

Ellis took a breath, feeling the adrenaline begin to wane, her emotions rising again to the surface. She tamped them back down again, there was too much at stake, and she had to maintain composure. This unexpected turn had upended everything she thought she knew about this investigation.

"He does have a free moment," the man said. "Our people will show you back."

The officer picked up the phone and spoke briefly before nodding and buzzing them through the security door. Another officer led them down a long hallway lined with heavy metal doors until they reached the administration offices.

Warden Baker was at his desk and welcomed them inside. "Detective Ellis, Detective McCallister, I'm surprised to see you. A phone call would've been nice."

"I apologize for dropping in," Ellis said. "I'd say we were in the area, but we weren't."

"Please, sit down." Baker clasped his hands on his desk.

"Tell me what I can do for you. I assume you're still investigating the Cochran House situation that involved your brother, Carter."

"And other inmates, yes, sir," Ellis replied.

Without wasting another moment, McCallister retrieved the ID badge, setting it down on the warden's desk. "This was found at the location we now believe was where Carter Ellis was murdered."

Baker slipped on his glasses and picked up the badge. Ellis quickly realized prints would now be difficult to pull, but at this point, she was running on the notion Fenton was a killer.

"This is my associate warden's badge." He set it down again, removing his glasses. "You say you found this...where?"

"Where my brother's broken phone was found," Ellis cut in. "And where I believe he was killed. Suffocated, then pushed into the stream—is my best guess."

"I see. That is troubling, to say the least." He eyed her. "What is it you'd like me to do, then, Detective?"

"We'd like to bring Fenton back with us, question him. Get his prints, DNA..."

"Are you charging him with murder?" Baker asked.

"That depends on what he has to say," McCallister replied. "We'd appreciate your cooperation on this, sir. As you can see, it would be difficult to explain away this badge ending up where it did."

Ellis tried to read Baker's face. He seemed to be weighing his options. But what she couldn't be sure of was whether he had any involvement. It seemed possible; this was, after all, his prison.

"How about I show you to his office." Baker stood,

walking around his desk. "Follow me. I'm sure he can clear up any misunderstandings."

Ellis followed, casting a knowing glance at McCallister. The good news was that the warden was allowing them to talk to Fenton. Did bad news still await?

Baker opened the door. "Bill, the Bangor police detectives are here again, asking to speak with you. I'd appreciate you giving them your undivided attention."

"Yes, sir." Associate Warden Fenton waited while they stepped inside. He shook their hands briskly and motioned for them to take a seat in front of his desk.

Baker remained in the background.

"How can I help the Bangor PD today?" Fenton asked.

"My brother, Carter Ellis, was an inmate here several months ago."

"I recall you were here before, Detective Ellis. I know what you're investigating. What I'm asking is, why are you back?"

Ellis set down the badge on the desk. "We found this where we believe my brother was murdered."

Fenton looked at the badge, and his face paled.

And for the first time since Ellis started this investigation, she believed she had her killer.

———

WARDEN BAKER and his top administrators accompanied Ellis and McCallister back to Flour Mill Dam. She had called Moss to send over a few officers who could secure the scene, allowing them to conduct a more detailed search. Associate Warden Fenton was in the back seat of the warden's vehicle.

"This is where we found the badge, Warden Baker." Ellis gestured to the tree. "On closer inspection, we do see footprints. We'll have our tech work on any other evidence in the area."

McCallister stepped in. "And you should have received an email from Detective Lewis with attached SARs reports, as well as your accounting department's records. All of this is currently being corroborated."

The warden seemed to be struggling to process the information.

"This is a lot to take in, sir," Ellis said. "But with this and what we have on DEA Agent Kroll, you'll see what's been happening inside your prison walls."

Baker glanced at Fenton still in the car. "Yes, I'm beginning to understand." He turned back to her. "But this doesn't prove murder, Detective Ellis. I'm very sorry your brother is dead, but all you've found is Bill's ID badge. He's already indicated that he misplaced it more than a week ago."

Ellis smiled. "That is convenient, sir. But we're here to find more evidence. And I have no doubt that what we find will be compelling." She squared up to him. "So what I'm asking you now is, will you agree, based on what you see here, to let us bring Fenton back with us rather than have Warren PD take over? This dam is in our city. This investigation should remain with us."

Baker appeared to mull it over. "Yes, Detective Ellis. Please, do what you need to do." He glanced back a final time at Fenton. "I'll provide whatever information you require to pursue murder charges."

BEVINS AWAKENED AFTER A SLEEPLESS NIGHT. Climbing out of bed, he pulled back the blinds on his bedroom window. Early morning light shone through the trees that surrounded his building.

He and Murph had gone to bed last night uncertain of the path forward. One that they hoped would see them escape from this nightmare unscathed. But there was only one person who deserved such an exit. And it wasn't Bevins.

No...as he lay awake, thinking of all that had happened, he knew he had been culpable. Regardless of Jack's part, something that felt like a dagger in his chest. The fact was, Bevins had let his father hide the truth. He'd let Lance Curry die without the justice he deserved. Part of that lack of justice hinged on the fact that Connor Bevins had also kept the secret. That was about to change.

He showered, dressed, and walked out of his bedroom to find Murph still asleep on the sofa. Bevins carried on into the kitchen to make a pot of coffee. He considered how best to ensure his friend didn't pay for what he had asked of him.

With the coffee ready, he poured two cups, carrying them back into the living room. He set one down on the table, rousing his friend from sleep.

"Hey," Murph said, rubbing his eyes. "What time is it?"

"Early. I have to get to work." Bevins took a sip from his mug. "Listen, I'm going to make sure nothing happens to you, okay?"

Murph sat up on the sofa. "How are you going to do that?"

"I have a feeling, when others find out what Jack has done, you'll be the last one they want to come after regardless of how you uncovered the information. The Army would be shooting themselves in the foot to come for the guy who uncovered a murder."

Murph tilted his head. "And what about you?"

Bevins peered down at his mug, the steam still rising from it. "I need to admit my part in it." He looked up at Murph again. "I let Jack cover it up. I robbed Lance of the justice he deserved."

"Jeez, man, are you sure about this?"

"I am." He took another sip. "I mean, it'll come to light anyway, but I won't use my dad to try to fix it this time. It's too late for that."

Murph glanced through the sliding glass door out toward the balcony. "What if you go to prison? Or get court-martialed?"

"Then that's what happens." Bevins drew in a deep breath, and for the first time in his life, he felt truly free. "It should've happened years ago." He got to his feet. "Stay here for as long as you like. I need to head into the station and submit my resignation. Then I don't know...I guess I'll have to turn myself in to the MPs."

He carried on through the living room, snatching his car keys along the way. "See you later, man. And thank you for everything." Bevins jogged down the concrete steps, glancing up at a partly cloudy sky. He reached his car and stepped inside, taking in the feel of her leather seats, the steering wheel in his hands. The power under her hood.

He smiled and drove on, heading toward the station house. Traffic was light this morning, and he arrived in no time. Stepping out into the parking lot, he stared at the building before him. This was probably going to be the last time he'd take in this view.

Inside, he offered pleasant greetings to everyone he

passed, climbing up the stairs that led to CID. But he wasn't going into the bullpen yet. Sergeant Abbott was who he needed to see first. Standing outside his office, Bevins rapped his knuckles on the doorframe. "Morning, Sarge. You have a minute?"

From behind his desk, Abbott set down his cup of coffee. "Of course. Come in." He narrowed his gaze. "You look... calm. Resolved."

He walked inside and took a seat. "I guess you could say that. Listen, Sarge, you know what happened now."

"I do."

"And I've decided that I can no longer, nor do I want to, hide behind Jack anymore. When this thing comes out, he'll go down, regardless. As for me, I intend to take my licks. Whatever happens, happens because I let Jack do what he did. I could've said something. He made sure the DUI charges disappeared. Everything."

"But, son, you ultimately weren't responsible for the accident," Abbott said.

"With respect, sir, I was. If I had been sober, I would've seen the wire in the road. I would've been able to avoid it. And Lance would still be here today."

"Well, I'm not sure about that. If you had been sober, it was still dark." Abbott raised his hands. "Point being, if that thing hadn't been in the road, worst case? You would've been issued a DUI, not faced murder charges."

"I can't change what happened..."

"No, but the whole story needs to come to light." Abbott leaned back. "All I'm saying is, this won't be the end for you. For Jack, yeah, I think his time is up. But it doesn't have to be for you."

"I suppose I'll just have to see how this plays out, sir,"

Bevins replied. "I allowed the cover-up. That doesn't make me look—or feel—great." He reached into his bag and retrieved an envelope. "For you, sir."

Abbott took the envelope. "What is this, son?"

Bevins swallowed his emotions. "A resignation letter, sir. It's what's best for the team."

THE WHYS and the hows still needed to be resolved. Ellis knew it all went back to the scheme they'd set up to feed inmates to the rehab center, introduce them to the cartel, who would offer them money and drugs, then turn them over to the halfway house, where Kroll pretended to be their friend. Insisting that if they acted as informants, they wouldn't serve any more time. Carter had believed it—for a while.

As for how Fenton got his hands in it...well, it had to be the money. The cartels had plenty of it. And maybe Carter had planned to take a stand. She knew they'd expected him to offer information on Bangor PD's operations. Maybe getting Fenton involved was how they'd planned to enforce their request. She would never know because he was dead, but it was a nice idea that he'd intended to do the right thing.

In light of Fenton's arrest, Warden Baker had been forced to issue a statement first thing this morning. Three more people had been arrested for their part in the kickback scheme.

But so far, no one directly connected to the cartel, besides Kroll, had been discovered. They had billions of dollars and the best lawyers around at their disposal. It saddened Ellis to know the sheer size and influence of their criminal enterprise. All of them. They played their turf wars on US soil now. It was a war Ellis wasn't sure the police would win.

But she would see justice for Carter, as the associate warden of the Maine State Prison was now being held without bond in Bangor PD's custody.

Ellis was supposed to take time off after Carter's funeral, but whoever believed she would actually do that didn't know her very well. Even Hank had insisted she go back to work this morning. After wagging his finger at her for not letting him in on the plan to go to Warren, he seemed to know she needed to work. Ellis had let him read the letter. She was grateful Carter had written it, and that she had found it, and so was Hank.

Her grief came in waves. The relationship she'd had with Carter was complicated, to say the least. His letter was unexpected and had changed how she perceived him. But there was much to work through. Forgiveness wouldn't happen overnight.

Now, she arrived at the station, returning to her desk, where McCallister met her gaze. "Good morning."

"I'd say I'm surprised to see you, but I'm not. Did you get any sleep?"

Ellis raised a shoulder. "Some. I'll be okay. I prefer to be here. Besides, there's still a lot to do with Fenton. In fact, I need to call Rivera about Carter's final autopsy report. He texted earlier saying he'd have it ready today. I'm hopeful he'll have found foreign DNA we can tie to Fenton."

"The nail in the coffin." McCallister returned to his work. "Lots of paperwork still to file."

"Yep." As she opened her laptop, she noticed Bevins arrive. "Hey, Con."

As he walked in, it was the look in his eyes that raised her guard. Sadness, maybe some regret. And it seemed she wasn't the only one who'd picked up on it. Looking around, the rest of the team seemed to be looking at him with a sort of expectation.

"I, uh, I need to talk to you guys," Bevins said.

Ellis and McCallister exchanged a glance as Bevins stood before the team, his eyes downcast. Though he tried to maintain a neutral expression, the sag in his shoulders betrayed his feelings.

"I wanted you all to hear it from me first." He unleashed a heavy sigh. "Effective immediately, I have resigned from the department."

A ripple of surprise moved through the room. Pelletier's brows shot up in alarm while Lewis leaned forward as though unsure whether she'd heard him correctly.

"What? Why?" Pelletier asked, bewildered.

Bevins raked a hand through his perfect hair. "It's complicated. But after recent events, I feel it's the best decision for everyone."

Though Ellis and McCallister knew the truth about the car accident years ago, they remained silent, letting Bevins speak.

"There are things in my past that I'm not proud of," Bevins went on. "Mistakes I've made that I can't take back. I let a lot of people down, including all of you." He looked around the room, meeting each detective's eyes in turn. "Fletch, thank you for helping me through this. You deserved better from me. And this department deserves better too. My resignation allows for a clean start."

Ellis leaned back in her chair, studying Bevins carefully as he spoke. She had suspected this might be coming ever since the truth about his past had come to light. Still, hearing him actually say the words aloud made it feel suddenly all too real. "Con, are you sure about this?" she asked gently. "We all make mistakes, especially when we're young. But you've become a great detective. The department needs people like you."

Bevins offered a gentle smile. "Thanks, Becca, but my mind's made up."

"I can't say I'm not disappointed to be losing you," she added. "But I understand why you feel this is necessary."

McCallister nodded. "We all have regrets. What matters is how we move forward."

Bevins gave them a faint, but grateful smile. "Thank you both. I appreciate you guys hearing me out." He glanced around the room again. "I know this comes as a surprise. And I'm sorry for any disruption this causes. I just hope, in time, you'll come to see this is for the best."

Pelletier still looked stunned, shaking his head in disbelief. "I don't get it, man. We're partners. If you were in some kind of trouble, why didn't you come to me?"

"It wasn't that simple, Bryce. Believe me, if there had been another way..." He trailed off.

"I wish things had gone differently," Fletch said. "But you're doing the honorable thing."

Abbott entered the bullpen, his face solemn. "So you all know Connor's leaving." He patted Bevins on the back. "You'll always have a place here if you choose to return."

Ellis locked eyes with him, knowing that part of his decision to leave was based on the selfless desire to protect the department. Bevins chose to put the team first. She stood to learn a thing or two from the young detective.

28

C onnor Bevins was family to Ellis, even if they weren't related by blood. Saying goodbye to him was almost as difficult as it had been to say goodbye to the brother she'd just buried. Now, as the day neared its end, reticence hung over the team like a cloud. A gathering at their favorite hangout was scheduled for later to offer an official sendoff. But loose ends still dangled before her.

Evidence had been gathered from the location where Carter had presumably died. The shoe prints left embedded in the soft earth near the water had belonged to William Fenton. His phone's GPS had proved his whereabouts at the time. But the reasons as to why Carter had had a meeting with him remained unclear. What was worse was that no physical evidence could yet tie Fenton to the act of murder.

Ellis got up from her desk, inserting a sheet of paper into an envelope. "I'm going to run downstairs to check in with Brown. See if he's gotten anywhere with Carter's phone."

"What's that in your hand?" McCallister asked.

She held out the envelope. "Oh, it's that letter I promised to write for inmate Perez. I'm going to drop it in the mail-room downstairs."

"That's good of you, Becca."

She shrugged. "I did promise him." McCallister had kept himself at a distance since the funeral. As though he might intrude upon her grief. Then again, she'd been doing a pretty good job lately of pushing him away.

Ellis walked into the hall and was carrying on toward the landing when Abbott emerged from his office. He caught her gaze, raising a finger to stop her. "What's going on, Sarge? I was just heading down to Forensics, hoping Brown had had a chance to take a look at Carter's phone, which we recovered at the dam."

"Listen, Becca, I just hung up with the DEA assistant director. Thought you should know that Agent Kroll will face corruption charges, as well as trafficking and money laundering." He pressed his lips into a tight smile. "You were right about him."

"Thank you, Sarge." While she was glad to hear Kroll would probably spend the next twenty years or more behind bars, something still pricked the back of her mind. "There is something that still doesn't make sense to me."

"What's that?"

She leaned back against the railing on the landing. "When Kroll and I met with the man who'd threatened Hank, Kroll offered to call off a raid in exchange for letting Hank go. At the time, I thought, yeah, you know, he's on our side."

"But he wasn't." Abbott nodded. "I don't have all the answers yet, but it's my understanding that Kroll was responsible for what happened with Hank."

"How so?"

"He wanted you to believe he was one of us. And the information he had on the raid was information the cartel already knew about. Part of Kroll's job was keeping the DEA off their backs. He was privy to operation details."

Ellis drew in her brow. "You're saying it was a setup?"

"I'm saying they used Hank as a way to keep you in line. And to keep you thinking that Kroll was on our side. Ultimately, I believe it was Kroll's job to gather whatever intel we had here to help further the cartel's causes."

"Which is why I'm certain Carter was targeted," she replied. "He was supposed to provide information. And when he didn't..."

He gazed out over the lobby below. "I should've done a better job, Becca. I could've dug deeper when Kroll wanted to join us. I didn't. I trusted him. But you saw through the bullshit. You did your job."

She raised her gaze to the ceiling, letting out a long sigh. "I had no idea the reach of these people, Sarge."

"We know now, and in fact, Moss, myself, and Lieutenant Serrano are preparing to meet with the state police. An official taskforce will be formed to tackle the problem of cartel activity across the border." He placed his hand on her shoulder. "Carter was in deep, and I'm sorry for that."

"Me too, Sarge." She thumbed back. "I need to check in with Brown." Ellis carried on downstairs, heading back to Forensics, but not before dropping off the letter in the mailroom. This meeting Carter had had...it started to make sense. But had he met with Fenton alone? Was there a chance Kroll had been present too?

She opened the door, stepping inside the lab.

"Detective Ellis," Harding began, "Leo's in the back. Go on."

"Thanks." She walked on until reaching Brown's office. Opening the door, she leaned in. "You have a second?"

"Of course. Come in."

Ellis stepped inside and noticed that Carter's phone was on Brown's desk. Smashed screen, dirt embedded into the frame. "I see you're working on the phone."

"Yep. I'm using our data recovery software now. In fact, it should be just about finished."

A smile spread on her lips. "You were able to get into it?"

"Oh yeah. Third-party software exists that can pull data off a phone in virtually any condition." He disconnected the phone. "Care to take a look at what's on it, since you're here?"

Ellis walked behind him, peering over his shoulder at the monitor. "Show me what you got."

While Brown scrolled through lines of data, he stopped at a row of files. "One of these appears to be an audio recording."

Her heart jumped into her throat. "Carter said he'd planned on recording the meeting."

Brown viewed the information for a few moments longer. "Okay. You want to hear it?"

"Please." She steadied her nerves, praying the truth was about to be revealed.

He played the audio file. It sounded as if someone was rustling around, maybe walking somewhere. Ellis continued to listen. Soon, voices could be heard, but they were muffled. Almost indiscernible. "I can't tell what's being said."

"He probably had his phone in his pocket," Brown replied.

She strained to hear. "Could be multiple voices." The

recording continued to play. "Come on, Carter. Tell me what's happening." Several moments passed. "Wait. You hear that?"

Brown stopped the recording. "Let me back it up and try again, lowering the ambient noise." He clicked on the file once again.

Ellis smiled. "Yes, I can hear them now."

"*You said you could get information from your sister, yet it's been weeks.*"

"*I told you it was going to take time. She and my dad, they don't know I'm out yet. I have to approach this carefully. Trust me when I say that my sister will get suspicious if I start asking questions.*"

Ellis closed her eyes, envisioning Carter as he must've been, standing near the stream.

"*You've had enough time.*"

It seemed whoever had been talking had stepped away.

"Is he going to talk to someone else?" Ellis asked.

"Hard to say," Brown replied.

It was then she heard Carter's voice calling out. "What's he saying?" she pressed.

Brown entered commands, soon isolating Carter's voice.

"*Don't do this. Give me more time, please. Both of you, I just need more time.*"

"Both?" Ellis said.

"*What do you think, Sean? I don't think he can deliver what he's promised.*"

"*You're the boss, Bill. I'll leave it up to you.*"

The names...it was Agent Sean Kroll and Associate Warden William Fenton. This was it, but which one had murdered Carter?

Footfalls sounded. He was running. Carter was trying to get away.

Ellis gripped the back of Brown's chair, leaning closer. "Come on. What's happening? What's happening?"

A sort of crash sounded; then the recording stopped.

Ellis pulled back. "Is that it? No. That can't be it."

Brown keyed in more commands. "I think it is. I'm sorry. I don't see another audio file."

She let go of the chair, her hand cupping her mouth.

"I'll keep looking," Brown said, his voice efficient, as always.

Ellis nodded, stunned into silence. She walked out of his office, disregarding Harding's goodbye, and entered the corridor. That was it. That was all they would find. She checked her phone as a notification sounded. Upon glancing at it, a final spark of hope ignited. It was an email from Rivera.

She quickly opened it, scanning the obligatory pleasantries until spotting the attachment. There it was. Carter's autopsy report. The summary. That was what she should read first. "Primary cause of death, hypoxia." Ellis continued to read, and then her shoulders sank. "No foreign DNA found."

The world spun around her. Officers passed her by in the hall. If they said anything to her, she heard nothing. Her entire focus was on that report. Everything else ceased to exist. And then it occurred to her. She was never going to know what truly happened. She'd been certain Fenton was her man, but all they had was circumstantial evidence. This report was supposed to prove he did it. But it seemed Carter had been in the water long enough to wash away the truth. She had nothing.

Nothing.

Her brother was dead. Someone killed him. But this time, the answers would remain out of reach. It was a case she couldn't solve.

———

ELLIS STOOD AT THE BAR, drink in hand, overlooking the team as they huddled around now former detective Bevins. The Waterfront offered a stunning view of the river. The early summer evening revealed a setting sun imbued with vibrant purples and oranges. Laughter sounded from the team as they relayed tales of their shared adventures.

It was a bittersweet moment. Everyone had seen how much Bevins had grown as a person and a detective. But Ellis was left feeling uncertain about his future, just as she had been about Carter's death and perhaps even her own future now.

McCallister approached her. "You sure you want to be here? Everyone will understand if you'd prefer to go see your dad."

"I'll stay for a little while longer. He looks like he's having fun." She turned to him. "You know, I didn't think I'd be this sad about it. All things considered."

"You were the only one who defended him for a long time. I think you saw yourself as his mentor, knowing what he was truly capable of becoming."

Bevins caught her eye and smiled.

She raised her glass to him. "He doesn't deserve this."

"Oh, I think his father will be the one to ultimately pay," McCallister replied. "But Connor's doing what he knows is right. What happens after this is hard to say."

"Isn't that the truth." Ellis went quiet for a moment, then felt his hand on her forearm.

"I know you wanted answers, Becca. I'm so sorry you didn't get them."

"Well, we don't solve every crime, do we?" She took a sip of her drink. "The important thing is that the people we know are responsible will pay for their other crimes. They'll be behind bars for a long time."

"Yes, they will. And you and Hank are safe. That's what matters."

"Are we? The problem didn't go away. The drugs are still going to come, and the same people will bring them." Ellis set down her glass. "But we're here for Connor. Come on, let's join them."

———

A FEW DAYS HAD PASSED. Ellis had done her best to care for Hank, staying with him while he overcame the worst of his grief. Those early days when nothing made sense. When anger seethed at everyone left behind. Angry they had the nerve to go on about their lives.

Now, the time had come to return to the station, to a team still getting used to the hole created by Bevins's absence. Though she felt invigorated by the notion of bringing on Officer Triggs in the near future. An idea Abbott had latched onto.

McCallister stood at Pelletier's desk, laughing over something. She studied his face, taking in the lines around his eyes when he smiled, the dimple in his cheek.

She thought about how much he had changed since he first arrived, after the shooting that drove him from Boston to Bangor. Closed off and brooding. Sticking to procedure as though it was gospel. Every case seemed to weigh on him heavily, as if he carried the burden for every victim. But gradually, glimpses of his warmth peeked through. His humor and empathy. Parts of himself he had previously locked away out of guilt and shame over what he'd done.

Now, watching him banter easily with others on the team, especially Pelletier, Ellis felt a swell of pride and affection. She had kept him at arm's length, wary of getting too close. Her failed marriage with Andrew, like scar tissue, making it hard to open herself up again. But McCallister had been patient. He let her set the pace, never pushing for more than she was ready to give.

Over time, the wall between them had crumbled. The connection she tried to deny emerged stronger than ever. Yet certain issues had cropped up. Decisions he'd made, sometimes undermining her own. He'd done so in the name of love and protection. But in this job, it was a dangerous path to walk. One that tilted the scales of justice. It had taken her brother's death for her to see it.

As she prepared to leave for the day, heading off to visit Hank, she knew the time had come. Ellis waited for McCallister to return to his desk. "Listen, I was just getting ready to leave. Need to stop by Hank's." She thumbed back. "Walk me out?"

"Of course."

It was just Lewis, Pelletier, and Fletch now. Walking by Bevins' desk, seeing it empty, gave Ellis a sense of longing. Longing for the way things had been before. Part of that was grief over the loss of her brother. Part of that was knowing the importance of finding herself once again. She would become a better detective. Bringing closure for others while she still sought it out for herself.

She led the way outside, pushing through the lobby doors, feeling the tepid summer air against her skin. The sun had already begun to set just a little earlier each night. A reminder that days like these never last.

"I wanted to talk about something." Ellis reached for her keys as they arrived at her car.

McCallister stood across from her, arms folded over his chest. "Okay…"

"These last several months, getting to know you, spending time together at work and in our personal lives…" She trailed off, not wanting to sound so clichéd. The last time she'd done something like this was announcing she'd wanted a divorce from Andrew. It hadn't gone any better.

His look shifted. The smile faded.

"Euan, I think we may have rushed into things."

McCallister remained stoic, keeping his eyes fixed on hers.

"I can't deny my feelings for you. But I've felt a change… in the way I work cases. The way I look at, well, everything." She tilted her head. "You must've felt this too. Being partners with someone you're involved with—"

"It changes your perspective," he cut in.

"Yes. And it's altered the dynamics of our partnership. Even that of the team as a whole."

"I'm not oblivious to your concerns," he said. "I guess I thought we could just work through them. But I'm sensing that may not be possible now."

"The decisions we make in this job, they need to be based on facts. Based on training." She glanced down, fiddling with her keys. "Not based on one of us wanting to protect the other."

He nodded, a gentle grin on his face. "I understand. In the beginning, I was objective. I told you what I thought was right, and you decided if that was what you wanted to do. Now, as I have before, I decide what I think is right for you." He chuckled. "Seems like you're the only one with the guts to say it out loud."

She wiped a tear from her cheek. "With everything going on—my dad's health, my brother, wrapping up this case with the DEA—I need to focus on work. *We* need to focus on work. And I need a partner who can be objective."

McCallister was quiet for a moment, seeming to consider her words. "You're not wrong, Becca." He took her shoulders and leaned in, kissing her cheek with the gentlest of touches. When he pulled back, he continued, "It'll take time for me to get over you."

Her lips quivered. "Me too. But it's the best thing for our team. For our careers."

"Goodbye, Becca." He took a step back, aiming a finger gun at her. "Hey, uh, I'll see you tomorrow, partner."

She smiled. "See you tomorrow." Ellis climbed into her Tahoe, taking a breath as she watched him walk away. It was the right thing to do. Wasn't it?

WE HOPE YOU ENJOYED THIS BOOK

If you could spend a moment to write an honest review on Amazon, no matter how short, we would be extremely grateful. They really do help readers discover new authors.

ABOUT THE AUTHOR

Robin Mahle has published more than 30 crime fiction novels, many, of which, topped the Amazon charts in the US, Canada, and the UK. Also a screenwriter, she has adapted some of her works into teleplays, which have gone on to place in film festivals nationwide. From detectives to federal agents, and from killers to corruption, her page-turning tales grab hold and refuse to let go. Throw in tense action and thrilling twists, and it becomes clear why her readers come back for more. Robin lives in Coastal Virginia with her husband and two children.

www.robinmahle.com

ALSO BY ROBIN MAHLE

Detective Rebecca Ellis Series

No Safe Place

A Frozen Grave

The Dead Lake

Leave No Trace

No Way Back

Printed in Great Britain
by Amazon

56940360R00189